W9-AXH-707

THE MAFIA WIFE

DAVID WEAVER

DAVID WEAVER PRESENTS 2020

To Darius.

For showing me the definition of a real friend during your time on earth. If only my storms could have subsided in time for me to carry the umbrella through yours. Every time I write a scene for Bullethead, I kept hearing him speak with your voice and demeanor. Although you're no longer here with us, may your spirit live on. #RIP

Darius Seltzer updated his cover photo.

March 13, 2016 at 11:09 PM · 🌐

1

AYOKI

The flicker of the candle's light caused a steady glow in the corner of the dark room. The window was open, and the breeze of the wind was just enough to keep the room cool, but not strong enough to eliminate the fire of the candle's wick. In front of me was a Bible– not a Bible app, and not the type of Bible that hotel rooms use for decoration in their rooms. I had a Bible that had been passed down to me from generations. From my great-great-grandmother, from my mother, and now to me.

The front cover was beaten from good usage. The pages thin and fragile, some of them no longer secured by the glue that once bound them. The Bible had an odor to it. The aroma of generations of blessings permeated from the surface of the script, causing my nose to tingle from the familiar inhaling of a night of prayer. The truth was... I was flawed, yet gifted– as was the generations of women in my family who came before me. Like my mother, I was a prophetess. Like my father, I had addictions. Like my mother, I could tell a stranger anything about his or her life.

But like my father, whom my mother couldn't get any type of insight into his life... was the way my husband was to me.

I could literally give personal insight to a complete stranger. In one meeting I've been able to tell them things about their child's mother, details about a new job promotion, answers to health questions, nearly any type of private uncertainty... But to the people I knew and loved the most, for some reason it was like God himself blocked and denied me access to their secrets and privacy. It made sense however, since they were who I saw the most and spent the most time with, I had no right having any type of thoughts that could potentially taint the pure love I contained for them, so I never got upset about it. Besides... The secrets that I was already able to pull from other people were enough to last me 10 generations. I'd seen some of the damnest things hiding behind the skin that enclosed a person's skull.

The Bible was open to 1st Corinthians, chapter 10, verse 13.

No temptation has overtaken you except what is common to mankind. And God is faithful; he will not let you be tempted beyond what you can bear. But when you are tempted, he will also provide a way out so that you can endure it.

I'd been praying for a way out of my temptation since I was a teenager. At 24, I hadn't found a way out– but a way to control it better, amongst the continuous fight to conceal my cravings from the watchful eye of my husband. To me he was perfect, and in my mind, I didn't think I was so deserving of such a great man.

The wind and its components swirled in, and blew against the strands of my Virgin Remy, my lip gloss blocking the dryness that came with a steady night breeze, my burgundy silk nightgown wrapped around my dark skin.

Sitting beside my Bible on the left side was my cell phone. My husband had gone out with friends, and I didn't expect him to come back until around 3, maybe 4 in the morning. He didn't go out much, but I urged him to get out of the house and have fun... Mainly because of what was sitting on the right side of my Bible.

The container read: *Breath Fresherizer*, but the liquid inside of the bottle was completely off limits to anyone but me. I made sure to keep this bottle locked away and hidden. I wasn't perfect, but I was certain that many women and men had drawers in their home that they wouldn't want their neighbors to slide out. This was that drawer for me.

I prayed for forgiveness in advance and closed my eyes. The door to my room was locked, in case I wasn't back to my normal self by the time my husband came home. I took a deep breath and picked up my bottle. Using the dropper, I put one drop of the tasteless liquid under my tongue. I blew the candle out and sat in the complete darkness with the Bible sitting in front of me.

From experience, I knew that the LSD was going to take me to another world, and I didn't need anything distracting me from the adventure I was about to be placed on. A few times I'd been taken to God and had full conversations with him while being on the drug. A few times I'd been taken to hell and fought with the devil himself over a hot span of 2 hours. I didn't know where the drug was going to take me this week, as I only used it on Saturdays before church– but I did know that I needed to be back to my normal self before me and my husband made it to church in the morning.

After about 30 minutes, the room started spinning, and even though I sat in pure darkness, the room was becoming brighter. Where the Bible once was, was my Grandmother's face. As I opened my mouth to talk to her, her face turned to a white midst of smoke and swirled its way into my mouth, causing me to choke. I tried to cough, and the devil grabbed my throat, preventing the exit of air. He was wearing all black and his skin was the color of a shadow. I tried to breathe but he pressed the skin on my throat harder.

I swung at him and missed, then jumped up and kicked him as hard as I could, knocking a chair over in the process. I knew I'd hurt my foot, but I needed to breath more importantly than I needed a foot. I kicked and fought until he let go, and I fell to the ground breathing heavily until I was able to catch my breath. In the next moment I was on a roller coaster... a real one... The cart I was in seemed to go all the way up in the sky, but I was ok because my husband was right beside me. We went all the way up... and it seemed like we were going all the way to the moon.

When the cart stopped, we both looked in front of us and saw that there were no more tracks for the cart to be guided on. We went into a free fall, both of us screaming... The cart flipping over several times... The distance between the sky and the ground being erased at a rapid pace... And right before we were to hit the ground, it all disappeared, and I was being choked again by the devil again. I kicked and fought... I punched him until my fist bled– until he let go of me. I lay there and repeated the passage of the 1st Corinthians verse.

I had to believe that God was going to take this addiction away from me so that I could continue to carry out His plan. I was so good to so many people... So many people saw me as an angel... But absolutely nobody was able to see my battles and the path of scars that led to my heart. I fought the devil that night until I was able to kill him... But I knew he would be back some other week. He always came back. If not next week, then surely the week after. I was happy though, because I'd been able to kill him before my husband came home, and that was the most important part of it all.

In a daze, I managed to somehow run my bathwater, take a bath, and get in the bed. I knew my dreams that night was going to be bad, as they were every night after taking my LSD trip. The good part was that I'd gone from taking it every two to three days, to taking it once every Saturday. I'd even gotten to where I could make it two weeks without going to face the dark dungeons of my soul. The bad thing was... chemicals of the LSD stored itself in my brain, and had been storing itself for years, so sometimes I'd randomly black out and not know where I was.

I felt too beautiful to have such an ugly addiction, but I knew that the prettiest colors on a spider were the deadliest, and as a human being I was also a part of the same rules of nature as any other creation of God's. I cried myself to sleep that night, and surprisingly my dream wasn't as bad as I thought it would be. I had a dream that I was a world class swimmer, swimming across the ocean and through the waves. I didn't know the purpose of that dream, but I knew that no dream was without meaning. I couldn't wait until morning so we could go to church. Even though many people at the church came to me for help, I needed the ministry more than most of all of the churchgoers combined. If I couldn't fight my demons in a more effective manner, then I was certain that my demons were going to kill me.

2

ZAEDAN

The average millionaire has seven sources of income.

That was one of those sentences that had been repeated several times through history and passed down from person to person pointlessly. Me and the people who followed me understood this to be a false statement, and I'd done everything in my power to exploit this phrase and everyone who believed in it. It was simply not a true thesis.

The secret to riches and power was knowledge– not knowing it all but knowing enough to distribute while still giving off the aura that you still had more knowledge left to give. I was passionate about education– a street guy with an above average IQ, but never to come off so intelligent that the average guy from the streets couldn't understand me. It was this one imbalance of the streets that made one person a boss over others.

I was a *boss,* and I was taught by the best of the best. My father.

At the age of 18, my dad sent me to Paris, France with the request that I study abroad in honor of my thirst for deeper education. I didn't understand his reasoning at the time, but I followed his requests regardless. Within 2 years, I was speaking French as if it was my primary language, and in the 6th year of living there, I'd befriended some guys with ties to the Milieu–the group of organized crime families in France. At the time I was working at a mobile app development company, and now that I think about it... maybe they targeted me specifically to help them with the problem that they were having. I'm sure they probably would have gotten turned down if they'd approached anyone else, since all of their issues were borderline unethical. Over time, I was able to help those guys through some serious situations that they were going through, and in return, I was introduced further into the French world of organized crime. Don't get me wrong... organized crime was never my goal. Me being so far away from my hometown, my intent was only to gain experience, make a little money, make a few friends from there, and return home with a really nice-looking resume.

I still remember the day I walked my black ass into the living room to shake hands with a high-ranking capo regime– who was the head of a "family," or group of soldiers. It was 3 capos in Paris, and each had several soldiers under them who took orders from an underboss. The underboss took orders from a Boss, and the Boss took advice from the consigliere– or advisor to the Boss. He didn't necessarily have more power than the boss, but his words were very influential to the most influential person.

After meeting the capo that day in Paris and helping him build an app so that he could operate an illegal numbers system, sports betting operation, and online blackjack operation, my life had been changed tremendously. Using a local attorney who was familiar with dealings of the mafia, he paid me 200,000 francs– the equivalent to a little over $200,000; but with the condition that I return to America immediately and never come back to Paris. I hated that I'd gotten myself into a situation like that, but his "offer," wasn't really an offer, but specific instructions to either follow and take the money or die and wish I had taken it.

It made lots of sense when I thought about it though. He couldn't afford to have a person living in his world who knew how his world operated. Initially I considered the fact that he was paying me instead of killing me to be a great thing, but as time went by, I didn't realize until way later what the real reason was that he didn't kill me, and what implications came with accepting $200,000 francs from the mafia. At that time period in my life, I barely understood what an implication was.

When I told my father what happened, he wasn't even upset.

"Son, as long as you've learned the main lesson here. Things are never as they appear, and always expect the unexpected."

I came back to Atlanta shortly after that, and never saw life the same again. Over the course of a few years, I'd been able to build a pyramid scheme of power and finesse unlike anything Atlanta had ever seen before. I was the perfect person to run such a powerful entity, being that nobody would ever expect it from me. I was 27 years old and had grown up entirely in the church. I was handsome and clean cut, dark-skinned with perfect teeth, I didn't drink or indulge in any drugs or alcohol. I participated in fundraisers, helped feed the homeless, and often gave speeches at troubled high schools in the area in an effort to convince young men and women not to fall victim to the streets.

They listened to me because I was popular in the city. I didn't club that much, but when I did go, I hung with and around all of the A-List celebrities and knew them on a first-name basis. I was always in some celebrities' Instagram photo getting tons of likes, and although I wasn't a flashy person, if I needed to make a statement, I always had access to the latest foreign cars, from Maybachs to Rolls Royces– although I only pulled those cars out when it was imperative that I do so. For the most part I was low-key, yet I had supreme control in a city that thrived on power.

I was a criminal. This was my way of life and it would always be. An organized street boss with several groups of men under me who obeyed and walked by the beat of my drum. Loyalty was our mantra– nobody would ever cross another member of our team and live to tell about it twice. Death was the penalty, and we didn't hesitate to enforce it whenever the situation called for.

Le secret des grandes fortunes sans cause apparente est un crime oublie, parce qu'il a ete proprement fait.

A French novelist by the name of Le Pere Goriot wrote that back in 1834, and it was the only phrase that I lived by:

The secret of great fortunes without apparent cause is a forgotten crime, because it has been properly done.

The idea that behind every great fortune lies a crime was the true secret to becoming a millionaire. A million dollars requires a significant advantage on your behalf in order to attain. You can leave it up to luck to bring you a million dollars– in which case you're gambling your life away waiting, or you can place the task in your own hands and go and get the million dollars you say you'd like to have. In order to get a million dollars, you have to be able to bend the rules a little to gain some type of edge. This doesn't mean you have to bend the rules to get the actual money, but you may have to bend the rules to achieve something in the process of getting to your destination.

Despite the fact that I loved my wife, Ayoki– I wondered what she saw in me that made her love me so much. I wondered what she saw in me that made her sleep beside me so comfortably at night, or smile at me when she woke up, or what she saw in me that made her hold my hand with so much passion as we walked into the church each Sunday. I didn't see those same things when I looked in the mirror each day, and I certainly didn't see those things in the eyes of the nigga I had tied to a wooden chair with an extension cord wrapped around his body. It was 11pm on the Saturday before church, and I was in the bedroom of a man named Michael Billy, making the same example that I'd made several times before.

Do not cross me.

"Pwease Zwaedan!" He slurred through the gap where I knocked out three of his teeth. Blood oozed down his chin and neck like it was only sweat from a hot workout. He was a light skinned guy with a shiny black mark on the side of his face, swelling from where I hit him with my baseball bat once he answered the door.

"Please Zaedan what?" I asked in a calm voice. I had on a custom-tailored business suit, navy blue with a white button up under the jacket. I wore a pink and red colored tie and had on a pair of red Louboutin dress shoes. I was a boss, but I still did the work of a soldier every so often, to let the streets know that I'm hands on and had no love for those who crossed me.

"Pwease gwive mwe another chwance Zwaedan! Um sworry! Pwease cut this wire off mwe! Pwease!"

I smirked and shook my head. "You see Michael... I'm

not able to do that. I loaned you some money... $20,000 specifically because you told me that you were going to pay me back $30,000 for helping you. I let you borrow the money and then you changed your number on me. You stopped texting me and became the person I always knew you were... but you didn't know that I was the person that you didn't know I was."

"Wait! Nwo! Swir! Pwease! Pwease gwive mwe another chwance! I have $13,000 wright now and I'll gwive you the wrest later this week! Pwease cwut this wire off mwe."

I reached in my briefcase and grabbed a pair of scissors and cut marks into the wire in several sections across the front of his body. I cut through the wire insulation, careful as to not damage the actual wiring, but diligently making sure to expose the live part of the wire. I couldn't cut too much of the wire, because it would only make it weaker, and allow him to eventually break loose with all of the struggling and wiggling he was doing.

I reached into my briefcase and grabbed a pair of hedge shears out. I smiled at him and quickly placed the tool around his left thumb and snapped that shit clean off. The snap sounded like the initial contact with the edge of a skillet and an eggshell. He screamed in agonizing pain, but he couldn't move much due to the way he was bound with the wiring. I stepped back so that his pouring blood wouldn't get on my suit and placed the hedge shears back into the briefcase. I then pulled out a syringe and medicine kit and withdrew liquid from the container. I squirted it in the air so that he could get a good visual for what was about to come. I slid the head of the needle into his right forearm and pressed the liquid testosterone into his body.

"I just gave you testosterone so that you can stay awake." I said with a smirk on my face. He should have been thankful that I was trying to help keep him awake instead of being upset at me about his missing thumb.

"You're going to need to stay awake in order to keep that blood from dripping on the open wiring on the extension cord..."

"Whyyyyy?" His screamed was muffled, his eyes like those of a sad child as he stared up at me in terror.

Amused, I picked up his loose thumb off of the floor like it was a lucky penny– then picked up his iPhone off of the table. I pressed his fingerprint against the fingerprint scanner to unlock his phone. I scrolled down and found the text message I was looking for. I opened it and showed it to him. He didn't even have a chance to react.

The blood was pouring out at a rapid pace, way more and way faster than I expected, and when it connected with the open cut of the wire, it was like I was standing in front of a barbecue grill. The odor from the burning of the flesh was strong, and quite frankly, I was disappointed. I thought I was going to be able to have a show for at least a few minutes and hated that it was over so quickly. I packed my briefcase while the electricity continued to jerk and slam his body against the chair from the electrically induced convulsions. The lights in the house flickered off and on, and eventually a fuse blew, and all of the power shut off for good.

Using the flashlight on my phone, I wiped my finger-prints off of his iPhone and lay it back on the table. My intention was to leave as clean of a scene as possible, but even if I did make a mistake, one of my top soldiers had finally made detective, and I knew he would make sure I'm good. That's the thing about me... Most criminals are constantly screaming how much they hate the police, but that wasn't me and never would be. I understood that the police were only out trying to do their jobs and make an honest living. It was nothing wrong with that, and that's why I embraced it, encouraging a few of my soldiers to join the force. The only way to beat something that's bigger than you *is* working from the inside out.

The way I was running my thing... I did everything I could to make sure it went as flawless as possible. I tried not to put extra pressure on the police department with too many murders... But at the end of the day... the only thing that was going to bring the murder rate down was if men started having character again. Long gone are the days when men meant what they said and had honor and integrity.

I coughed as the odor of burnt flesh permeated the room. I gave it one more glance over and walked out of his house as though it was a normal night– as if I'd just come to say hi to an old friend. I didn't play about people trying to disrespect me or play games with me, and I learned in Paris a long time ago that personal honor was always the only thing a person had to stand on, and as long as a person stood on that, he or she would always stand tall. I also learned that you have to protect what you stand on, whether it be by your life or another person's life. The moment you allow another person to kick or tilt what you stand on or for, is the moment your balance in life is in jeopardy.

My stomach was weak from the memory of the smell of the man's burning flesh– it was a smell that I wasn't yet familiar with. I made a mental note to choose a different way the next time I had a similar issue. I stopped and took a deep breath, suppressing the urge to throw up, and trying to gather myself so that I could get out of the area without leaving any unnecessary evidence. I wasn't quite feeling like myself that night, so I was going to just go home and lay up with my wife so I could be on time for church tomorrow.

I always felt guilty after my deepest sins, and always told

myself that I would never do it again, but once the memory of the sin started to fade, it was like the incidents had never taken place. My phone rang as soon as I got in the car and closed the door.

"Hello."

"Hey Zaedan..."

"Why are you calling my phone?" My blood pressure elevated quickly every time she called me.

"Are you around your wife? Is that why you have the attitude?" She replied.

"I got the attitude because you're a trifling, lying ass bitch. But you already know that. You thrive on drama and ignorance... It's like you can't live your life normally without creating a negative cloud."

"How nigga? Nobody told you to fuck me raw. You can't get mad because I refused to have an abortion. Nigga this is my body, and my child. It's my right."

"Bitch you a fuckin liar. Clear as day, you told me you had your tubes tied. I told you I didn't even wanna fuck you without a condom but your trifling ass talking about you allergic to latex. Fuck that... what's your address? I wanna' see the baby."

"Nigga if I haven't let you around me and the baby at this point, what the fuck makes you think I'ma give you the address now for? I'm not stupid, and you're not about to send your goons at us. Nigga I just want what's mine."

"*Be clear!* What is it specifically? What *do* you want from me?"

"You know what I want... I told you... I want you to marry me... leave your wife... You know that bitch ain't–"

"Watch your fuckin' mouth bitch!" Don't you ever call my wife out her name. Fuck wrong with you?"

"Nigga awl boo. Shut up! If you were that concerned

about her you would have never stepped out on her. I don't wanna hear all that save a ho shit tonight. Either you're gon marry me, or you gon give me 5 million dollars cash. Straight like that."

She had me pissed, but I'd done it to myself. It was the first and only time I'd ever stepped out on my wife, and I'd regretted it since the moment it'd happened. I still didn't even know why I did it, because Ayoki gave me everything I could ever ask for and more. The other woman didn't even give me the same vibes as my wife, and yet I was still in the streets being a weak ass nigga. I guess even the most brilliant men were prone to make the most boneheaded decisions. If a woman could get a glimpse into our minds just once, I think they'd forgive us for more of our mistakes... Well not all of us, because some of us are beyond ruthless. We are permanently flawed as men. We have our strengths, but boy did we have our flaws.

"Well don't worry about it nigga. I'ma make your life pure hell until you realize that I'm not bullshitting with you. I'll see y'all in church tomorrow, how bout dat?"

"Aye! You better never–"

Before I could reply, she hung up on me. An unmarked car drove by me, and it scared me because I hadn't even moved but a couple of hundred feet away from the residence of the murder scene. I started my car up and began my drive. I turned my music up to rid my mind of the stress– I couldn't take these emotions and bad energy home to my wife. I couldn't go home caught up in my feelings with Tarralla– the one-night stand that I wished I could give back to the devil. I was a boss in the streets, well-respected in the church, admired by the youth, a friend to the celebrities, and a pillar of the community. I had some fucked up shit going on with me, but that was the one thing I wished that I could take back.

I'd tried to pay her some money to get rid of the baby months ago when she first told me she was pregnant, but it had already been too late. Her grimy ass had waited until she was past the abortion deadline before breaking the news to me. She didn't give me any say-so in the matter, and that's when I first knew that she was on some bullshit with trying to trap me.

I didn't know how I would ever be able to allow that type of news to be broken to my wife, especially when me and her had been trying to conceive for the past few years. I wasn't going to allow that woman to break up my marriage, and I definitely wasn't about to let her blackmail me for 5 million dollars.

I was the nigga doing the extorting in Atlanta, she was not going to extort me. I had to figure out a solution to the madness, but in the meantime, I needed to get some rest so I could be alert and make it to Esekel Baptist Church in the morning. Everything was going to be ok; I was sure of it.

3

AYOKI

My dreams actually became pleasant that night, surprisingly. I dreamt of a little boy who looked more like my husband than me. A beautiful little baby with his slanted eyes, thick lips, and plump cheeks. For some reason I could only see the baby from a distance, as if I was window shopping through several panels of impenetrable glass. Even though there was glass, I was able to reach through it without the glass stopping me. It was as though I was invisible– as if the glass was just an open door, but for some reason, I still wasn't able to touch the baby.

I saw my husband in the dream, and he was able to touch the baby, but I wasn't fortunate enough. Maybe it was God's way of telling me what I already knew... That my husband was fertile and waiting, but as long as I kept doing LSD, I would never be able to give him the child he wanted. I sat in my make-up chair and exhaled. It was only 6 o' clock in the morning, so my husband was still sleeping, lightly snoring. I glanced at him in the reflection of my mirror and admired everything that he was. A handsome chocolate God– one that God had designed for me and me myself.

He was brilliant. He'd started his own successful chain of internet cafes in Atlanta and had been able to make it popular when everyone else thought it would fail. It was called *Free Wi-Fi*, and the name alone had proven to be an attraction within itself. I admired his thought process and all of the knowledge that he'd absorbed on a regular basis. He was always reading books, watching documentaries, working, and above all else... right back by my side for church every Sunday with me. He was flawless, and here I was, just as flawed a creature as God could possibly create.

An alert dropped down from the top of my phone. It was from a conception app letting me know that today was the peak day of my fertility. I knew it was of no use though. I swiped the screen to the right, held down the icon for the app until the x appeared, and deleted it. I didn't need to hold on to false hope; and didn't need to worry about anything that God already had the answers to.

Mac Pro Longwear Paint Pot in Soft Ochre was the base for my eye shadow. I was going for a dramatic look, and me knowing how many people were going to approach me to pray for them, I wanted to look my most serious best, but down to earth and approachable. After applying, I used Makeup Geek Eyeshadow Pan in Mocha to trace out the cut crease before I defined it with a darker shade. I pressed the brush into the hollow of my eyelid and lightly ran the color against my eye socket line.

I used a black eye shadow and lightly traced over the shadow I'd just applied. I started at the outer corner of my eye and moved inward, applying it along the crease, and creating a wing-like shape at the outer corner. I picked up my blending brush, and my mind went blank. My thoughts began to cloud, and I lost track of what I was doing. It was happening again, and it was nothing I could do about it.

"Not right now, please God." I whispered softly, pleading, begging. I put the brush down and walked into the bathroom, shutting the door behind me softly. I locked the door and turned the shower and the sink on, as a sound proofer between what was happening to me and my husband's ears. This was the reason I'd started using LSD. It was the reason that I couldn't get a grip on my life and the reason I'd been spiraling out of control since I was 18. I'd been running from a mistake for years.

A mistake that had snatched the soul out of my family and caused me to be out casted forever. There was no number of apologies that I could speak that would cause them to forgive me for my error. I closed the lid on the toilet seat and sat there with my face in my palms. An agonizing terror originated from the pit of my stomach and lurched outward through my body like sound waves with knives attached to them. A cry of pain seeped out of me, and the tears were threatening to flood the work I'd done to my make-up with no remorse or emotion.

For my mistake, my own tears never forgave me.

For my mistake, my only sister never talked to me again.

My heart had been hurting for 6 years, and I was sure that I would never be a normal woman again.

Memories attacked me. Hit me in the face hard, treating me like the punching bag that I was. My family didn't deserve what I'd done. No family deserved to have a person like me around. I didn't intend to do what I'd done. I didn't do it on purpose, and if I could have had those moments back, I would eagerly trade places in the situation.

I was 18 years old when it happened. That evening was a breezy one. The sun was out, but it was still colder than normal since it was the end of fall. I'd grabbed my mother's keys to her Expedition so that I could go get some hot dogs from the store for dinner. It was a Saturday, and since she always cooked a big Sunday dinner, it was no need to eat big the day before. I backed up the truck and heard a crunch and a muffled scream, and instantly felt my soul being snatched away. Panic seized my body at that moment and had never let go of me to this very day.

I didn't know whether to go back or forward, but I knew I had to do something immediately. I went back forward. I jumped out of the truck and screamed when I saw my 3-year-old nephew crushed from the weight of the truck. It was a pain deeper than anything I'd felt before, and just as bad as he was hurting from what I'd done to him, was just how I was hurting as I stood there. No woman should ever have to experience such a deep painful mistake. I let out the loudest and deepest scream I'd ever had in my life. I'm talking true pain. I passed out.

The next memories were of me waking up in a hospital bed in a room alone. I was suffering from shock, and as soon as I woke up and replayed my memory and realized that what had happened wasn't a dream, I started screaming until I passed out again.

Besides two police officers, nobody from my family came to my hospital room the whole time I was in there. When I called my mother, she didn't answer the phone for me. When I called my sister, it was the same thing. The only person who seemed to accept that I'd made a mistake were the police officers, and even they left me alone and never returned. Nobody wanted to be around me again. I was bad luck.

From there I was never able to gather up enough nerve to return back to my mother's house. I cried and cried and wished I could just live in the hospital forever. I wished that it was me instead of the baby. God why couldn't I have seen him behind the truck trying to get his basketball? I prayed for forgiveness from God, I begged, and pleaded, and the more the weight of my mistake started eating away at me, the more I started to become suicidal. I didn't want to live anymore. The moment I realized my family hated me was when they didn't allow me to go to the funeral. I understood it though, because who wanted someone as bad luck as me to be around them?

Every day those memories haunted me, attacked me... beat at me mentally– and I fought them as best as I could until I started looking for ways to create new memories. Hard drugs and hard liquor were the only things that could help me through those dark times. If it wasn't for me meeting my husband, I was sure that I would have been dead by now; for he gave me a reason to desire to breathe. This was more of the reason I loved my husband.

I jumped up, pulled the toilet lid up, and threw up the entire contents of my stomach. I didn't notice how many tears had been running down my face until some strands of hair got stuck in my face.

"Baby you ok?" My husband called out from behind the bathroom door. He tried to open the door, but it was locked. I took a deep breath and blocked my problems as best as I could. I knew I couldn't let him see me this way, and knew I had to fight the way I'd been fighting. I was a strong woman, and everybody in my current life knew this about me.

"Yes, I'm good baby. I'll be out in a second."

"Aight... I was wondering because you locked the door... Didn't know what that was about..."

"Oh, yea I'm sorry. I did it out of instinct. I didn't mean to."

"Ok... Well I'm about to cook us some breakfast. You relax when you come out of there. Alright?"

"Baby you know that's my job."

"It can be your job, but I wanna do it today. I just wanna feed my beautiful wife. Let me cook for you baby. *Je veux juste nourrir ma belle femme.*"

It was nothing I could really say to that. Anytime he spoke French to me it stirred my emotions and swayed my thoughts and opinions towards his favor. My husband wanted to cook for me, and I was about to let him. With as many deep, dark secrets as I was holding on to, he still loved me and still treated me like a queen. He was my motivation for wanting to be a better woman. He made me want to increase my value as a woman because I always saw him raise his value as a man.

"Well who am I to stop a husband from treating his wife to breakfast? Thank you, baby."

He walked away from the door and I took a deep breath, trying to gather myself so that I could have a productive day at church. I turned the shower and sink off, wiped my tears, and walked out and grabbed my Bible. I put the Bible on the bed and got down on my knees.

"God, I ask that you guide me today in your honor Father Lord. I ask that you move me to help others and continue to shine the light in my spirit so that I can reveal and heal the darkness in others Father God. I ask that your revelations be given to me for the ones who most need it God. I ask that you use me how you see fit God. I ask that you help me do your will God. God, I ask that you heal the hurt of my family Father God. Heal the hurt from my mistakes Father God. Show them that I loved my nephew and that I would never intentionally do anything like that Father God. Please forgive me God. Thank you, God. Thank you for everything, as your mercy is sufficient Father God. Amen."

It was one of several similar prayers that I repeated each Sunday before church. A woman of God can only walk when her steps are ordered, and even though I'd made great mistakes, I knew God was a forgiving God, and He still loved me no matter what I'd been through or experienced. After saying my prayer, I knew that everything that I'd been worrying about was about to be resolved.

As I got up off of my knees, I couldn't help but to notice a small red spot on my husband's shoes. It looked like blood, and I needed to make sure that he was ok. I picked the shoe up and walked into the kitchen.

"Baby... Are you bleeding somewhere? Are you ok? It's blood on this shoe." I held it up by the tongue so that he could see it.

"That's ketchup. I bought a hot dog from the food truck outside the club and I must have wasted it while walking and trying to eat. Babe, why you worry so much? Everything's good."

"Ok." He was right, I didn't need to worry so much. I guess I always felt like God was going to take away the person I loved since I took away my sister's son by accident. I was always worried that God was going to teach me a lesson in case He didn't think I'd suffered enough.

"But why is your make-up smeared? You been crying?" He asked.

"Nah, I was in the process of wiping it off to switch the color up and saw your shoe..." I told a protective lie. I didn't want to have our energy off on the way to church, but I knew I was going to come clean with him about my fight at some point. I loved Zaedan, and I didn't want him living a lie, or not knowing who he was married to... But a part of me felt like if he knew the real me, he would probably leave me. It was difficult to get myself to the point where I could make such a gamble.

"Baby I'm almost done, so go relax and I'll bring your plate to you. Voulez-vous du jus d'orange ou du café?"

"I'll need the coffee today; I'll get orange juice next time." I smiled.

"You're a good student." He said as he returned my smile.

"It's all you Zaedan. When my teacher is as fine as you, you can count on me being on principal's honor roll every semester."

He walked over and kissed me on the lips softly. That one kiss brought me back to reality. I was strong again, even if only just for a day. I needed to find the strength to push through, and I had found it through God and my husband. I was so happy he saw a wife in me, and equally happy that God saw fit for me to be one to Zaedan.

4

ZAEDAN

verything was great on the way to church that morning. I was dressed to the nines, as sharp as I could possibly get. Despite my street status, all of the mafia members under me understood that they needed not to disturb me on the day of worship unless I contact them. I was flawed but I still gave the glory to God, and I would always be the man to do that. My wife was as beautiful as she'd ever been, and never had I ever seen a woman more beautiful the whole time I'd been living. It was like God placed a golden circle around her, signifying that she was the one.

We were sitting on the front pew absorbing Pastor Gihanna's words when my wife suddenly screamed out and put her arms up. She dropped to her knees and let out a scream, and I picked up a fan and started fanning her to keep her cool. I stood up to make sure that she understood that I was right there for her. She screamed out louder, so loud that the pastor walked over to us, smiling.

"Brother Montez, Sister Montez are a God send to our church." The pastor spoke softly.

"Amen."

"Yes, they are."

"Amen."

Many members of the church spoke in agreement to what Pastor Gihanna was saying about us. It humbled me to know that me and my wife had the respect of the church, and it make me want to change my ways, however, I knew that if I did, I wouldn't be able to support as many people as I did. It was a catch-22."

"Prophetess Montez... Do you have anything on your heart today?"

The congregation applauded when my wife stood up and took the microphone from the Pastor. I applauded as loud as I could and stared at her in amazement as she walked down the aisle and stopped in front of a woman who seemed like she had it all together.

The woman was holding a designer purse, had on designer shoes, and extremely expensive jewelry. I remembered seeing the woman when we pulled in, because she came in a new Porsche Panamera.

"What's your name?" My wife asked her.

"Bonita."

"Bonita God has a message for you..."

"Hallelujah." The congregation spoke and applauded as they watched my wife in action. We all knew that she had a special gift, a psychic level gift but nobody truly knew how good she was except God, her and the person she was she speaking to.

"Bonita... God says you don't have to struggle no more."

"I'm not struggling." Bonita said defiantly, an embarrassed look on her face.

"Bonita... Oh Bonita... God told me to tell you... That the

house note that you missed... It's going to be paid but under one condition..."

"I didn't miss no house note." Bonita said in disbelief.

"God said go back to Madison Wisconsin and GET that little 9-year-old that you gave up to her Daddy. God said that 9-year-old girl needs her mama in her life! God said you don't have to allow what your mama did to you stop you from being a mama to your daughter! He says He's gon guide you in the right direction and He's gon take that tax lien off of your account if you go get your daughter! He said he's gon drop that lawsuit that you think you're going to lose! He said he's going to DROP it! Even though you were in the wrong and you burned that lady's ear by not paying attention, God is going to help you, so you KEEP your beauty salon! Your 9-year old daughter, Brielle.... She has a birthday coming up and God say he NEED you there with your daughter! Go GET YOUR DAUGHTER Bonita!"

Bonita was in tears listening to my wife speak to her, and my wife was in a zone like no other. She was spitting complete facts out of the thin blue sky as if she knew Bonita before today, when in fact, we'd never seen Bonita a day in our lives. Bonita was crying hysterically, her guard broken down because she knew that God was talking to her through my wife. She stood on her feet and reached out for a hug. My wife wrapped her arms around the lady while she cried in her embrace.

Once the lady sat down, my wife stood and stared at the door to the church.

"It's a spirit outside this door that wants to come in. It's an evil spirit, and it exists inside of a broken young woman. I see a woman with a baby. On the other side of this door in her car, and she's fighting God's words, and fighting the devil's words too. She's broken and torn, and she doesn't know what to do because of all of her wrongdoing. If we can get her to come on into this church, God has a message for her. Someone open the door please..."

I began to panic because I knew she wasn't just making stuff up, and based on the description of the woman, I knew was potentially talking about Tarralla. My blood pressure elevated to the max, and I was sure that my life was about to be over. Two ushers opened the door and there she was standing there with a baby in her arms.

Tarralla.

I knew I had some explaining to do.

"You can come in... It's ok..." My wife said to her.

"Oh, I'm sorry, I was looking for another place, I'm sorry." Tarralla said and turned around.

"No, you're in the right place baby..." My wife spoke through the microphone.

Tarralla walked faster; ran to her car and put the baby in the car seat. My wife started walking towards the door and I started walking after her. Tarralla got in her car, started it up and had the car in reverse before my wife could make it to the door.

"Her spirit is torn! God has a message for her that I have to give her, but she's fighting the devil so bad that she doesn't know right from wrong right now!" My wife spoke as she stared into the admiring eyes of the congregation.

She walked back to the front of the church and stood before everyone. "Those of you who need personal prayer, come see me."

I knew when my wife dealt with extremely deep spirits that it took a lot out of her emotionally and physically, and today was one of those days. I went and stood beside her and pulled out my checkbook. I reached for the microphone and she handed it to me.

"I would like to donate $50,000 to the church today. Pastor will get with any of you going through any hardships, and he'll help those that are in need. This is on behalf of *Free Wi-Fi*, and on behalf of my wife and me."

The congregation applauded and screamed, but it wasn't about that for me. I genuinely wanted to give back and help as many people as I could whenever the spirit called for me to do so. I didn't have the talents that my wife had, but we definitely worked well together. Not just in church, but in life in general. I sat down on the pew and watched the line of people go to my wife for personal prayer, knowing that I needed to be one of those people.

A guy walked up to me and reached his hand out for a handshake. I shook it.

"Hey Zaedan..." He said.

"Hey deacon."

"Y'all gon have the casino open tonight?"

"Yea, I'll call your phone and let you know which warehouse it's going to be at."

"I can't wait. Will ya'll have blackjack and a craps table tonight?"

"We'll have everything deacon."

The gentle sound of dice tapping against each other, the sound of disappointment from every loss, and the occasional win for a short-lived victory. The aroma of stress sticks– cigarettes and marijuana depending on your plant of preference, both decorated the abandoned warehouse. Ten electric generators powered the pop-up casino in the middle of downtown Atlanta. It was a brave move by Zaedan, but it was expected, as he was known for making fearless decisions.

It had taken him and the team three hours to turn an abandoned warehouse into a fully functional Las Vegas style casino. Club speakers were aligned along the walls, and there were waitresses walking around topless, wearing nothing on their entire bodies but G-strings and stilettos, and carrying trays of Hennessy, Patron, and pre-rolled blunts. Zaedan opened a casino once per week, and on a typical night he made between $1 million to $2 million in revenue. Most weeks, there would be a decent profit to be made, but then there were some weeks where he broke even with the revenue vs payouts. He hadn't been running it long, plus his location changed each week, so he knew that once the word got out about it a little more.

Some weeks he made a huge profit from some of the ballers from the city. In order to keep the ballers coming to gamble with him, he had to also make it attractive for the people who could barely afford to gamble. Nothing spelled disaster like an empty casino, no matter how illegal it was. So, to help those who couldn't afford it, he gave payday loans to those who asked for it, regardless of their credit. He wasn't worried about them paying him back, because they all knew what would happen if they didn't.

The casino chips had to be purchased at the door, and all had serial numbers and a digital imprint on them so that they couldn't be cloned. The cashiers had been instructed to cash in chips without hassle or argument, and it was this ease of collecting money that made it a trustworthy operation for anyone with aspirations of getting quick money.

Zaedan sat in a gold chair at a table with 3 trash bags full of money sitting beside him. His most trusted– his right-hand guy, Bullethead, sat across from him with his sunglasses on. He was cock-eyed, and hated when people looked at him funny, so he decided to save their lives by eliminating the possibility of all jokes. Maclente, Zaedan's main lawyer, sat at a desk in the corner with his laptop open. Antonio, Zaedan's tax attorney sat beside him writing down some of the keypoints that Maclente was mentioning to him. Brizzo, Zaedan's handy man, paced back and forth by the window. He had a headset on, and Wilburt, who was handy man number 2 was on the other end, reporting any and everything that took place on the casino floor.

"Zae. How was church?" Bullethead asked as he shifted in his seat. The big man leaned inward intensely to hear what his boss had to say.

"Church was church..." Zaedan answered nonchalantly.

Bullethead nodded. He knew when his boss didn't want to discuss something, so he left it alone. Instead, he sat back in the seat and rubbed his finger under his chin, deep in thought.

"What?"

"Huh?" Bullethead asked, caught off-guard to Zaedan's question.

"You're thinking something. What is it?"

"Oh, it's nothing honestly…"

"Honestly it's obviously not. So, tell me what's up." Zaedan said firmly.

"Oh, I was just wondering about the girl with the baby. If she came to church… Or if you need me to get somebody to go talk to her."

Zaedan shook his head. "See I knew it was something… And nah, don't worry about it. It's personal, it's not official family business."

"Boss with all due respect…" Bullethead began, "I think I speak for all of us when I say this… and forgive me for being out of place… but whatever you go through, is what *we* go through. Your personal business is our family business, and we're willing to solve any problem, especially somebody that needed a good talking to."

"Somebody needs a good talking to?" Brizzo asked enthusiastically. His senses were elevated upon hearing that phrase. In their world, talking to meant a few broken bones, and a good talking to, meant that that was the last conversation a person would ever have on this earth.

"Brizzo… relax. Bullethead, chill. I'm good. It's just a small misunderstanding. It's something I'm going to handle soon, I promise."

Zaedan knew that every decision he made set precedents for everybody under him. He didn't want a woman who got pregnant to die or get hurt even though she was trying to blackmail him. There were certain limits he placed for how his organization moved, and many of them were drawn from standard mob rules, yet many of them were new and improved. He didn't want any hurt for kids or women, they were always innocent of the sins of their fathers and husbands. And as far as a woman who wanted to see if she could blackmail him… he wasn't worried in the least bit.

Zaedan glanced at his watch and walked over to the window facing the casino floor. He watched as some of the local hustlers and working-class men alike stood around the dice tables and prayed that they hit their numbers. He'd seen enough dice games in his lifetime to know that the dice could never be controlled. No matter how two dice were tossed, it would always hit the number 7 more than any other number. And as long as that science was a fact, people were always going to lose on dice tables.

He glanced around at the familiar faces in the casino and stopped when he saw a light skinned guy with a large pile of chips in front of him, and an equally large crowd standing around his particular table.

"Who the hell is that?" Zaedan asked as he pointed at the guy in confusion.

Brizzo walked over to where Zaedan was standing and squinted his eyes as he looked in the direction that he was pointing. "That guy with the purple shoes on?"

"Yea. Him."

"I never seen him before."

"You never seen him before? Well who let him in?" Who invited him?" Zaedan asked, concern draping his voice.

Bullethead made his way to the window. "I think y'all talking about Pretty Tony. I think he had on purple shoes today. I invited him if that's who y'all talking about."

"Who the hell is Pretty Tony?" Zaedan asked as he watched the man win another huge pile of his money. "What the fuck. Aye, Brizzo go check on that situation. Make sure his dice ain't trick dice. Make sure everything's on the up and up."

"Zae that's Pretty Tony from the singing group." Bullet-head said with a smile on his face.

Zaedan looked at Bullethead curiously and returned an

all too knowing smile. "What? Oh hell. Well don't worry about it. Brizzo, tell WIlburt to ask Pretty Tony if he needs anything. They were on the Forbes list a few months ago as one of the highest earning singing groups. I'd love to keep his business. Let him play. Even if he gets a good win today, he'll bring it back and more the next time we open the casino up."

Zaedan smiled as he stared on at the casino floor. It was a genius idea. The casino itself wasn't his most profitable line of business, but the payday loan service that was attached to the casino was dependent on the lure of the casino– *that* was one of his most profitable businesses. If most people just ignored the dream of getting rich quick and making fast money, they would have way more money to do things with. But instead, they couldn't stay away. They were addicted.

"Boss, did you think about the thing I mentioned?" Brizzo asked as he put his hand in his pocket while waiting on Zaedan to reply.

"Thing you mentioned. What thing? I thought I asked you to check and see if Pretty Tony needed anything."

"My fault Zae. I'll be right back." Brizzo said as he walked out of the room and made his way to the casino floor.

"Zaedan. Come here a quick second please." Maclente, Zaedan's lawyer spoke out while holding his hand on his forehead. The way he was looking, Zaedan knew something was wrong. He exhaled as he approached the attorneys, dreading thinking the worst.

"What's wrong now?" Zaedan shook his head as he stood in front of the computer and the lawyers.

"Well, I'm afraid we have a small issue... You've been reporting that you've made this amount of money, yet you've been spending out this amount of money... At the moment, the paperwork isn't adding up, and the government is going to see fit to wave a red flag."

Zaedan frowned. "Oh, fucking K, so fix the shit. That's y'all's job. Why the hell y'all bothering me with this shit?"

Antonio, the tax attorney spoke up with anger in his voice. "It's our job to advise you when we spot an error being made, and– "

"Yo who the fuck you think you talking to?" Bullethead said as he walked up to him. "Lower your fucking tone."

Antonio exhaled. He was passionate about his job, despite the fact that he was directly working for the black mafia. But he knew he couldn't risk being fired, being that the black mafia was his only client at the time. And in order to not be fired, he had to keep the paperwork in order so that his client could continue to prosper and handle his business.

"Nah, you're right. Both of you are right." Antonio said. "I can fix this... But Zaedan... You'll have to let me handle all the paperwork from now on. All of this stuff has to be done to perfection with the FBI and IRS constantly breathing down your neck. We can't afford any flaws."

Zaedan exhaled and walked away. He'd prided himself on being able to handle all of his own paperwork, and to his recollection, he couldn't recall any such moment of being distracted enough to commit an error. Men from the streets were already aware that Zaedan was just as book smart as he was street smart. Men from corporate America was unaware of this fact, and in fact, he found himself becoming at odds with more men from corporate America than men from the streets. He found out over time that men from the streets knew they were breaking the law, and they owned up to it. Men from corporate America thought that nobody could see through their bullshit. While there was a slim chance that he'd made an error, there was an even slimmer chance that he didn't.

He wholeheartedly trusted Maclente, but it was Antonio who he still had questions about. He made a mental note to dive deeper into the issue later.

"Maclente, you gon handle that?" Zaedan said once he reached the window again.

"I think this is more of something Antonio specializes in more than me." Maclente said with a confused look on his face.

Zaedan looked at Antonio. "My fault. I said the wrong name. I was meaning you Antonio. You gon handle it for me?"

"Oh, it's ok. Yes, I can handle it for you. You may have to make me the power of attorney over your main account so I can move some stuff around for you."

Zaedan looked at Maclente, who looked at Bullethead, who looked at Zaedan. It was such a bold statement, so arrogant that it came across as though it made sense. But Zaedan knew it made no sense at all. Instead, he decided to play along. "Yea. Aight. I'll hop on that tomorrow after lunch."

Antonio picked up the 20 pages he had been working on, slapped the bottom against the desk so that they made a neat stack, took a stapler to it and placed it inside of his briefcase. The door opened and Brizzo peeped his head in. "Zaedan... lemme speak to you for a second."

"Speak."

"In private please."

"There is no privacy amongst us. What you say to me, I'll eventually say to them."

"You're right." Brizzo felt foolish for even requesting a

private conversation. He walked in and closed the door. "Well... I asked Pretty Tony if it was anything, I could do for him– anything you can do for him... He said if he can get some white girl, he'll be able to stay all night."

"Come again?" Zaedan frowned.

"White girl. Pretty Tony wants some white girl."

"What the fuck? He wants a bitch?"

"He wants cocaine."

"Nigga do I looked like a fuckin drug dealer? We don't sell no fuckin drugs. Why the fuck would you even come repeat that shit?"

"Well that's what I wanted to speak to you in private about Zaedan. I wanted to see if you would allow me to start a new division so we can really increase our money and power."

Zaedan looked at him with a face full of disgust. He looked at Bullethead, who was just looking out of the window and shaking his head. He walked over to Brizzo and stared at him. "My nigga listen to me clearly. Never in your life approach me talking about some damn drugs. You hear me? I don't run no fucking drug cartel. I don't peddle no cocaine. I'm not no got damn low-level kingpin. Nigga I'm a real boss. See... niggaz who move drugs only control the city for a few months, and then they graduate to prison. This happens every year, every season, and every single time somebody gets busted, some new stupid nigga wants to be what the old stupid nigga was.

As long as you've known me, I've been preaching real power, real elevation, real ideas. Look how many laws we break each day. We got all kinda shit going on except for drugs. We got the FBI sitting around taking pictures of us every time we walk to the mailbox. But can they fuck with us? Ask yourself why... It's because they don't have something as stupid as drugs to connect us with. They think black mafias can't exist. They think we don't have the mind capacity to run the streets without drug money. But I've been proving them wrong for years now. You tell that nigga Pretty Tony, that if he needs anything else... Cash, women, a kidney, a liver, a new car, a credit card, a new identity, a new driver's license, a new house, anything besides drugs– he can get anything else he may so desire."

Brizzo nodded his head and walked out without further comment.

Bullethead shook his head. "I'ma have to keep my eye on that young nigga. This isn't the first time he's mentioned wanting to sell drugs. He's mentioned it when you weren't around in the past, but I'm guessing this is the first time he's mentioned it to you. He's tripping something terrible."

"Yea but it's going to be all good." Zaedan checked his watch. "Aight, aye... Bullethead I'm about to head to open up the hookah lounge for the night. Have this place shut down in the next 90 minutes."

"I know the routine. How long will you be at the lounge tonight? You opening and leaving, or you staying through the night?"

"I'm opening and leaving. You know I got that thing..."

Bullethead nodded. "Right. I remember you told me you had that thing... Ok. Well be safe, and you know... hit me if you need me."

You know I got that thing– was one of Zaedan's favorite phrases. He would use it when in front of others to make it seem as if the person he was talking to knew something that other people didn't. The reality of it was that nobody ever knew what the thing was. Everybody assumed it was just personal business in general, and that he didn't feel like going into details about it.

Even though Zaedan owned some expensive cars and clothing, it wasn't a part of his day to day usage. He drove a new Honda Accord with dark tints and wore suits from J.C. Penny. It wasn't that he didn't have style, or that he didn't have money, he just found that he had better use for his money instead of spending it on impressing people whose opinions meant nothing. He walked out of the back exit of the warehouse and locked the door. As he walked to his car, two federal agents in plain clothes got out of the car parked right beside his.

"Zaedan. How are ya?" The short agent smiled.

Zaedan smiled back. "I'm great. I'm having a much better day than you two are."

"Huh?" The taller agent asked. "What makes you say that?"

"Well... it's a fact. For the past two years y'all have been following me around taking pictures of me. That's a terrible life what it sounds like to me. I'd be pissed if I had to dedicate my life to taking pictures of a nigga who didn't give a fuck about me."

The short FBI agent shook his head and put his hands in his pocket. He watched as Zaedan walked to his car and opened the door.

"Is there anything I can help you with? Or y'all just like when I acknowledge your miserable existence?"

"Well... We were hoping you could help us out with something."

"I doubt it, but I'll listen to it. Why not get free information from the government? It's not like it's doing you all any good." Zaedan laughed as he continued teasing the FBI agents.

"Yea... Well... two pieces of information actually." The tall agent started as he walked up to Zaedan. "You know anything about who brought in the latest fentanyl shipment? Our sources estimate that it's been nearly 1,000 pounds of that shit in Atlanta. It's pretty important... There's been many overdose deaths being reported off of bad drugs."

Zaedan looked at him like he was a lame. "Do I look like I fucking know? Do I look like a damn drug dealer?"

The short federal agent shook his head. "Zaedan. Our sources have painted you as one of the biggest kingpins in Atlanta. We know for a fact you're moving drugs, and it's only a matter of time before you slip up. Us asking you about this fentanyl will actually help you out in the future once we bust you and you're facing life."

Zaedan looked at him like he was the scum of the earth. "Well if your sources knew so much, then you can find out all the information you need to know about the fentanyl. Why the hell would you ask me instead of your source?" He smiled as he mocked the agents.

The tall agent exhaled. "Ok that's fair. Well... I had another question for you. You ever heard of Peter Blacklou?"

Zaedan shook his head. "Nope never heard of him a day in my life."

"That's funny you say that... See back at the office, we have a picture that you two took not too long ago, but you say you've never heard of him."

"I take a lot of pictures with people I don't know... I'm a celebrity."

The short agent was tired of the back and forth. "Yea well do all of your fans end up missing, or just him? He's been missing for about a month now, and a few people said one of the last people he was supposed to meet with was you. So, where's the body?"

Zaedan smiled at the agents. His teeth were perfect, his smile was bright, and his aura was powerful. He was never intimidated in any situation, and that situation was going to be no different. "I've never heard of him a day in my life. But I'm running late. I have a thing to do. However, I know y'all still got questions for me, so I can send my lawyer down to grab the other questions from y'all while I go handle my business. How's that?"

The agents turned and walked away from him and towards their car. They stood at their car and watched as Zaedan got in his car and drove off. They'd been investigating Zaedan for two years at that point, yet they had been unable to indict him on any major charges. That was causing a lot of tension amongst the agents especially because his name had come up in everything from murders, kidnapping, and weapons sales; although no proof of any wrongdoing had ever been presented. It was nonstop hearsay.

The agents got in the car, put their seatbelts on and just sat in silence. The short agent was the first to speak. "What do you think Bobby?"

The taller agent closed his eyes for a second to let the anger dissipate. "What do I think? I think he's fucking full of shit. That's what I think. He's definitely selling drugs, probably more drugs than anybody has ever sold in the state of Georgia. There's no way a person could rise to power so fast, have so many men under him, have so much money without selling drugs– I mean... It's possible... But a black man from Atlanta? Heavy in the streets like he is? And with all of the fentanyl that keeps popping up here with no explanation? We have to get to the bottom of this if it's the last thing.

The short agent, Frankie T, nodded his head as he listened to his partner speak. He took it all in, processed it, and exhaled. "Bobby... What if we're wrong about this one?"

"Wrong? Wrong how?"

"What if we're wasting our time? What if he's not selling drugs? What if he's not even breaking any laws?"

"What? No chance in hell. Don't let the bosses hear you say something like that. You're an FBI agent. We– are FBI agents. We got to bat for our colleagues, and we investigate what we're told to investigate according to our assignments and resources. We don't put down our own intel, we're the best in the world. You should be ashamed."

"Yea, you're right Bobby. I won't say it again. We're going to get to the bottom of this case once and for all."

5

BRIZZO

I stood by Pretty Tony and watched as he continued to toss dice and win money. He was on a helluva lucky streak, and everybody at the table was cheering for him. I checked out his diamond watch, diamond chain, $1400 pair of Amiri Jeans, $1400 Off-White purple sneakers– and I couldn't help but to envy his style. He had three women with him, all drop dead gorgeous, and all with at least one hand on his body. The power that Pretty Tony was commanding in the casino seemed to rival that of the electricity that lit the place up.

"Hell yea." He yelled as he rolled another 8, winning him another $5,000. He held two hands up and high-fived two of his female companions, and then used the same two hands to high five– high-ten rather– his third female companion. The first female took a blunt from out of her purse and placed it in Pretty Tony's mouth. The third companion took a lighter from out of her own purse and handed it to the second female, who lit his blunt for him. In my whole lifetime, I'd never seen something so simple as lighting a blunt be done as breathtakingly complex and beautiful as what I'd just witnessed.

Damn. I actually had to wipe my mouth– I was drooling just looking at another man's life. Pretty Tony glanced at me. "Yo... You got that for me?"

I was so confused; I didn't even know what he was talking about. "Huh? Got what?"

"You forgot already? Don't worry about it. I'll get it."

As soon as he replied, I remembered exactly what he was talking about. I remained silent as my thoughts beat against Zaedan's words. I knew Zaedan meant well, and I knew Zaedan had my best interests at heart, but sometimes I just think he was unaware of the potential we could have if we expanded to selling drugs as well as everything else we had going on. I mean... the shit we were already were doing was some of the most heinous shit in the world as it was. I just felt like... if we added drugs to the shit we were already doing, we would be making a million dollars a week at the worst. Sometimes I thought that Zaedan just wasn't aware of the power he really had. Us– as a crew, we would be the most powerful crew in the world. The most powerful in the world in my opinion was always the ones who controlled the products.

I watched as Pretty Tony continued to play, and he eventually crapped out, hitting a number 7 with the dice, and losing nearly $40,000 that he had placed on the table in bets. That was a small loss for him though, because he'd been up financially since he'd been winning the entire night. When he lost, they passed the dice to another shooter to roll, and Tony put more money on the table to bet on the new dice roller.

He leaned over to the girl who took the blunt out of her purse and pointed at a guy who was playing blackjack at another table. I glanced and new it was a local dopeboy and figured that he was going to make a drug purchase regardless of who he bought it from. He peeled off a few thousand off of his bankroll and handed it to her. She walked over and whispered something to him, and he whispered something back to her. He got up from the card table and let her sit at his spot to play his hand out while he walked outside. After a few moments, he walked back to the table and took over his hand and handed her a brown bag. She glanced inside, handed him the money, took the brown bag to Pretty Tony and the other girls, and they all glanced inside it. There were huge smiles on all of their faces.

"Hell yea." Pretty Tony expressed as he threw a deuce up to the local dope boy. "Aight this my last game y'all. We about to really go have a party."

Uneasily I made eye contact with one of the girls who was with him. She stared at me and it made me nervous. I had no idea why... Hell I was one of the worst men on the planet. If anybody should have been nervous it should have been her ass. I couldn't explain the feeling though. It was as if I just knew better and still engaged.

"You wanna party with us?" She asked and laughed.

Her question caught me by surprise. I didn't wanna be rude by showing any type of interest to another man's woman, regardless of how many he had. I knew better than that.

"Oh nah, I'm good." I spoke nervously.

Pretty Tony laughed. "Bro you can come. You might as well. Shit all we do is party anyways, and we appreciate you tryna look out for us. Shit if you want to just come down to Lockwerk Studio in Buckhead later on tonight after midnight. Knowing us, we'll probably have a few more bitches around and you can fuck with one. Or two." He laughed as if he'd just told a hilarious joke.

As I was about to reply, Wilburt walked up and tapped me in the center of my chest. "What's up Will?"

"Damn lil one. You haven't heard nothing I been saying through your headset? I been saying let's wrap it up for the past ten minutes bro."

I glanced down and realized I'd turned the volume down and forgot to turn it back up. "Man, my fault Wilburt. Aight, I'm on it. Let's shut down. My bad bro."

I started to walk to grab the microphone when Wilburt grabbed my arm. "Aye bro... You gotta focus... I don't know where your head has been lately, but you know we gotta do better. We gotta stay alert."

I nodded my head because he was right. Me and Wilburt had been running with the crew for years now, and we both considered ourselves handy men– Basically soldiers; if you will. Most of the stuff that Zaedan or Bullethead didn't handle was stuff that we handled. To clarify it... if it was simple or private, it was something that Zaedan or Bullet-head handled. If it was messy or complex, it was something we handled. To simplify it even more... If you fuck up, do something wrong, and piss Zaedan off... If you were alone or with one person present, Zaedan or Bullethead would put a bullet in your head. If you were in the presence of 3 people, or in the presence of a large crowd of people, me and Wilburt might open fire on your whole damn crew.

Me and Wilburt were airtight, and nobody knew me and my tendencies better than him. We understood each other because we were the same type of people. Men who did whatever it took to accomplish their goals. I announced the end of the casino for the night and watched as Bullethead came down to help us make sure nobody was left behind in the warehouse. The camera man walked up and gave us his footage. Bullethead gave him an envelope with some cash in it and a hug. The camera man walked back to his camera crew and they took the equipment out to their trucks.

Zaedan had rented the warehouse claiming that he was going to be shooting a rap video in there, so by him hiring the actual videographers, it made everything he was saying seem just that much more legit. In actuality, we were about to burn the tape and go help count up what was probably close to a million dollars in cash. We had a pretty unique way of going about things on casino nights. After we finished our count, we would leave the money behind stashed away and hidden, and since Zaedan always rented the warehouses out for three days at a time, he would always arrange for one of us to come back and get it either a day or two days later. We would all leave the premises carrying empty briefcases, so in the event that anybody wanted to try something funny, their results would be even funnier. For the most part though, people knew not to try us because they knew we didn't play out here.

When we got outside to our vehicles, we all noticed the FBI surveillance, but we had become so used to it that we didn't even mention it. They had been following us for years, but they knew not to do anything stupid because we had our attorney *on hand* at all times. That was one situation that made their jobs a living hell. They probably would have moved recklessly had it not been for that, but they knew they had to come correct, and since we weren't going to make any dumb mistakes, they'd never get the opportunity to come at us. I approached Maclente, about to give him our customary handshake, but he ignored me and opened his car door. I smirked. He knew I liked living on the edge sometimes, and I'd been dying for the FBI to get our handshake on camera so they could try to decipher the meaning. It wasn't like it meant anything, but I guess Maclente felt it was just another way to identify us as one. I didn't feel that way because hell... all the footage they'd had of us already... They already knew we were one.

"Drive safe Maclente. Antonio." I tossed the deuce at his stuck-up ass and went and opened my car door. I was about to get in, but a thought hit me. "Aye Wilburt. What you bout to get into?"

"What? My bed. I gotta handle something out of town for boss in the morning."

"Oh yea, I forgot tomorrow is Monday. You need me to come witcha?"

"Hell nawl, you know boss always want me to handle this trip solo."

I nodded my head. Me and Wil were tight, but not tighter than him and Zaedan. He had been making a trip out of town every Monday to handle something for the past year straight, and I never had even so much as a clue where he was traveling to or what he was traveling for. The only thing I was sure of, was that his trip always generated a lot of money. I was bound to find out one of these Mondays, but apparently not that Monday.

"Cool. Well drive safe homey. Hit me if you need me."

"Bet. Where the hell you bout to go? Why you ask what I was about to do? Don't get in no trouble bro."

"Ah hell naw. I'ma go post up and see if Zae need anything... Go fuck with him a little at the spot... And then I'ma go head home too. Nothing really going on. Just a slow-motion Sunday."

"Dig that. Aight say no more. I'ma hit you tomorrow bro."

"Aight bet."

I was the last one to finally leave the warehouse parking lot, and I noticed the FBI were deciding to follow me that particular Sunday night. I was surprised they weren't following Bullethead or Zaedan per usual, but I guess they wanted to see what activities I was about to get into. I didn't mind at all. I knew that having the FBI follow me would provide me free security guards courtesy of the United States government. They thought they were slick, but I was a little slicker. I was most definitely going to hit a club or two now that I had free security. But first... I was going to drop by the studio in Buckhead and see what kind of party Pretty Tony was having.

ZAEDAN

E very Sunday after midnight, my hookah lounge was packed to capacity. Not only was it a source of legitimate business, it was also a place for me to show my face to the streets for a few moments. The way I was getting money, it required me to be able to speak to the everyday man or woman, plus this was going to help me out with my longterm goals of one day getting into politics. I was aware that that could be a longshot with the kind of shit I had going on, but hey... a man can dream right?

I sat behind my bar as the crowd came in a few people at a time. My security made sure that nobody brought in weapons and the DJ had it feeling like a nightclub environment. I didn't plan on being there long, I just wanted to show my face for a little while and get home to my wife. I grabbed my phone and sent her a text to let her know I was thinking of her.

I love you. I'll be home soon.

Right as I hit send, a young lady walked to the bar and sat on one of the stools. She was light skinned, had long hair, a typical Instagram model shape– typical Atlanta nightlife. I was sure that if I were to look at her social media profiles her pictures would average about 6,000 likes each. Since I'd just opened the doors not long ago, my bartenders were in the back preparing themselves for the night they were about to endure. People didn't typically want drinks as soon as they came in the door. Most people wanted to feel it out first and decided later if they needed a drink or not. She was different.

"Hey excuse me." Her voice was lightweight, weak almost; kinda like she was just exhausted from talking and only had a few words remaining in her to speak. I got down off of my seat and walked over to her. "How can I help you?"

"Give me a double shot of the strongest cognac you have to offer, but mix it with something sweet. And give me a sugar rim as well."

"Aight. I got you." I didn't want to turn down any customers, even those who wanted to drink alcohol earlier than normal. I turned and sent a text to my top bartender—letting her know to bring her azz in there to make the woman a drink and climbed back into my chair so that I could get back to minding my business.

"Damn it's like that?" She said as she frowned at me.

"Huh? What's like what?"

"You're not going to fix my drink?"

I smiled at her just to let her know that I meant no harm concerning the choice of words I was about to use. "Baby... I'm not the bartender, I'm the owner. But I tell you what... If my bartender doesn't have your drink made in the next five minutes, I'll give you a free $300 bottle on the house."

She gave him a smirk, exhaled, and nodded her head. After about twenty seconds had passed, she looked at him hesitantly. "Well I have a better idea."

I was starting to get irritated. I liked people, and was

generally a people's person, but at that moment I'd had a few things on my mind and didn't feel like making pointless small talk. Especially after what I'd just saw being shared on Facebook– there were a few people sharing news links about a man who'd been electrocuted on Saturday night at his home. The way the media reported it– it was a particularly heartless, heinous crime.

"Alright... What's your better idea?"

"Let me be one of your bartenders. I promise I'll never be late... And I need the job honestly. I'm a single mother trying to raise my kids here in Atlanta."

I don't know why that sentence startled me... maybe because I'd judged her completely different based on how she looked, and I immediately felt bad about it. "You wanna bartend here? I'm not open every day... just a few days a week, so this would be a part-time position... and the bartenders make their living off of tips... Which might not be good or might be good; just depends."

"I don't care. I'm really doing bad right now. This would help me take care of my little one." She grabbed her phone and fumbled with it for a second and started scrolling until she found what she was looking for. She held it out for me to see.

I reluctantly got up and walked over to see what she was trying to show me. It was an Instagram picture with her and her kids, with a caption attached to it that read: *It's just us against the world.* I wasn't too far off with my first guess either, because that photo she was showing me had 4,000 likes. Maybe she would bring more business just based on her following. I guess it wouldn't hurt to let her bartend.

"Have you ever bartended before? Do you have a license?"

"Yes, and yes."

"Can you start Wednesday?"

"I was actually hoping I could start now."

I nodded my head. "Ok, I'll let Blue– the manager know that you're hired. He'll be with you in a little bit. I wish you the best, and hopefully you do great tonight."

"Ok sir. Thank you so much. I really appreciate the opportunity, and I won't let you down ever."

"Not an issue. Wait, what's your name?"

"Ares."

"Huh? Arrest? Like jail?"

"No... A-R-E-S. Just... Ares."

I couldn't even say it was nice meeting a lady named arrest. It was nothing else for me to say to her at that point. I walked off and glanced out of the window at the parking lot on my way to the office. I had quite a bit of traffic outside waiting to come in. Tonight should be profitable, which was always the point. I called Bullethead, and he answered on the second ring.

"What's up family?"

"Hey, nothing much, seems we have a decent sized crowd here at the lounge tonight; what's good your way?"

"Ah man... Well we wrapped up at the casino, and tonight we ended with $630,000."

"That's it?"

"Yea... I think that Pretty Tony cat made a nice little profit off of us. Unless people just didn't go big tonight, I'm not sure. I'll look at the tapes later."

"Cool cool. Where you at right now?"

"I'm almost home right now. I wanted to come to the lounge, but I gotta get up at 4 in the morning to handle that thing you wanted me to handle."

"Oh yea, get your rest so you can be sharp. That guy needs a good talking to."

"And I'm going to definitely talk to him real good family."

"Say no more. Respect."

"Respect. Family if you need me for anything, my ringer will be on."

"Nah, all should be fine at this point. I'm about to go home to my wife. Oh yea... did those people follow you when you left? Or did they follow Maclente? I was surprised they didn't follow me when they left, but I don't see them outside. Or maybe they took the rest of the night off?"

Bullethead paused for a second. He was so used to them following him or Zaedan that he didn't even think about what he'd seen when he left. "Actually... Oh yea, Maclente text me and told me they followed Brizzo tonight."

I felt my heart skip a beat. Brizzo was not only younger, but younger-minded as well. I knew that if Brizzo wasn't Ayoki's cousin, I would have never had a guy like him around me. I also knew that he was going to get in the streets whether he had me guiding and protecting him or not. So, for the sake of my wife; who asked me to give him a job some time ago... I decided to try to limit his errors so that he wouldn't be his own downfall; and especially so he wouldn't be mine. Over time, he'd shown me he was a dependable soldier, but at times I could tell that he would need to switch occupations and do something different. Something about how he moved and thought told me that he wouldn't have real longevity in the streets.

"Family you there?" Bullethead asked, breaking me out of my reverie.

"My fault. Yea I'm here. Let me hit Brizzo up. I'll check in with you in a minute."

"Bet."

7

AYOKI

My mind was frazzled, and I couldn't think straight. It started at church when I laid eyes on the lady who was holding the baby. I couldn't see her face because of the way the sun was shining, but she felt so familiar to me, close to some degree. I didn't know what kind of battles or demons she was facing internally, but I could tell she was going through some things, and I knew God had a message to give to her... I just couldn't get her to come to God. That was going to bother me, because every time I had a message from God, I made sure to do all that I could to deliver that message to His intended recipient. I never held back because I never knew how badly another person needed to hear it.

The yellow car I saw in my vision, I didn't know why I kept pointing across the street when I was trying to show my husband my vision, but I'm glad that he realized that I was having a long day. A part of me felt like the LSD had me tripping for a minute, but my husband seemed to be ok with chalking it up to me just needing to rest. Still I felt a sickening to my stomach that I couldn't completely explain. I had a bad feeling about Bullethead, my husband's friend, and I knew that he was who my husband spent the most time with, so I needed to make sure that he was ok.

I called Zaedan's phone, and he answered it right away.

"Hey."

"Baby... I want you home with me... Please?" I asked him gently.

"You never have to beg me to come home bae. I'm headed home now. I can't wait to make love to you, spend some time with you..."

It was as if there was something else he wanted to say, but couldn't; and didn't. "Were you about to say something else?" I asked him gently.

"No... That's it... I just wanna spend some time with you... I'm headed home right now."

There was a brief pause, then I asked the question that had been sitting on my spirit.

"Is Brizzo ok?"

There was another pause, and then a deep exhale, as if he was measuring the words he was about to tell me. Zaedan got like that when he was in deep thought or coming out of deep prayer.

"Baby... I think it's time for us to get out of Atlanta soon. I think we should finish up our ministry here and move to Miami so we can get us a beach home like you've always wanted."

His words made my heart so happy. I so wanted to escape the darkness and start over. I always told myself that maybe if I started over in a brighter place that it would erase some of the darker memories that I had to fight away so often. I'd always expressed that I wanted a beach house with an ocean front patio. He'd worked so hard with building his businesses, and I wanted to embrace the rewards while we were able to. Also, with me being in a new place, it would make it harder for me to have access to drugs.

"I agree Zaedan. I'd love to do just that. That's a great idea."

I was so happy. I was smiling so hard that he would have thought I was unhappy with my current life, and that was definitely not the case... it was just that I was about to be sooo much happier than I was currently.

"Well I'm headed back right now. I figure I can wrap up everything here in the next 3 months, and we'll be on our way to Florida; for good."

"Alright baby. I'll see you when you get here."

He had no clue how happy he'd made me, but I was surely about to show him. The way he'd just excited me— I didn't even realize that he'd just skipped over the questions about Brizzo until I'd hung up the phone. All of my bad thoughts left my mind, and I jumped into the shower. I used the Sparkling Moon bath and body gel and put on my red panties with the black fur strings. I put on the matching red bra with the black fur strap— these were garments that were only suitable to be taken off; and I knew that's exactly what he was going to do the moment he arrived.

I told myself that I was about to go to the living room when he arrived, but instead, I ended up laying down for a quick 2-minute nap and ended up falling asleep well beyond 2 minutes.

8

BRIZZO

The FBI continued to trail me from the southside of Atlanta, all the way until I got downtown. Even though they tried to disguise that they were following me, they knew I knew, and they knew I didn't give a fuck. I was in my blue Corvette convertible, and even though it was wintertime, I considered letting my top down to really let them know I didn't give the first fuck. As I drove, I suddenly had an idea. Zaedan always taught me to use every situation to my advantage, and always think ten steps ahead of my competition. He always made me study chess strategies, and at that moment I'd thought of one of the best chess moves ever.

There was a group of niggaz I went to school with who had been calling me out and talking shit about me recently. Not only was it me they were talking about, they were talking about us— my crew. When I mentioned it to Bullet-head or Zaedan, they always said... *Since we don't have any business with them, we ignore them. That's not a problem we'll entertain.* But I knew that everything in the streets isn't about business, no matter how much Zaedan kept trying to act like it was. Shit is real out here, and for people that *don't* have business with us, their currency was respect. If they feel they've disrespected you and got away with it, that was worth a million dollars to them.

I made a quick detour and started driving to Decatur where the young niggaz were running a chop shop and trap house all on the same block. I slowed down to let the FBI catch up to me, not to be obvious, but just to be certain. There was no way I would ever drive down them young boys' block without them alphabet boys following me. The last time I had an encounter with them, I'd taken my girl-friend to the dine-in movie theater with me in Buckhead. They were saying all kinds of slick shit throughout the movie, really being rude and aiming it towards me even though they were trying to play it off. At one point I stood up and told my girl I was about to head to the bathroom. When I stood up, three of them stood up; and my girl, when she realized what was happening, pulled my arm and asked me not to leave her.

They were jealous of me. I guess because we were all the same age and I was doing better than them despite me not having to sell drugs. But what they didn't realize was... I was doing shit way more extreme than anything they could ever sign up for. I had real bodies under my belt and knew there was no stopping in sight. Killing a person was like having a drink of alcohol for the first time. You do it, and it's nasty... And you don't understand how people do it a lot, because that one time sucked. Then later, especially if you had a reason to kill that person, your reason makes you feel better because you've solved a problem. So, the next time you have a problem, you take another shot.

I sped up slightly when I saw that the agents were still following me. I knew they were going to want to document this trip because they've never seen me drive to Decatur as long as they'd been documenting us. We had no business there due to some prior events that had taken place involving us. But oh well, I was there. I exited and took a right turn off of Candler Road and drove to an area named Shoals Terrace. They had a neat lookout system. Once I got on the street, the first house turned on some really bright lights, and I'm guessing to do a quick identification of my car. After a few seconds, all the lights on the street went off. It was like they had somebody on the breaker switch for the whole block. That shit made me nervous because I wasn't expecting that. Suddenly my idea no longer seemed like a bright idea. I pressed the gas pedal to the floor and used all the horsepower my Corvette offered so that I could get off of their street. Right as I was about to turn the corner and be gone I heard a series of gunshots that sounded like I was listening to a special about the war in Iraq. Shots ripped through the neighborhood, but I was fortunate to make it out of there in one piece. I jumped back on the expressway and sped off to Buckhead.

After driving for a while, I realized the FBI were no longer following me. I guess they found something better to do. I started laughing as I relaxed behind the wheel. I knew them niggaz was about to be pissed, but hell, that's why it's not a good thing to have drama with people for no reason. When you have unsolved tension with a person, it just gives the other person all types of time to plot and plan against you. Why would a person want another person plotting and planning against them continuously? That made no sense. Zaedan always told me that we had enough problems in the world without inviting more to us. I understood it completely that night, and I smiled one of my biggest smiles as I pulled into the recording studio's parking lot.

There was a sparkling red Mercedes sitting outside, with the vanity plate reading PRT TONY. I looked at it closer as I walked past it and saw that it was next year's 2020 model. I guess it wasn't a surprise that he was able to grab whips like that before they dropped. He had that legit money and wasn't afraid to spend it. I was going to get like him one day, whether I'm going to use legal or illegal funds.

I walked to the door and stood there looking for a bell or button to press. I didn't see anything, and even more surprisingly, the door didn't even have a handle. I balled my fist up to see if I could bam on the door, but it was hard concrete and produced no sound when I hit it with the bottom of my fist. I picked up my phone and the door popped inward. I put the phone in my pocket, walked in, and was greeted by one of the producers.

"Yo. Pretty Tony said bring you on through." He said as he speed-walked through the building. He was walking fast and dressed like some type of college student. I didn't know why he was dressed like that on a Sunday night. Wasn't no class that night. He walked down the hallway, took a left, and then walked up two flights of stairs.

I was surprised that I was so out of shape. I hadn't even done anything. "Y'all need some elevators in here." I said jokingly.

"We actually do have elevators, but the noise from the elevators have been messing up some of the studio sessions we have going on. We have to get that repaired, but the soonest they're saying they can get somebody out here will be in January of next year."

"What? Why?" I asked curiously.

"Well the elevator companies– when they install custom systems, they don't like to go behind other people's work; especially being custom. And the company we got this install from, they sold it to another company whose head-quarters are in New York. They told me it'll have to wait until they set up their new Atlanta branch in January. It's been hectic with no elevators, especially being that we have 5 floors worth of studios. It makes our business seem unprofessional on nights when we have a lot of major recording artists come through."

"Yea?" I asked, my mind spinning. "I could probably talk to them for you... Get some strings pulled and have it fixed for you this week."

The producer's eyes widened. "Man, for real? My boss would be happy as hell if you could do that. He was forecasting a revenue loss because he's used to having all floors accessible. A lot of major artists are diva's and divos, and if they don't feel like walking up flights of stairs, they'll just record at another studio."

"Aight, cool. Yea, I'll see about talking to them."

He opened the door leading to the studio where Pretty Tony was, and as soon as I glanced in it looked like something out of a wild porn movie. The producer walked right back to the mixing board and had a seat. He had an instrumental playing– the sounds of trumpets, pianos, and pounding bass vibrated at loud decibels in such a tight space. I understood why he was dressed the way he was... This man was just trying his best to mind his business and do his job.

There was a wine-red sectional along the back wall of the studio, and on the sofa was the girl who asked me to come party with them. The only thing she was wearing was a tattoo– a tat of a butterfly right above her left breast. I looked closer and it seemed like a coverup tat of some sort. Her legs were wide open, and two women were both on their knees eating her at the same damn time. Her face was of pure ecstasy– she looked like she was having the time of her life. At first, I thought it was Tony's other two girls who were eating her, until the door opened behind me and they walked in.

"What's up my man? I see you made it." Pretty Tony extended his hand. I shook it.

"Yea bro, I wasn't doing much else. Decided..."

"Yo. What you say your name was again?" He asked me. "I know you told me at the casino, but I met so many people... You said your name was... Rizzy? Blizzy?"

"Brizzo." I corrected him. He was close enough. That showed me that he at least tried to remember.

"Brizzo. Nice to meet you brother. I appreciate you for asking me if I needed anything back there. There were so many people walking up to me asking me for shit. That went a long way with me."

I wanted to tell him that it was Zaedan who offered, but he probably had no clue who Zaedan was, and if he did know, then hell Zaedan didn't need any more credit at that moment. Hell, Zaedan knows I love him, and anybody who knows me knows exactly how I feel and how I rock.

"That casino was so lit. Man when y'all gon open back up? Will y'all open tomorrow night?" He asked as he slid his iPhone into his pocket.

"Nah, not tomorrow, but certainly this weekend. Sometimes we did it on Saturdays, but most times it took place on Sundays."

"Aye man, count me the fuck in. Everytime y'all having something, I'm coming through. I'ma bring some other heavy hitters too. I told some of the rappers I knew, and next weekend I'll probably be bringing the who's who of Atlanta through there."

That made me feel great. I loved when I had good news

to report to Zaedan. I liked when I could feel beneficial towards the greater good of our operation. Most days it's just Zaedan telling me how to increase our money, and the only idea I'd ever contributed was regarding us selling drugs. In theory, I guess that would have brought us more money, but not the type of money Zaedan wanted to deal with. I understood him in that aspect. I'll be able to make up for that suggestion when I tell him what Pretty Tony said. That was one of Zae's goals anyways– he wanted to have the who's who of Atlanta gambling at his establishment. Once he did that, he knew we would have a tremendous amount of power over the city. Not that we didn't have power right then, but Zaedan had plans I don't think anybody's mind was strong enough to focus on except for his.

"Bet that up bro." I said as I dapped Pretty Tony.

"You cool folks Brizzo. You rap? You sing?"

"Hell nah. I just handle business. Nothing else."

"Ah come on man, everybody raps in Atlanta."

I smirked and looked at him. "Everybody except for me." The arrogant undertone, and the cold steel delivery of how I delivered that sentence was enough for him not to mention it again.

His short girlfriend pulled a small bottle of Hennessey, a small bottle of what looked like cough syrup, and that packet they'd gotten from the guy at the casino out of her purse. She walked towards the sofa, and everybody's attention switched to her as she started putting the stuff on the table in front of her. The door opened and three more girls walked in, all gorgeous, and all barely clothed. The girls stopped eating the other girl out and sat upright as they stared at the table. It seemed like everybody was staring at the table except for the girl who they were eating out. She was staring at me. I blushed, but I was sure she didn't know.

Normally I would never care for a wild ass chick like her, but for some reason, I was drawn to her wild ass. She wasn't wifey material, but she seemed like pure fun. I wondered how different it would be to go out with a chick who seemed to love other chicks. That shit just seemed so different.

The producer stopped working on the music, but left it playing. He grabbed a stack of cups out of a small cabinet located under the mixing board and computer. Everybody grabbed cups, and Pretty Tony handed me one too.

"You drink Brizzo?" Tony asked me.

"Yea." I lied. I was 22 years old and had never really liked the taste of liquor. I guess it wasn't a lie, because I do drink, I just don't particular find it interesting. But with everybody else falling into the moment, I wasn't about to stand out like a sore thumb and ruin shit. It felt like I had Pretty Tony's trust and attention, and even though it was Bullethead who initially invited him to gamble with us, it was me who was going to be responsible for bringing his business and the rest of the ballers from the city. I knew once the stars came and gambled with us once, that's all it would take for Zaedan to work his magic. Then he would be able to network and have popup casinos in different cities, and he would be guaranteed to have ballers present.

They poured a shot of Henny in my first cup and spread the shots out from person to person until the bottle was empty. That really wasn't going to be enough to get anybody drunk, but it didn't matter since that wasn't my purpose anyways.

"You sip?" Tony asked after I downed my shot of Henny. I was just trying to get it over with. I frowned because it was actually my first time drinking Henny. Normally when I did drink, it was always a clear liquor. Ciroc preferably, since they at least tried their best to make it taste better. No matter what the flavor was– watermelon, peach, it was all disgusting to me. Hennessey– that just tasted like I tried to siphon gas from a gas tank and accidentally swallowed it. It literally had no point to it whatsoever.

"Brizzo. You sip?" Tony repeated.

"Oh yea. I sip." I responded. They handed me two more cups, one stacked inside the other, and poured some of the red syrup mixture in the cup. I was about to do it the same way I did the Henny shot when Tony put his hand up.

"Hold on, hold on." He said. The girl took my cup and poured soda and dropped a pill in it. She then did the same thing for everybody else in the room. When she was done, everybody started making their way over to the sofa to sit down. I sat at the end initially, when Tony threw his hand up. He waved for me to sit beside him. I relocated, and two of the girls slid over to my left so that I would be between them. The girl who was getting eaten out when I walked into the room was sitting right next to me, still naked; her cup with more syrup than mine, and her Hennessey shot three times as much as I drank.

The producer played another instrumental, and everybody started nodding their heads. The music sounded good, and I was enjoying the vibe even though it was different than anything I'd experienced. Pretty Tony downed his cups and started vibing harder to the music. I saw him move his lips as if he was saying something, and then he jumped up and went to the door of the recording booth. The producer looked up and smiled at Tony, Tony nodded his head as if to say this is it, then opened the door and went in.

Pretty Tony's smooth singing voice took the vibe of the room from level 10 to 10,000. The women were really feeling it, and anything the women were really feeling, I was really feeling. I took a few sips of the syrup mixture from my cup and was surprised at how sweet it tasted. However, it was blended was like it came from a master bartender. I could drink that like Kool-Aid. I sat there for a minute, lost in my thoughts, lost in the vibe, lost in the music. The bass from the speakers were vibrating in the room so hard that I didn't even realize my phone had been vibrating the whole time. I didn't realize it until the instrumental stopped for a brief moment.

Once the instrumental started back up, I pulled my phone out and saw that I'd had 20 missed calls. Five of them were from Zaedan, two from Bullethead, and the rest of my calls were from my girlfriend, Sila. I glanced at the time and was shocked at how much time I'd spent in there. It seemed as if I'd just arrived, but when I checked my phone, I saw that I'd been in the studio for 3 hours already. I looked up and Pretty Tony was sitting beside me. That was weird because I swear that nigga was just in the booth doing a song.

"You finished the song already?" I asked him.

"Huh? The song? Where you at bro? I've recorded 5 songs already."

I looked at him without replying. The girl with no clothes on took her soft hand and started rubbing it up and down my left thigh. I looked up at her and saw nothing but lust in her eyes. I was turned on by her and didn't even know her. I decided to ask.

"What's your name?" I leaned in and said to her.

"Really? You've asked me that three times tonight." She laughed, and I looked up to see if Pretty Tony was going to laugh with her, but he was going back in the recording booth, this time with three women.

"My name is Jazil." She whispered to me gently. "Say my name to me."

"Jazil." I repeated.

"Yes. Jazil. Brizzo?"

"Yes..."

"Do you wanna taste me?"

"Yes..."

"Do you wanna fuck me?"

"Yes." Her erotic vibe was turning me on. She was like pure electricity being injected into my hormones. She rubbed her soft hand across the crotch of my jeans and grabbed my dick. I didn't think I could get any harder than I was, but it was feeling like I was about to burst through my jeans.

She stopped and reached into the pouch that was sitting on the table. All of my movements were slower than normal, because it seemed like I was seeing things in segments. I would see something, and in the next moment, whatever I was seeing was like it had been fast forwarded 3 minutes forward, leaving me in the past with every passing minute. I was getting confused, so I closed my eyes for a little.

When I opened them again, Jazil had my jeans open and was on her knees sucking my dick. Another girl was sitting where Jazil was sitting prior to her being on her knees. The girl beside me was naked too. I looked around the room and noticed Pretty Tony, the producer, and the other girls had left the room.

"They went for some privacy." The girl beside me whispered. I was about to reply, but Jazil's warm mouth kept wrapping around and massaging my dick. She was sucking me like she wanted me to give her my soul. I lay back on the sofa, my body feeling drunk, my movements slow, my thoughts slower than normal.

"Can I do this line off of your dick?" Jazil asked as she reached for the packet that was on the table.

"Line?" I asked.

"White girl. Can I snort it off of your dick? I'll lick it all up after I get it off." She replied confidently.

The other girl looked in my eyes and smiled. "Ooo me too. Can we both do lines off of your dick?"

"Y'all do cocaine?" I asked, confused.

"Hell yea. You never had it?" Jazil asked.

I frowned and shook my head. "Fuck no. I don't fuck with no shit like that." They were trippin for real to even ask me something like that, but they definitely didn't ask me anymore. Jazil poured some of the powder on the top of my dick and sniffed the entire line up as if it was never there to begin with. She was like a vacuum cleaner. She poured some more, and the other girl did the same thing. I was expecting them to go crazy or something, expecting them to be tripping, but to my surprise, they seemed to be turned on even more. They started sucking my dick together, taking turns sucking it down each other's throats, then got on opposite sides of my dick.

Jazil was running her mouth up and down the left side, and the other girl was doing the same thing from the right side, occasionally French kissing each other in the process. Their hands were rubbing across each other's bodies, and my hormones were on full blaze. Pretty Tony walked in the room wearing only a pair of boxers. He went in the bag, poured some cocaine into his palm and walked out without saying another word. I was curious.

"Fuck it I'll try it."

Just as soon as it came out of my mouth, she went to the bag and cupped some of it inside her long fingernail. She got up off of the floor and sat beside me. Using her other hand, she pointed to the floor. "Get down there."

I did. I got on my knees and watched as she dumped the

substance on the top of her clit. "Hurry up and get it off." She said as she pulled my head towards her pussy. I sniffed it, and immediately started coughing uncontrollably. I stood up looking for some water, and as I was standing up, the other girl sniffed the rest of the cocaine that I left on Jazil's clit. My nose was burning, and once again, I didn't understand why people used such a drug. There was a bottle of water by the producer's computer, and I didn't care whose it was at that point. I drink half the bottle.

After a couple of minutes, something happened to me that I'll never forget. My brain literally started tingling– as if it was being tickled with the softest feathers. It tickled me constantly– massaged my brain, my whole body felt like it was in the middle of busting a nut, but with no nut about to come out. At that moment I was in love with Jazil, the other girl, the whole world. It was the happiest I'd ever felt ever in my life. I was speechless as I sat down next to the girls. I stared at the wall in amazement of how happy I felt. I put my arm around Jazil and pulled her to me. I wanted to tell her I loved her, but I didn't want to sound foolish. I felt so damn good it didn't make sense.

The tingling sensation I was feeling went from the top of my brain to the side of my brain, it tingled all across the top of my head and up and down my back. I was erotically stimulated, and it had nothing to do with sex. Well not yet at least.

"Damn... let me sit on that..." Jazil said as she put her hand around my dick. I couldn't even remember when my pants came off, so I definitely couldn't remember when Jazil actually climbed on top of my dick and started riding me. Sex combined with the combination of the drugs was so mind-blowing. The only way I can describe it– it felt like I was busting a continuous nonstop nut with every stroke, and every time she lifted up and went back down on my dick. The only thing was... My nut wasn't coming anytime soon.

Both girls were riding me back to back, having orgasms back to back, and I still hadn't had my first nut. My dick was harder than I'd ever felt it get, and it seemed like it was only getting harder as the time went by. I thought about when I was tired going up the stairs of the studio and couldn't even compare that moment to the moment I was experiencing with the women. I had infinite energy, and it seemed as though I would never run out of it. I pulled Jazil off of me and made her bend over. I started stroking her like a real-life porn star, kept pumping her like she was going to be the last time I had sex in my life. She came, and fell flat, convulsing, shaking, twisting, her body balled up in the fetal position. I looked at the other girl and she was laid back against the sofa with her knees pulled up close to her chest.

"I can't take anymore." She said as she shook her head at me. She reached down, picked up her small skirt and started putting it on. She reached down and grabbed Jazil's short skirt and handed it to her as well. "Girl we gotta go." She said to Jazil. "It's getting late."

I glanced at my phone and my mind started racing. It was 4 in the morning and I'd been with them at that damn studio all night. Before long, the effects of the cocaine wore off, and I hated myself for even trying the shit. I was even more disgusted as I looked at the two thots put on their skirts while whispering to each other about their responsibilities.

"It's Monday so I gotta go get my lil one ready for school." Jazil said to me.

"You have a kid?"

"I have three. The other two are with their dads, but I

have to get this one ready. I gotta go pick him up from my sister's place. Take my number, hit me later."

I put her number in my phone and didn't even save it. It wasn't her fault though; it was my fault for not asking questions. Had I known she had three kids, I wouldn't have even allowed her to have drugs in my presence, let alone doing it with her and enabling her. I felt terrible. I put my clothes on and watched as the girls grabbed their bags, purses, and cups. I grabbed my phone and sent a text to Pretty Tony to see what they were up to.

We left an hour ago. I'm at the crib sleeping.

I shook my head. I was never going to do no shit like that again. I felt bad for losing track of time, and I knew I needed to get my shit together with the quickness. I got my clothes on and left out of the studio. I followed the signs that said exit, and they all led me to what looked like a waiting room. I went and pushed the door to leave and it wouldn't budge. I shook my head. I knew damn well I wasn't locked inside of a studio. I pushed the door again and it didn't budge at all.

A voice came over the speakerphone system, apparently speaking to me. "Your balance in order to exit is $7,000."

I sobered up real quick. "Come again?"

"It's $7,000 to exit. That covers your studio time.

"What are you talking about?" I'm not a singer or rapper." I thought maybe he had the wrong person in mind the way he was talking.

"Pretty Tony said you were his manager, and that you were going to pay for booking of two studio rooms for 10 hours at $350 per hour."

It suddenly all made sense. I'd been used and set up so his lame ass could get some free studio time. $7,000 worth to be specific.

"How do you wish to pay? We accept debit, Visa, Mastercard, or cash."

I took a deep breath. "Aye my man... Look right... I'm not nobody's fuckin manager ya heard?"

The whole night had pissed me off, and I couldn't wait to see that fuckin nigga again so I could give him a really good talking to.

"I understand, but it's our policy to call the police in the event that we have someone failing to pay for services."

"Yo... I'm actually going to have somebody fix y'all's elevator later this week. That doesn't count for anything? Damn."

There was a brief pause as if he was considering what I'd said to him.

"I tell you what... You pay us what's owed right now, and when you get the elevator repaired this week, we'll just give it back to you. Deal?"

I exhaled. I was beyond pissed at how my night had gone. A part of me wished I would have just gone home, but another part of me was happy that I'd had the experience I'd had. In all of the madness I was able to experience the drug that so many people went crazy over. Now that I knew how it worked, the next thing for me was for me to learn the best way to sell it. There was no way possible I could experience something so mind-blowingly pleasing and not try to sell it. From experience, I knew it would do me no good to tell Zaedan of my thoughts on the matter. He wouldn't want to hear it, and I wasn't going to change my mind anytime soon. I was locked in on this idea. I was sure that once he saw what his cut was going to be– he would definitely be ready to make this a major part of our family hustle.

I paid the bill using my credit card and left out of the studio. The cold fresh air was relaxing, invigorating as I made it to my car and started it up. I glanced across the street, and there they were, a fresh set– two more FBI agents who'd been sitting up doing surveillance. I turned the music up and drove to my home. I wasn't far away, so I was happy about that. I made a mental note to catch up on all of my phone calls the moment I figured everybody was out of the bed. I was about to put together my greatest plan ever, and I wasn't going to let anybody stop it. I was already taking federal risks every single day, so if I'm going to go down, I might as well go down for being the man, or at least for being a major player. I knew exactly how I was going to pull it all off too.

9

ZAEDAN

One of my major pet peeves was when I was trying to check on somebody and they don't answer the phone or text messages to let me know they were ok. That was especially true when it was applied to the line of business that I was in. At any given moment, I had to be able to accept that anything could happen. I would hate for that anything to happen to one of us, but it was nothing that could be done about it at this stage. It was me who chose to accelerate my income beyond any limits set forth by any lawmakers or constitution writers. The reason I'd even taken this path was because it was the same path that most of America's favorite companies had taken.

BIG COMPANIES like Coca Cola is worth billions today, but they had drugs in their soda in the beginning in order to get people hooked. Trace amounts of cocaine specifically. This went on for years until it was outlawed– but by the time it was outlawed, they'd laid the foundation for what was to come. A household name that everybody recognizes as a success story. I was never going to be fooled into thinking I could start a billion-dollar company without breaking any laws. It wasn't realistic. This is the reason that most startup companies end up spending all of their hard-earned money trying to get their new companies off of the ground, until they eventually fail.

I KNEW that if I wanted it that level of success, there was going to be some extreme risk taking in the initial stages, and risk is what had me worried about Brizzo's crazy ass. I'd already called his girlfriend, and she said she thought he was with me. I'd talked to Bullethead, and he said that Brizzo told him he was headed to come kick it with me also. So, the fact that I hadn't heard from him after hearing the FBI was following him had me worried. I called my lawyer, Maclente, and had him check and see if he'd been arrested. When that turned out to be a negative, all I could do was just wait to hear from him.

I WAS DRIVING HOME, but driving slowly, trying to give Brizzo a chance to hit my phone, but by the time I finally made it to my driveway, he still hadn't called or text me. I turned my cell phone off and put it in my glove compartment. I always made sure to give my wife my complete attention whenever I was in the house with her. That relationship was more important to me than any other relationship I had, and that was another reason my stomach was hurting about not hearing from her cousin, Brizzo.

. . .

I TOOK a deep breath and cleared my mind. I made it a point to leave everything from the outside on the outside. I didn't bring drama or worry into the house, and I definitely never discussed anything I had going on in the streets. She knew nothing about a mafia, a crew, a gang, a street family; none of that, and I was going to keep it that way. She did know that the FBI followed me and stalked us, but she compared me being powerful in the community to a young Malcolm X, and I left it just like that. I put the car in the garage and locked the doors. That was as far as the outside world could get to my home, and I meant that.

10

AYOKI

I awoke to pure darkness, with light R&B music playing, and a light tongue painting heavy strokes across my womanhood. The panties were gone, and I didn't know if he'd pulled them to the side, pulled them off, or cut them off with scissors. How they came off of me didn't matter not one bit though, because the things he was doing to my womanhood was something that could only be done by a husband. No boyfriend, no lover, no baby daddy, no fling, or one-night stand could do the things to a woman's body as a husband could.

A husband put extra care on your womanhood, and not just because it's his; but because he felt deep down in his soul that he could be as nasty as he ever wanted to be, and it still wasn't a sin. The way he ate me... the way he sucked every piece of me, from the tip to the *toota*, the way he licked every crevice, fold, the way his tongue explored every surface and every hole. I wrapped my hands around his head like I was holding onto a steering wheel. I had my hands on the 10 and the 2, and his tongue rotated across the 12 like it was midnight in *Orgasmville*.

My husband loved me, and I loved him right back. He slurped my juices gently, carefully– going slow enough so that I could feel the juices lift off of my skin and flow across the crevice of his lips. Going slow enough so that I could hear him swallow between extended slurps. Slurping me so slow... the orgasmic straw that he was sucking me from had my entire body tingling and shaking.

"Baby!" I screamed as I shuddered and pulled his head closer to my womanhood.

"I love you." He whispered to my womanhood in a language that only it understood. It rattled, jumped, squeezed, and erupted.

"Baby I'm about to–"

I couldn't even get it out verbally because my body burst into a million explosions of pleasure. I squeezed myself as tight as I could to prevent from squirting in his face, and I loved how he knew my tendencies. As I squeezed myself, I felt him separate me with his mass, causing a strong passion to weaken me– I squirted all over his manhood, and the more it came out of me, the deeper he pushed himself into me. It was as if he was digging the juices out from the bottom of my well. He kept pushing in and pulling it out, causing buckets of passion to spill out and onto the bed we slept.

I kept coming. Arrived, left, and came back with more.

"I love you Zaedan."

"I love you too Ayoki." He said as he returned the liquid back into me with his own well. I wrapped my arms around his body as he came into me, and my eyes rolled into the back of my head as I orgasmed with him– a soul shaking experience that could only be shared with a person sent to you by God Himself.

My husband, oh how I loved him so.

I knew that eventually I was going to have to come clean with him with all that I've been through, and regarding my little problem, but on second thought, maybe I could get it all out of me in the next few months and leave it all behind when we left Atlanta for good. That way I would never have to see the disappointment in his eyes once I told him what was going on with me.

I fell asleep moments after he fell asleep. At some point he woke and put his arms around me, pulling me close to him as he slept. He always did this, and I loved it every time. I felt protected with his arms around me, felt loved and invincible– in these moments, I felt like he was the only drug that I would ever need. Felt that he had the only chemicals that could achieve those levels of euphoria. He was my bliss. My future, past, my life. God knew what he was doing when he sent us each other. It wasn't a surprise because He was all-knowing. My weekend was complete. Our weekend was complete, and I looked forward to waking up and beginning a new day with my husband. Life had never been better for me.

11

BULLETHEAD

I 'm a different breed of man. When I was growing up, I had a learning disorder; and therefore, I spent most of my childhood years in special classes. Yea... I guess you can say I rode the short bus. Crazy thing was... I was the biggest kid on that bus, so it made things even harder for me. I wasn't dumb, but I just had a problem remembering shit the same way everybody else did. As you can guess, I wasn't very popular in my high school years as a result of that. Of course niggaz ain't have the guts to laugh at me in my face for taking slower classes, but they always stayed doing some underhanded sneaky behind my back laughing. This went on all through my junior year in high school.

See, in my junior year, I was allowed to take some regular classes along with the special classes I took. One class in particular is the one that changed my life. Gym class. I never gave a damn about sports, never cared about gym, so during that class, I always tried my best not to participate and to stay out of everybody's way. One day the gym teacher came and brought out a basketball. I never understood the excitement everybody had about that damn ball, because it definitely didn't excite me.

Me and Zaedan took the same gym class, and me and him were complete opposites. Whereas I was in the slower classes with people laughing at me behind my back, he was in advanced classes, a chess club captain, with all the girls gushing behind his back. We did share some qualities though. He didn't just talk just because he had a mouth. He was reserved, as was I. However, I had no idea that he was going to pick me to be on his basketball team that day. It made no sense to me. He'd never seen me play, nor did he even know if I could play at all.

"How you gon pick him to be on your team?" One of the other popular guys asked Zaedan after he picked me.

"Why can't I?"

"Because... that nigga... nevermind."

"That nigga what?" Zaedan asked. "Do you know him?"

"Nah, but... bruh, ain't you in the slow class?" He asked me. Everybody in the gym class burst out laughing as if it was the funniest thing anybody had ever said. I can't say that didn't hurt my feelings, but I can say it didn't make me feel good. I didn't reply, but Zaedan did.

"Nigga you an authentic bitch."

I'll never forget how the entire gym class gasped at the choice of words Zaedan used towards him. Even the guy himself was caught off-guard. That moment changed my whole way of thinking. I thought guys like Zaedan looked over guys like me, but that wasn't even the case. From that day on, we became best of friends, and as we progressed midway through our junior year, it was as if my learning problem had never existed. Things started clicking with me mentally, and halfway through the semester I was taking regular classes, and in my senior year, I was passing tests and had scores at such a high clip, that many teachers thought I'd been cheated out of a gifted school path.

Zaedan had that air about him. It was a level of confidence that if you came into contact with, it wrapped you up and made you possess it. I can honestly say that my path would have been completely thrown off if it wasn't for him. See, when he came back into the United States from studying abroad, I was in the streets doing some wild shit just because I could. I was just wilding out really because I knew I was smarter than the average criminal. When Zaedan came back around, once again; he helped me elevate things mentally.

I would forever be loyal to Zaedan and his wife, and I knew he knew that. It was the same way he would be for me, no questions asked. I knew if I needed something, he would give me his last– that's how we were, and that's how we would always be. This thing of ours... It was something special, immeasurable, something rare for black men to experience. Yet we were in it, and in it deep.

At 4 AM, my day was just beginning. One of the police officers that belonged to our organization was about to start trial in a few days. They were charging him with obstruction, fraud, and accusing him of aiding and abetting of a felony. See what happened was... the police were building a murder case against one of our members, and after the prosecution secured the evidence that would make or break the case, our officer removed it all from the evidence room; preventing the case from going on. The issue was, there was a witness who claimed they saw him remove the evidence, and they were charging him with a felony and trying to give him 25 years because it was a major murder case that they really needed a conviction from.

A conviction for a murder of that magnitude would give

them the leverage they would need to start to make arrests in our crew. And of course, we could never allow that to happen. I was about to send a vicious message to them all to let them know that we will never be the ones to be played with. They'd sealed the names of the jurors and had them under heavy security, but that was pointless. We didn't mess with innocent jurors because it wasn't like they woke up and wanted to put their noses in our business– that's what the old-fashioned mobsters did. They were being summoned and threatened to bring their noses in our business. See whenever we operated, we went to the real sources.

I had on black no-slip gloves, and boots with no traction on the bottom. My prints would never exist for anything I touched or stepped on. I had an old pistol, one that had been passed down from my great uncle. It was a gun that had been made back in the 1930s, and one that I insisted on keeping in the family for generations to come. I would never throw that gun away no matter how many bodies were on it. It was a family heirloom.

I'd invited one of the managers from Security One to the casino the day before, which was a local home security company out of Atlanta. I gave him a free $10,000 worth of chips to play with, and I helped him have a really good time. Later on that evening I told him what favor I would need from him, and although he didn't want to do it, he knew that he had no other choice at that point. I called the manager once I made it to the house I was going to. I made him stay on the phone until the man's wife left out, got in her car and left.

This was the house of the person prosecuting the case against our police officer. He needed this conviction in order for his career to elevate, but I knew he needed to let this conviction go if he wanted his life to continue. The wife left out each morning at 4:10 to go take an early morning yoga class at the 24-hour fitness center located 30 minutes away. This would give me an hour to handle the things I needed to handle. Their kids didn't wake up until 6AM, so the timing was perfect.

"Aight, disable the alarm system on 9627 Hutchlime Drive." I whispered into the phone.

The man got quiet on the other end of the line.

"Did you fuckin hear me? Don't play with me!"

"Nah I'm doing it. I'm doing it yo. Chill." A few minutes went by, and soon he had it configured in my favor. "Ok it's done. You need me to do anything else?"

"Yea. Answer the phone when I call you."

I walked through the bushes, through the yard, and up to the door. I had a hot mold key kit made out of a magnetizing solution. So basically, what happens... I take a blank key and insert it into the hot press for 15 seconds. It was like a mini microwave; it made the blank key so hot that I could literally fold it into a bow if I wanted to. I took the hot key and slid it in a straight line into the lock, then I slid it out quickly in that same straight line. On the surface of the lock was the shedding of the blank key. It was stuck to the surface due to the magnet. I snatched the shedding off and put it in my blank bag.

I waited about 30 more seconds for the newly made key to cool off, then took the key, slid it back into the lock and unlocked the door. That shit worked to perfection every single time. Technology was way too advanced for us to be kicking in doors. The black web made so many things possible, it was unbelievable. I walked in and shut the door gently. I'd cased his house a few times, watching him enter his house and watched which light he turned on first. I'd done this on 4 separate days, so I knew at that point which room was his bedroom.

I walked up the stairs gently, carefully not to cause any random noises. Went straight to it like it was my house. When I approached, I could hear him snoring loudly. That was going to help things out, and then I heard his heater turn on, which helped things out even better. That would help in muffling some of the sound of me approaching. I walked into his room and kept walking until I stood over him. He was literally out like a light. I could have killed him in his sleep, and he would have never known what hit him. The problem was, I needed him alive. If I killed him, they would just assign another prosecutor to the case, and I needed the case dismissed.

I stood over him with my pistol out, glanced at my watch, and saw that I had plenty of time to get my point across. I walked around the bed and got in the bed with him. This woke him a little. He was still half-sleep, mumbling.

"Honey. You're about to work out?" He mumbled in the darkness.

I didn't say a word. I just laid back on the pillow and stared at the ceiling. Moments like those were razor thin. There was always the capacity for error, but there was always the capacity for perfection as well. Before any execution ever took place, we have a choice in if we're going to ensure perfection or ensure error. I would never ensure anything that would harm me or our organization. I was a professional, no evidence of me ever attending a slower class existed in my efforts.

The prosecutor reached over and flipped on the lamp. With the speed of light, I wrapped my hand around his throat and stuck the barrel of the old rusty gun in his mouth. His eyes got wide and he was twisting, panicking, and trying to move my hand from his throat. He quickly realized my power was that of 4 men, and he had no chance of preventing me from doing whatever the fuck I wanted to. I slacked up from chocking him and whispered in his ear.

"Listen. I could have killed you; I could have killed your wife before she made it to her yoga class, and of course your kids were in danger as well. I know you're just doing your job Mr. Prosecutor, but here's what you're going to do... Today you're going to tell the judge that you'll dismiss all charges against Norman Smith."

He nodded frantically, tears coming from his eyes.

"See... I know you're nodding, but for some reason, I don't really believe you." I lift my hands off of his throat and he gasped for air desperately.

"I promise. Fuck that case. They're not paying me enough anyways. Believe me man, I'm not about to risk shit." He squeaked.

I reached into my pocket, pulled out a knife, and pressed a button for the blade to pop out. I took the sharp blade and slide it across his head, giving him a haircut in the process. He shook like he was having an orgasm, and I didn't know if he liked the shit or was afraid of it. It put the hair that I cut off inside the bag to let Zaedan know that I'd talked to the prosecutor.

"Aye... And this is my all-out promise... Don't try to be some type of national hero Mr. Steve Williams. If you care about your family's well-being, you'll take this warning very seriously, and you'll be thankful that I spared you today."

The prosecutor nodded, tears rolling down the side of his head and into the pillow. "You have my word sir. I promise."

I heard footsteps in the hallways, and I was really hoping that I wasn't going to have to kill this man's entire family that morning. I took a quick, harsh, irritated deep breath and stared at him.

"It's probably my son going to the bathroom. Sir please... I'll keep him in the bathroom, and you can leave us? Please."

I got up and held the pistol to the back of his head. "Go." I whispered. He walked into the hall, into the bathroom and closed the door.

"Good morning Daddy. I thought I heard you talking. Is Mom up?"

I went down the stairs and out of the house, disappearing into the early morning darkness. Leaving him alive as important, but it would be up to him if he didn't value this importance the same way I did. I'd have no problem with providing his demise if he ever felt like life was too difficult to live without trying to be a hero. I called the security manager back, but he didn't answer the phone. I was hoping I wouldn't have to knock his ass off too, but that wasn't my concern that morning. One problem at a time was the best way to solve them.

I went to Dunkin Donuts and ordered a sausage croissant with strawberry jelly and an orange juice. I tossed the egg out the window when they gave me the sandwich, applied the jelly, and blended in with the morning rush hour. It was amazing what stories were taking place behind the seal of the Atlanta windshields. There were honest workers, crooks, politicians, athletes, entertainers, police officers, killers, robbers, prostitutes, pimps... The list was endless. In life, it's common knowledge that you get in where you fit in. At least you do this until you outgrow the life you fit in, or until somebody pulls you out of it.

12

ZAEDAN

I woke up at around 10:30 AM. Kinda late for me because I like to be up at 8 o'clock handling business, but I knew it was also important to listen to my body. I'd had a long weekend and was sure the week itself was going to present even more challenges. My wife wasn't in the bed when I woke up, but I didn't have to guess where she was. I heard the shower running in the bathroom, and although I thought about joining her, I knew that would only put me to sleep longer than I intended to sleep.

I checked my phone and saw that everybody had been calling me, Brizzo, Bullethead, Wilburt, Maclente, and Antonio. I was going to call everybody back, but the first person I called was Maclente, my lawyer.

"Hey."

"Hey. You heard what happened?" He said enthusiastically.

"No... What was it? I slept late this morning." I yawned.

"So... they dropped the charges on the officer. The prosecutor claims he found out some things about the witness that weren't deemed credible, and he feels he's unable to proceed in prosecuting the case."

"Hell yea!" I yelled into the phone. "That's good shit!"

The lawyer laughed. "Hell yea that's good. But honestly, my team wasn't going to lose the trial. I felt confidently about it. I guess we'll never know." Maclente said.

"Right. Right. Well that's still a win. He's not guilty and can go home. It's a win. He probably saw how hard your team of lawyers were defending him and just realized he couldn't win the case anyways."

"Yea... maybe..." Maclente said, brushing it off.

"What do you mean maybe?" I asked.

"I mean... it's really convenient ya know..."

"What's really convenient?"

"I'm saying... like this was like some last-minute stuff... Like something happened or something."

"Maclente... Are you accusing me or..."?

"Hell no. I wouldn't do that... I know you would tell me if something like that was amidst. It's no biggie."

He was irritating me at that point. "Tell you what? And tell you for what even if I'd done something? Even though I haven't done anything."

"I'm just saying man... You know... Dealing with lawyers, prosecutors... They never lay down... They always come back later in some other form... ya' know? I wouldn't wanna be caught off guard, I guess. But if you say you had nothing to do with it– "

"You have a good day too Maclente. Don't ruin my morning with that kind of nonsense."

"My apologies sir."

I hung the phone up and nodded my head. For that reason alone is why I didn't tell every person every single thing. I would explain stuff as needed, but there was no reason to explain that. It was self-explanatory anyways. My wife came out of the bathroom in all of her elegance and perfection. She had a smile on her face, her skin glowed like a soft brown candle, and her eyes shined as bright as the skin of the sun.

"Good morning." We said simultaneously. I smiled at her. "Baby what you up to?"

She walked to the closet and pulled a red, black, and orange polka dot sweater out and a pair of black jeans. "Well first I'm going to go check on the order of turkeys and hams. If they've arrived, I'm going to make sure the church is open so they can be delivered for our giveaway tomorrow."

The giveaway had almost slipped my mind. I'm glad she reminded me. "Where are they going to store them if they're dropping them off? 1,000 turkeys and 1,000 hams won't fit in a refrigerator."

"Well they're dropping off portable refrigerated trailers full of meat, and they'll just pick the trailers up after we're done with everything."

I nodded my head. It made perfect sense. Doing things for the public was my true passion, but I knew it was going to be a work in progress because I had huge dreams I wanted to execute. Not just doing stuff for the city of Atlanta, but doing stuff for the entire United States, in every hood, in every city.

"Then I'm driving to Macon, GA to go visit your Grandma. You know I told her I was going to come see her."

She made me feel bad because I knew my Grandma was going to wonder why I wasn't there. I made a mental note that I was going to do whatever I could to make it up to her the moment I could get a break with work.

"What do you have to do today Zaedan?" She asked as she put her clothes on.

I gave her my customary answers. "Some paperwork for the business, gotta handle some street marketing, and of course I gotta go talk to a few people who needs talking to." As many times as I'd uttered those words to her, to that moment she had never thought to require me to break down what I was talking about, neither had she ever questioned me. She was amazing in the fact that she allowed me to work without difficulty, and that alone was the encouragement I needed to get out of the game and seek a fresh start for us.

She got dressed, came over and gave me a kiss while looking into my eyes. "I love you Zaedan."

I sat up in the bed and pulled her close to me. Her warm body caused fire to build in my loins at a rapid pace. I let go and exhaled. "I love you too Ayoki, and I always will."

She smiled that perfect smile again, grabbed her jacket and keys, and left out of the house. The moment I heard the door close, I called Bullethead.

"Everything good family?" I asked as I listened intensely to his end of the line.

"Not really Zae."

I was confused. How could things have gone bad if the situation worked out perfectly? I thought to myself. I was expecting him to just say... *Yes, everything's fine bro;* but I definitely didn't have that coming.

"Alright. Then what's up?" I asked curiously.

"The FBI followed me home this morning. They've been outside of my place all morning just sitting there."

"Ok, that's nothing new. Why you tripping about it?"

"Yea... well I don't know how long they've been following me this morning. I really wasn't even paying attention. I didn't know they were following me until about 10 minutes after I left Dunkin Donuts."

It felt like my heart was about to explode. I couldn't be hearing what he was saying at that moment. It was almost as if he was speaking a language that I wasn't privy too. That could mean...

"Man fuck them Bullethead. It ain't like you did anything wrong anyways. Think about it. You're good bro. Keep handling your business and don't stress it."

"You're right. I'm tripping. I haven't done shit... Yea you're completely right. I don't know why I let them stress me this morning."

"Hell, me either." I started laughing, and he started laughing in reply. "I'm about to hit up this crazy ass Brizzo to see what happened to his ass last night. I'll see you this evening though bro, let's say around 6 PM."

"Definitely. Say less family."

I got out of the bed and went to take a shower before calling Brizzo. I needed to cool-down because I was almost sure he was going to rile me up. He was the most unpredictable part of our organization. It was almost guaranteed that he was going to drive my blood pressure up. I took my shower, got out, got dressed, and ate a cup of sweet mandarin. Then I called his phone.

"Man, what the fuck?" That was the only way I could greet his ass that morning after having me stressed most of the night.

"I know Zae man I'm sorry man. I was working on something for you though."

"For me?" I was confused as hell.

"Hell yea. I was working on building a relationship to increase business."

I shook my head. "Bruh... I didn't ask you to work on any relationship to increase any type of business. That's not your responsibility Brizzo. I appreciate you trying, but I got this handled."

I heard him mumble but I couldn't make out what he was saying. "Huh?"

"I said well it's done anyways. I got invited by Pretty Tony to the recording studio. Cool peoples man. He said he was going to bring the who's who of Atlanta to the spot this weekend."

That made me nervous as hell. From experience I've known for people to always try to take advantage of the nice side of Brizzo. One thing for sure though, they never tried to take advantage of the other side of Brizzo. When he meant business, he really meant business; but when he thought he was being either slick or a friend to somebody, I have yet to see it become a success. I could tell based on how his voice was shaking that he was at least trying though. I wasn't going to be hard on him.

"Aight that's what's up. Good work with that. I guess we'll see how it works out then Brizzo."

"Good. Good." He said in the phone, I could tell he was

speaking through a smile. "Zaedan... Man we need a crew name."

I frowned. "What the fuck are you talking about?"

"Man... A name bro. Like... the Black Cartel, or Cartel Gangsters, or the Black Mob... hell I was thinking we could just call ourselves Mafia. What you think?"

"Fuck no. The fuck are you talking about? We're not building a brand here. Why the hell would we give ourselves a name? That's stupid as fuck. That's the reason y'all young niggaz keep going to prison every other day round this bitch. Y'all so fast to wanna brag and get these people's attention. Why the fuck do you want to have their attention to the point where they can identify us all with one name? That's stupid man."

"Well they already know us. The FBI already follow us. I don't understand why not just give ourselves a name... That way when it's all said and done, people will remember the work we put in."

He was pissing me off. "Nigga we ain't putting in no got damn work to be remembered. You act like we're a fucking recording group. This ain't muthafucking Jodeci my nigga. We do not sing nor do we entertain. We don't wanna be remembered, nigga we wanna be forgotten. Dismiss yourself of this crazy ass thinking. And you better show up at 7 this evening with a refreshed mindset."

I didn't want him showing up the same time as Bullethead. I needed to clear my mind with Bullethead before he came through with them crazy ass ideas.

"Aight. My fault Zae. We don't gotta call ourselves anything then."

My blood pressure was through the roof just because he was still trying me. He had sadness in his voice as he said that. He just didn't understand anything I was saying to him and it was infuriating me. "Bro... Do you understand what I'm saying to you?"

I listened as Brizzo exhaled. "Nah, yea I get it... It's just that..."

"Just that what?"

"Even the old school mafia, the 5 familes; BMF, everybody, they all had names to represent their legacy. It wasn't just for memories; it was to warn people not to fuck with us. Like if we mention the name, they should automatically know the reputation. Like... The name could be used as a warning."

I hung the phone up without replying. I really did have a headache at that point, and I went to the kitchen to find some aspirin to take. I opened up the medicine drawer in the kitchen and saw a bottle of Tylenol. I took two of the pills with no water, just downed them on the spot. I needed them to start digesting immediately. I would grab a bottle of water on the way out of the house.

13

AYOKI

After leaving the church and making sure everything was intact for our giveaway, I stopped by Red Robin to buy two large cups of freckled lemonade. For some reason, that lemonade made me feel better about life, even when I was feeling down. From the perspective of most outsiders, I had no reason to feel down, being that I had a loving husband and the life a woman could only dream of. Although I was extremely appreciative of what God had done for me, I still felt like I had a hole in the bottom of my soul where all of my happiness would drain to during certain moments.

That was the reason for me going to see Mrs. Irena, Zaedan's grandmother. She was the only person who I'd told everything I'd endured. She understood me and never judged me, and I loved her for that. She always told me to either call her or come by and see her as often as I liked, and I took advantage of that invite as often as I could. It was burning me up keeping my secrets from Zaedan, but I always felt a huge release whenever I could express it all to Mrs. Irena. I got in my red Audi truck, opened the sunroof;

and turned the music up as I got onto the expressway headed to Macon, GA.

Midway through my trip, I thought I saw someone following me, but I was pretty sure it was my crazy imagination playing tricks on me like usual. I was listening to Summer Walker's album as I drove, just enjoying her melodies and thinking about the similarities we had in common. I was shy also, and I definitely suffered from anxiety. The only time I wasn't shy is when God was speaking through me. By myself I'm just me, but when He used me; I was fulfilling my purpose.

My stomach dropped when I realized I was running low on gas. I was mad because I never put gas in my car, it was always something Zaedan did for me, and I'd completely forgotten about mentioning it to him that morning. It wasn't that I couldn't do it, I just hated any situation of where I had people walking around, behind, and in front of my car. I wasn't going to hit anybody, but I wasn't trying to hit anybody all those years ago. I exited the moment I saw a sign and followed it until I was parked at a Pilot gas station on pump 11.

I got out of the car, and my anxiety seemed to take over my body immediately. The gas pump was on my left, but my gas tank definitely wasn't there. Panic was eating at me because I knew I would have to turn around and back up to get gas since all of the other pumps seemed to be occupied. I got in the car, started it, and the moment I put the car in reverse, I saw a kid get out of a car right beside mine and start walking towards the store. I put the car back in park and sat as I watched the kid go in the store. I was about to put the car back in reverse when I saw another group of kids come out of the store. I didn't know where they were headed but I didn't want to take any chances.

I decided I wasn't going to back the vehicle up, and instead I was just going to wait until the cars in front of me left, and I would just drive forward and loop around the gas pumps. I sat there breathing frantically. I felt like I was drowning underwater, and I held my breath trying to stop from dying. After holding my breath for as long as possible, I broke through and took a large deep breath, suddenly remembering that I wasn't underwater, and was instead just sitting at a gas station. My heartbeat against my chess as my anxiety attack ate at me.

Then a horn blew behind me frantically. I Looked behind me and there was an angry white lady with her hand in the air. I had no idea how long she'd been behind me, and that made me feel even worse. I could have easily run into her car and hurt her, or accidentally ran over her and killed her. Tears filled my eyes and I panicked as I sat there trying to figure out what to do. I grabbed tissue and wiped my eyes as the lady kept blowing her horn behind me, wanting me to move. Kids kept walking out of the store and getting in and out of cars and I just didn't wanna live anymore. I couldn't understand why my life had become so hard in such a brief amount of time. I cried as I looked around for help and jumped when a white man in a suit approached my car.

"Hey. Are you ok?" He asked me through the window.

I didn't want to seem like something was wrong with me, but indeed there was something wrong in that moment. I rolled the window down, and when I felt his vibes, I almost rolled my window back up. He had harsh vibes, really negative, almost as if he knew me or knew someone I knew. The horn blew again, and he reached his hand in the air and yelled at the woman behind me.

"Aye, go around!" He yelled.

I was thankful that he was helping me, but I was worried because something wasn't right about his vibe.

"I have anxiety really bad..." I said as my hands shook uncontrollably. "I just wanted to get some gas, that's all. My tank is..." I felt horrible as I watched my hands continue to shake. For one moment he watched my hands and saw that I was having a difficult time. He stepped back and looked at the side of my car. When he realized that the tank was on the other side, he gave me a long and exaggerated reply.

"Ohhhh I see what's going on."

I literally was about to just hand him the keys and let him handle it when he walked to the pump and grabbed the handle. He then walked around the car and to the gas tank opening holding it. I was surprised that it reached that far, but I was definitely happy that it was all over.

"Yea they make these gas station hoses really long for some reason. Everything's going to be fine." He said as he pressed the button on the pump. I realized that I forgot to tell him what kind of gas to put in, but when I glanced up, I saw that he'd already known what kind to put in. I relaxed for a moment as the worst of my panic attack subsided. I lay my head back against the headrest until he finished pumping my gas. When he finished, I frowned because I didn't even give him my debit card or tell him how much gas I wanted and he'd filled it up. I glanced at the amount and reached into my purse and grabbed a $100 bill. I handed it to him and he nodded.

"I'll be right back." He said as he walked into the store. I'd honestly never seen a store give up a full tank of gas before payment, but again; I didn't pump gas anyways, so what would I know. I thought about letting him keep the change as a thanks for him helping me. I was about to call Zaedan when he walked out with a smile on his face. He walked up to my car, handed me the change, and when the skin on his hand brushed across my hand, I felt nothing but heat, causing me to drop the money.

"Ma'am. Are you ok?" The guy asked as he looked downward to see if he could see the money I'd just dropped.

"Yes. I'm fine." I answered abruptly.

"Good." He said. "I know this is awkward, but do you mind sending a message to your husband, Zaedan?"

All of my senses were on fire at that moment. I knew for a fact that something was up with him from the very beginning, and I couldn't place it until his skin brushed across my own. I saw a glimpse of him trying to hurt my husband. Saw him trying to hurt me. I looked beyond his eyes, saw his soul and waited on God to speak to him. I knew the words were coming, knew I was about to have some choice words to tell him.

"Sure. I'm good at delivering messages." I replied.

"Good." He smiled. "Let him know that Agent Schiffner is onto him. You tell him he might want to schedule a meeting with me before it all goes down. Not to scare you though ma'am, but just give that message to your husband. Not that you have to pass the message along though, because I'll be there to take both of you down when it's time."

He started laughing in a sinister way, and the words hit me like a tsunami. "God told me to tell you that you have to ask him for forgiveness if you expect to have any success in this world. He told me to tell you that your past is just as bright as the nearest billboard for as long as you continue to run from it. He told me to tell you that you're wrong for what you did to your ex-wife all those years ago. He says you may have thought you got away with killing her and blaming it on a home invasion robbery, but God's power is the ultimate power. Yes sir you've been a really bad man. You think because of your status in the FBI that your word is the almighty word, but I'm here to tell you that God has the final word in all that you think you've hidden from this world."

More words hit me but when I looked in his eyes, I could see that God didn't want me to say more. I could see that God had allowed me to say all I could say in order to keep me safe. He was furious as he stared at me, jaws open, nose rising and falling like the stock market– my anxiety had jumped off of me and took over his body instead. He balled up his fist, and for a moment I thought he was about to hit me; but he didn't. He backed away from my car and stared at me and stood there like the lost demon that he was. I didn't waste time. I started my vehicle and got out of there with the quickness.

FBI agents were always bothering my husband. They were afraid of his power, of his dream, of the things that God called him to do. They should be afraid. Anybody who sided with the devil should always be afraid of God's will. Simply because no matter how a person or group of people tried to prevent it, His will would always be done no matter how you slice it or cut it. I got on the expressway and realized that that's who was following me when I thought someone was behind me. I wasn't going to call my husband with that nonsense because I knew he already had enough going on. There was no need to add more worry. I was a messenger for God. I didn't send messages for the devil.

"Hey Grandma!" I screamed as I walked into her living room.

"Hey baby!" She said, enthusiasm falling out of her pores, happiness covering her face.

"Grandma I missed you so much. I meant to come back by here yesterday after church, but I was so tired after dealing with those spirits. I'm sorry."

"Baby you don't have to 'pologize to me. Anytime you spend with me, I appreciate it everytime." Mrs. Irena said as she wiped some sweat off of her forehead with a small towel.

"Grandma why you got it so hot in here?" I didn't notice the heat until I saw how bad she was sweating. I'd just been happy to see her when I walked in the door.

"I don't know... It's cold outside, so I turned the heater on. It always gets real hot like that, but I have to ask myself if I wanna' be real hot or real cold. So, I choose real hot."

I got up and walked to the thermostat. "Grandma nobody showed you how to use this thermostat?"

"Nah, they didn't tell me how to use the thermometer. Well they told me how to turn it on and turn it off, so that's the way I do."

I grabbed the dial and slid it away from 90 and stopped it at 74 degrees. "Ok Grandma. I fixed it for you, and you can keep on turning it on and off the way you've been doing, but if you get too cold or too hot, you give me a call and I'll get down here and adjust it again for you."

"Baby I don't want you driving way down that road to fix no heater. I thank ya', but I wouldn't call you for nothing like that."

"It's not an issue Grandma. It'll just give me another reason to come see you." We laughed together as the words left my tongue.

"I just don't feel right to call you for something like that though. You know I worry about you when you take that great long drive to Macon. I worry about that Grandson of mine too. How's he been doing?"

I went and sat beside her on the sofa and put my arm around her. I didn't have a family because they wouldn't forgive me, so she was everything to me and I loved her for it. "Zaedan is doing really good. He told me to tell you he loves you."

"Tell him I love him too. Tell him I wanna see him soon as he can take some work time off."

"I sure will tell him. You know he still has a dream of being the people's president one day Grandma."

"I know you was telling me that one time or another. How does that work?" She asked me that everytime, and I never got tired of explaining it to her.

"Well, he doesn't wanna be the real president, he wants to be the president for the people Grandma. So, he'll have to save up a whole lot of money, millions of dollars; and then every time it's a natural disaster, or hurricane like Katrina, then we're going to show up and start helping people out. It don't gotta be any natural disasters though. He just wants to show up and start helping people. Just trying to fix the world, tryna help us all because it seems like nobody else cares about us."

"You sholl' right about that baby. You tell my Grandson I said I'm proud of him, and I do hope he can be the president one day. That old Donald Trump just as crazy as he wanna be ain't he?"

I laughed, and she laughed too. "Yes, he's truly crazy Grandma."

"Ain't he?" She laughed harder and shook her head. "How you been doing though baby? Has things been bothering you still?"

I got quiet and closed my eyes. She could sense the shift in my tone and mood, and apologized. "Baby I'm sorry. I don't wanna hurt your feelings, I just want you to be happy. You know?"

I nodded because I knew she meant me nothing but the best. I exhaled and bit my tongue so that I wouldn't start crying. "Grandma I had an episode on Saturday night before church." As soon as I spoke those words, tears flooded my face. I couldn't help it.

"I'm so scared Zaedan is going to look at me different when he finds out Grandma. I'm just a mess. A lot of days I feel like I'm not good enough for him with these problems that he doesn't even know about. Look at what I've done Grandma. I ran over a little kid!"

Tears fell down Grandma's face as she wiped my face with the small towel she was holding. "God has forgiven you baby." She said through her tears. "God has forgiven you many times. I know it's really hard, but I want you to know that God has already forgiven you for what you've done. He knows that's not who you are. He knows you're a beautiful queen and he's going to show you that."

"Grandma you keep telling me that but why does it hurt me so bad every time I think about it? I can't even make it through the week without suffering because of what I've done. I don't know what to do. I'm really hurting Grandma."

Grandma Irena sniffled as she listened to me cry out in pain. She'd been trying to help me with my problem for almost a year at that point, and each time she would give me a different perspective. She was always praying for the words required to try to help fix my pain, and that time was no different.

"Baby... I prayed about this through the week, and it's like I never got an answer back. It's funny because I didn't even know what I could say to you until just now, maybe a few seconds ago. God says that you He's forgiven you for what you've done, and he wants you to prosper and be happy. He wants you to be stronger so that you can reach your full potential, but the only way you're going to be able to do that is if you forgive yourself baby. I don't know what it's going to take for you to forgive yourself, but you must figure out how to do that. You have to handle that no matter what it requires of you baby."

I put both hands over my face and cried into them, and Grandma wrapped her arm around me and pulled me close to her. "It's going to be ok baby. I promise you it's going to be ok. Great long years ago, my mother told me I needed to leave that man of mine that I was supposed to marry. I didn't listen to her at first because I just didn't understand. I had low self-esteem, and I didn't know how I was supposed to get another husband. See this man was abusive, but he was the only man saw fit enough to marry me. She kept telling me... Irena, you need to leave that man. You're not happy. He's abusive, you need to leave."

Mrs. Irena wiped her face and finished her story. "I didn't know where I was going to go with no money. This man had told me that I wasn't worthy of a husband. Had me feeling like God didn't even love me, made it seem like the only man who could ever love me was him. I didn't have a place; I didn't have a job or nothing. You know... My mama kept telling me to trust God and He would make a way. I left that house in the middle of the night and met the husband

God wanted me to have by lunchtime the next day. See... I forgave myself for my thoughts that night, and by the next day, I was exactly where I was supposed to be in this world. That man loved me from the moment he met me until he died 45 years later, and I loved him just the same. You and my Grandson got that same kind of love, but you got to forgive yourself and let God come into you."

I was so appreciative of Mrs. Irena for her wisdom, and I always loved hearing the stories she told me about her life. There was so much to learn, and I'd never had anybody else to teach me the way she'd done. I was forever thankful. I had lunch with her and adjusted the heater's thermostat for her one more time before I left. When it reached 74 degrees it was just a little chilly, so I increased it a couple more degrees. We had such a good time, and we said a prayer before I got back on that road. She was such an amazing woman, and her words inspired me to try to make some progress with my own family. Maybe since time had passed, they wouldn't still hate me for what I'd done. God knows I didn't mean to do it. I was going to reach out to them in a couple of days. Since me and Zae were going to be giving away turkeys and hams the following day, I knew I was going to be tired from dealing with so many spirits.

"What?"

"What you mean what? Nigga what what?"

"You heard me bruh. You might as well get down with the Blood Money Gang and get some of this real money. You see the chain, don't you?"

I was outside of the barbershop talking to one of the little niggaz from my hood. He wasn't but about 17 years old and had a chain so shiny and with so many diamonds in it, nobody could tell him he wasn't getting real money out here. It actually made me jealous just looking at the way he was shining. His chain had a bag of money with red diamonds flooding the word blood, green diamonds flooding the word money, and white diamonds flooding the word gang. I shook my head.

"I'm serious bruh. We can use a few old heads for real for real."

"Old heads? Nigga I ain't even 22 years old yet, I'm damn near your age. How you gon call me an old head?"

"Old head like I said nigga. You say you out here getting

money but ain't nobody seen nothing. You ain't got no chain on, you ain't representing no crew, shit sound like an old head to me." Him and one of his homies started laughing. I didn't even know that was his homey until he laughed, and I definitely didn't see no chain on his neck.

"Where yo chain at nigga? Since y'all getting so much money. Y'all sharing one chain or something?"

He laughed and lifted his lip up at me like I was the scum of the earth. He pulled his keychain out and pressed a button. An engine roared to life from about ten feet away. I looked over and couldn't believe what I was seeing.

"Man, that ain't yo shit man. Fuck no." I refused to believe it.

"Yes the hell it is. I ain't want no chain. I bought that new Range Rover and a new house in Jonesboro. But I'ma get a chain anyways now since you think it's a game."

They had me speechless. These were two young kids, both under the age of 17, and were out here looking better than me. I was honestly embarrassed and felt like I had to save face. "What you spent on that chain?" I asked the one with the chain on.

"$120,000 from Icebox Jeweler."

I couldn't even argue with him. It wasn't like he told me the price and didn't tell me who he spent it with. Being that he'd named the price and who he spent it with, he knew it could be easily checked out. Niggas didn't volunteer extra lies when they were getting money. Niggaz that lie only give you one lie at a time. I knew he was being honest, and it definitely made me feel some kind of way.

"That's cool... But shit I can't wear no jewelry because I'm a part of the Mafia." I couldn't help it. I had to say something to save my reputation.

Both of them looked at me with their eyes wide. "The

Mafia? Like the real mafia? Like the Italians? Because I know an Italian who's in the Solumbert Mafia. You talking about like that?"

"Man fuck the Solumbert Mafia." I was really showing out then. I really didn't have a reason to downtalk another mafia, but I was trying to show that I really belonged to something.

They stared at me wide-eyed. The one with the new Range Rover whispered to his friend. "Man, he said *f* the Solumbert Mafia bro."

"Nah, I said *fuck* the Solumbert Mafia. Get it right. I'm on some whole other shit right now. We got the biggest guns, bombs, we getting in all the dope, we got all the money, nigga everything in the city y'all touch gotta come through us first. Same thing for the Solumbert Mafia. They can't do shit without our permission." I was going off like I was performing in front of a crowd or something.

The one with the Range Rover seemed ready to instigate some shit. "Man, I'm gon tell them you said fuck the Solumbert Mafia man." He laughed, half-jokingly.

I guess he was trying to see if I was going to back down off of my words or something. Everybody knew the Solumbert Mafia because they made headlines every day or so for murder, robbery, kidnapping, human trafficking, you name it they did it. They made headlines so often, it was as if they were trying to get caught in order to bolster their reputation. I didn't understand their power though, because they also got convicted and went to prison a lot. If something happened to one of us, Zaedan had us out of there no matter what the charges were. I wasn't afraid of them at all.

"I don't give a fuck if you tell God I said it." I laughed, but they didn't laugh with me. "See... it's like this... When you tell the Solumbert Mafia that The Mafia said fuck em', they know they gotta just eat that shit. My nigga Zaedan went to Italy and got connected way deeper than any of the little baby mafias in America."

With that being said, I went into the barbershop and got my haircut. With all the work I'd put in in the streets, I felt better now that I'd represented some of it. I knew they didn't really know anybody from the Solumbert Mafia, and even if he did tell them I said fuck them, they wouldn't know who the hell I was anyways. Fuck that. I wasn't worried about that shit at all.

15

WILBURT

One of the most lucrative divisions in our organization was ran by me. It was a CDL class. Now, I know what you're thinking... How the hell is a group of hoodlums running CDL classes? And how is it profitable for them? Hold your horses, allow me to explain. See... Me and Zaedan have been friends since the 3rd grade. I'm talking about the type of friends that would go over each other's house and walk past their parents and go in the refrigerator type of friends. When Zaedan came back from overseas with his new plan to run a street organization, I had the perfect situation going on to help make it all run smooth.

I KNOW most people would ask... If you already had a way to make the money yourself, why would you split it or even bring it to Zaedan? It just *seems* that way to an outsider. If you were in my shoes, you would have done the same thing. See... when a person breaks the law, it doesn't give you a normal feeling. It makes you feel taboo, as if you were completely wrong, which you honestly are... And it made you feel like it's you against the world by yourself. Technically it is. The moment you got caught it really was going to be you against the world by yourself. It was better to include someone, preferably someone smart who could help you work your way out of whatever brick wall you may run into. If you're a working-class man or woman, and you yourself need help sometime, then imagine the type of help professional criminals may need to keep going.

THE PROBLEM WAS, most guys in the streets lacked honor and couldn't be trusted, so that's where the saying comes from: I do my dirt all by my lonely. But those same people usually do their time all by their lonely too, and it hardly ever takes a long time for them to get caught. You can turn on the news and see solo criminals getting caught every single day. But how many times do you turn on the news and see organized criminals all going down at the same time? It's rare. Most of the times it's unorganized criminal groups that you see doing the dumb crap on the news.

IN THE HOOD where I'm from, I know quite a few guys who desire to be truck drivers. Along with that statistic, I know even more guys who desire to be able to own their own trucking company. I mean who wouldn't? It's a lot of money involved, and there's the American Dream of one day living the good life. I mean... It's not hard to get started... You simply take a course, pass the test, get your CDL license and now you're driving trucks. The problem was that the people I knew from the hood were always looking for shortcuts and ways to get money way faster than it was coming. This is where I came in at.

THE AVERAGE STARTING pay for a new truck driver could be from $40,000 to $60,000 per year; maybe more, maybe less depending on where you got hired at. If you work with us, we can get you $150,000 in a week, maybe more, maybe less, almost the same rules apply. I had a sophisticated system in place of where I help men from the hood get their CDL and help them get placement at certain companies. Most of the time I tried to target the startup trucking companies, but every now and then I mixed it up to deal with a major company. It really didn't matter honestly, because both of them worked out the same exact way.

It was Rafael's 7th month on the job working for the Sunbow Family Trucking company, and it was the day he had been anticipating since he'd started working. He had what was considered a High-Value-Load, and in his case; he had a truckload of new iPhones still in the box with a value of $5.3 million. Per the protocol of his job, he wasn't allowed to stop for at least 200 miles of the point of pickup. Considering he'd picked the iPhones up in North Carolina and were transporting them to Birmingham Alabama, he was well beyond the 200-mile mark when his truck was ambushed in broad daylight in Atlanta, Georgia.

He'd pulled into a Pilot gas station in order to gas up, and the moment he hopped down off of the stepladder, goons ran out of the bushes with rifles and pistols, wearing masks and armored vests. One of them hit him in the forehead with the butt of the gun, splitting his forehead open; and then hit him again so that it was guaranteed that he would need stitches. Two of them pulled out two small square devices with mini satellites on the end of them. The first one aimed it at the truck itself and pressed a button, and the second one aimed it at the trailer, and pressed the button on his.

After about 3 seconds they both nodded at each other. They looked at the man who'd hit Rafael with the gun and nodded at him.

"The GPS tracking devices have been disconnected from the trailer and the truck. You're good to go."

The man jumped in the truck, started it up, and drove out of the gas station parking lot while the other men started kicking Rafael in the face, chest, stomach and throat. They beat him until he could barely move; until he was almost unconscious, and they ran back through the bushes the route they'd come. They had vehicles parked down a dirt road path about a mile out, and they ran with their body armor on with the weapons in their hands.

Rafael tried to get up off of the ground and passed out.

Rafael was questioned at the hospital about the robbery, and he offered as much information as he knew. He had no idea he was going to get beat so badly, otherwise he wouldn't have even gone along with it. He was pissed.

"Did you know the guys who attacked you?" The detective asked him.

"What?" Rafael managed to squeal through all his pain.

"I'm just asking if you knew them. Are they friends of yours?"

"No." Rafael started crying as he answered, which was exactly what Wilburt told him to do.

The detective instantly felt bad for treating him like a criminal when he was just a working-class guy trying to do the right thing in life. He was so used to dealing with sneaky criminals that he had to treat everybody as if they were criminals until he learned otherwise about them.

"My apologies sir. You understand why I have to ask these types of questions right?"

"Yes." Rafael cried harder. "But I'm just a hard-working man trying to do the right thing for my family."

The detective nodded his head. "Ok. I understand and I apologize. How many kids do you have?"

"I have a daughter, she's 9, and a son, he's 7. They're my whole life. I could have been taken away from them today." He cried harder thinking about his reality.

"You're going to be ok. Don't worry. We're going to find the scumbags who did this to you. Is there anything you can offer about them? Anything you can recall that would be helpful for us to find these crooks?"

Rafael shook his head. "It all happened so fast. I got down off of the truck and there were guns in my face."

The detective nodded his head. "Ok. We'll check out the surveillance footage and see if we can nab these scumbags. In the meantime, here's my number should anything come back to memory... Just give me a call anytime day or night. Ok?"

"Yes detective. Thank you."

Wilburt watched as the goons unloaded the trailer full of iPhones into the warehouse. It had been almost a year since the last high value load he was able to secure, and even then it wasn't as valuable as the load that he'd just secured. Zaedan was going to be excited when he found out, and that made Wilburt happy because even on months when he wasn't able to produce, Zaedan still gave him more money than he could dream of just because he didn't want to see anybody struggle. Zaedan had multiple sources of legal and illegal income, so he never relied on any particular cash flow stream. This kept everybody motivated because nobody wanted to be known as the person who was freeloading and not pulling their own weight.

Wilburt watched as the last box was placed into the warehouse. In total there were 36,000 iPhone boxes, and the unloading process had taken up most of the day. He paid the goons $2 per box each for their work and smiled when he saw how happy they were to receive the money. That was $72,000 each, and nobody complained getting a bag of money that large in one day. They didn't care that the value of the total truck was $27 million, as they knew the bigger money came with way bigger responsibilities.

"Leave the trailer, leave the truck. My driver Gondon is going to take y'all where y'all need to go. He's parked up front in a black van."

Wilburt watched as the goons exited the premises and checked the time. Rafael was supposed to have been calling him from the hospital, but for some reason he was a few hours late. Wilburt exhaled. He knew it was important that he hear from him, because anything else was going to signify that he was too busy snitching. And if that was the case–

His cell phone rang mid-thought.

"Yo."

"Wilburt. Everything good on my end. They believed me."

"Aight good Rafael. Good job. Where you at? Still at the hospital?"

"Yea. I'm still here. Hey, so when do I get paid?" Rafael asked. He had been thinking about the money for months now, and now that he'd done his part, he was anxious to get it.

"Did you get a package from me on Friday from UPS?" Wilburt asked.

"Yea. You sent me a book."

"Right. I figured you wouldn't open it because niggaz rarely did. Anyways, just go to pay 180, and there's instructions on where we put the money at. People will be following you so be mindful. But the good thing is, you don't have to worry about meeting up with us. You can just give the instructions to your wife and she can pick it up, that way you won't draw any extra suspicions. My advice though is to be patient before you get the money. It's not going anywhere. And don't call me anymore for any other reason. Got it?"

"Yep. That's all good with me." Rafael said as he hung up the phone. He smiled as he thought about the things he would be able to afford with money of that magnitude. It was going to be a great holiday season for him, he was sure of it.

Wilburt drove the truck and trailer to what he called the Vehicle Graveyard. It was a secluded area that only him, Zaedan, Brizzo, and Bullethead knew about. The Vehicle Graveyard was a long strip of chemically protected land with a glossy surface designed by chemists from the underworld. He got out of the truck and walked over and pressed a button on what looked like an irrigation system. The moment he pressed the button, a white foamy liquid sprayed and covered the truck like snow. He stood watching patiently for a moment, allowing the foam to soak into the truck.

After a few minutes, he pressed a red button on the machine, and another liquid sprayed on top of the foam, and almost instantly the two chemicals fizzled like soda being sprayed out of a can. In minutes the chemicals reduced the entire truck to a puddle of liquid. The liquid sat atop the chemically protected land as if it had just rained. Wilburt picked up a vacuum and collected the liquid, sending it back into the reservoir for it to be recycled for further use.

There was a huge difference when a mafia was run by a genius compared to when one was run by an average crook. Zaedan had made sure to take advantage of every technological advantage that he could find, and they certainly came in handy for when it was time to execute the biggest of jobs.

Wilburt placed a call to his Indian buyer, who was going to drop off $8 million in cash for the $27 million worth of phones. He wasn't going to bother Zaedan about it until it was completely handled. There was no need to discuss something that hadn't happened. That was a bad way to get people's hopes up for no reason. Wilburt walked around to the opposite end of the compound and into a little room that looked like an old beat-up outhouse.

He put a code in on the door and it unlocked. On the inside there was no toilet, and anybody who walked in would have no idea of the value of that outhouse. Wilburt lifted up a wooden lid covering the floor, which exposed a set of stairs. He walked down the stairs and into a small underground room equipped with surveillance from cameras set up around the compound. He sat back in his recliner chair and studied the surroundings. He checked to make sure all of the goons had left and that nobody was laying behind. Then he checked to make sure there were no FBI agents hiding somewhere planning a sweep.

When his phone vibrated, he checked and saw that his Indian buyer, Arjun; had arrived. He watched as the Indian pulled up in a Jeep Cherokee. He frowned. If he was pulling up in a Jeep, then there was no way he had the $8 million they'd discussed. Wilburt was getting mad. He didn't have time to play. He called the Indian and watched on the screen as he answered the phone.

"Hello Wilburt. I'm here, but it's a small issue."

"Clearly it's a small issue... I don't see how you put that much money in a Jeep."

"Can you come out so I can speak to you in person?" Arjun asked.

"Speak to me in person? Man, you need to speak to me now. Just speak, my phone is secure." Wilburt exclaimed with an irritated voice.

Arjun exhaled. "Alright. Well... I do have the money as discussed. The entire $8 million, but I brought it a different way... That's why I wanted to speak to you in person to show you."

Hearing that he had the money was music to Wilburt's ears. Nothing made him happier than a man keeping his word. "Aight cool. I'm on my way."

"Wilburt you're being paranoid buddy. You know me right? Yea? You know me, I'm your buddy. I'm good people. We're good man."

WIlburt thought about what he was saying but dismissed it. There was no such thing as a good crook. If you had fucked up ways, then you had fucked up ways in whatever you were involved in. The only reason they had been in good standing for so many years is because he hadn't given Arjun a chance to cross him yet, nor did he plan to.

"Yea I hear you. I'm on the way." Wilburt walked across the yard through a secret underground tunnel that led to the inside of the warehouse. He checked his strap to make sure it was loaded and ready. He hadn't ever had to resort to anything like that with Arjun, but one could never be too safe when danger was forever a possibility.

Wilburt walked out of a side door and greeted Arjun. "What's up my guy?"

"Hey my buddy. Good to see you WIlburt. So, look at this... I have the money, but I wanted to show you how I had it." Arjun took his phone and started scrolling across through his apps until he found what he was trying to show me.

"To avoid the paper trail and to make things a little easier... And I don't know how you're going to feel about this, but I wanted to at least just present it to you... I wanted to know if I could give you the $8 million in cryptocurrency. I could give you $8 million in bitcoin instead of the cash?"

WIlburt frowned at him. "Man that's what you're tripping about? Hell yea you can send it in bitcoin. But you can't get access to the warehouse until it's confirmed in the network and is sitting in my bitcoin wallet. You're late Arjun. We've been dealing with bitcoin for years now. How you think we were able to start legit businesses without the paper trail leading to the streets?"

Arjun wiped his forehead. "I should have known buddy. You're high tech I should have already known that. Forgive me buddy."

Wilburt ignored all that damn buddy talk and pulled his phone out. He scrolled through until he found his bitcoin wallet and quickly generated a receiving address. "Here. Scan this QR Code with yours and send it over." Wilburt said as he held his phone up.

Arjun scanned it and sent it over. "Ok my buddy. It's sent."

Wilburt smiled. When he thought about all of the business transactions he'd made with Arjun through the years, he knew he had to give him more credit than he was giving. Everytime he did business with him, Arjun never asked to see the product before he paid. He was a different breed, and as he thought about it, he started to lighten up towards him.

"Thanks buddy." WIlburt said as he extended his hand to him.

"No it's thanks to you. Not me. You help me plenty buddy. This is going to get us good profit through our networks." He shook his hand and smiled.

WIlburt opened the door to the warehouse and flipped the light switch on. When Arjun stared at the huge shipment of iPhones, his mouth dropped to the floor.

"Yes my buddy. You always come through. Always good

business with you. Yes yes." He said as he opened a box and pulled a new iPhone out. "Perfect."

WIlburt's phone vibrated, the bitcoin app letting him know that the cryptocurrency had been transferred to his wallet. He smiled. "Aight Arjun. You picking it up after midnight like usual?"

"Yes buddy. I'll be coming with a crew and an 18-wheeler to load up. Will you be here?"

"Nah I won't be here. But you know how we do. You've paid me, so the door is wide open for you to handle your business. Let me know if you need anything else Arjun."

"Yes. I'll let you know. I have to talk to bossman and see what else and I'll let you know."

16

AYOKI

I was full of emotion by the time I made it back to Atlanta. Who am I kidding? I was full of emotion before I left Atlanta. I was just a crybaby when it came to family and dealing with people. Which is why even though Zaedan's grandma told me I needed to forgive myself for my past, I knew I wouldn't be able to do that. If I was able to do it, God was going to have to force me through the journey. I was vibing and listening to music on the radio when breaking news took over the airwaves.

"An Amber Alert has been issued for a 2-year-old African American toddler who was kidnapped at gunpoint in front of Wal-Mart in South Atlanta. The alleged kidnappers are described as a black man in his mid-40s and they were said to be driving a blue Chevrolet Equinox. If you have any information leading to the arrest, please call us at..."

I felt my chest tighten as I listened to the lady discuss the kidnapping of that poor baby. My stomach was hurting, and I knew I was going to throw up soon. It didn't take much to make me relive the worst day of my life, and it couldn't have come at a worse time. As I drove, I began to get dizzy, and my headaches had begun to seize control of my brain. I'd planned to make a few stops before heading home, but all of those ideas evaporated the moment I heard about the kidnapping. At that moment I wish I could help them, but it wasn't my business to jump in, and I knew what type of trouble I could get in if I just approached them and started offering unsolicited information. Authorities didn't react kindly to those with psychic or prophetical gifts. The moment your words checked out; you instantly became their top suspect.

I TURNED the air conditioner on high even though it was the middle of winter. My panic attacks could take freezing cold temperatures and make me feel like it's the dog days of summer. Sweat formed on my forehead, and I knew I needed to hurry home so I can escape my reality. LSD. Every time I felt trapped in this world, the LSD always gave me the escape I needed, always took me on a trip so I could forget about the madness. As I drove towards home, I thought about something Ms. Irena said and I decided to just try it. I grabbed my phone out of the center console and exhaled. I wasn't going to be able to do it while driving, so I pulled over at the very next exit. I followed the signs and stopped when I made it to Barnes and Nobles' parking lot.

I SAID A QUICK PRAYER, gathered my composure, and made a phone call I'd been afraid to make for years. I was afraid, and rightfully so. The last time I tried to call my Mother, she hung up on me right after I said hello. My sister changed her phone number, but my number was the same as it's always been, yet nobody had reached out to me since the incident happened. That was enough to let me know that everybody hated me. Motivated from Ms. Irena's conversation about self-forgiveness, I called my mother's phone number to try to begin the process.

"HELLO?" A soft feminine voice answered on the 4th ring.

In my mind, I had it figured out what I was going to say to her, how I was going to apologize and beg for forgiveness. In my mind... I had planned this conversation for years... But the moment I heard my mother's voice, I broke down in tears.

"I'M SORRRRRY MAAAAAA." I couldn't stop the tears from flowing the same way I couldn't stop the hurt from affecting me. "Mommyyyy please forgive me! Please! Please tell Eyoki I love her and I'm so sorrrrry!" I was crying uncontrollably, but I didn't care. I just wanted my mother and sister back. I wanted a chance to repair the bond with my family and heal from what I'd done in the past.

"MOMMYYY PLEASE! Say something! I love you and Eyoki with all my heart, and I'm begging you to forgive me for what I've done. I know it's a terrible thing, and I've been hurting every single moment, every day and every month since it's happened. Please forgive me Ma. Please." My face was soaked with my salty tears, my heart heavy and yearning– praying for my families' acceptance again. There was a silence on the phone, and for a second I thought my Mom had hung up on me.

"HELLO? MOM? YOU THERE?" It had taken a lot of courage to make that phone call. My heart was fragile at that point, and I'd held off from contacting her for so long because I felt like my heart would shatter into a million pieces if she hung up on me. Instead, what she did was much worse; much deeper and colder than hanging up on me.

"FORGIVENESS IS between you and God. You've crushed this family irreparably. That baby was only 3 years old– an innocent baby Ayoki. Just the thought of that poor baby not being able to stop that heavy vehicle from crushing him... That's inexcusable. You say you've spent years suffering since that accident? Well I say you haven't spent enough years suffering from it. You committed one of the vilest acts of any human on this planet, and I don't care if you meant to do it or didn't mean to do it. My family has not healed, and you are not to call here anymore you hear? I'm not your mother, and as far as I'm concerned... I don't know who you are."

"MOMMY!" My heart hurt so bad that I had to take a deep swallow so that I wouldn't vomit in my car. Tears ran down my face like I was standing in front of the shower head, and no matter how many tears fell down my face, I still felt dirtier and filthier by the second.

. . .

"As far as your sister... You have no idea how you've ruined her. But since it is your burden, you should go check on her. She's in Central State Hospital, in the mental asylum down in Milledgeville, GA. She's been there for 3 years now and she's lost her mind since you took her world away from her. And to think... you had the nerve to call me talking about forgive you. You're pathetic."

She hung the phone up on me, leaving me with the guilt of a thousand nations. I was sick to my stomach thinking about my sister locked away in a mental asylum. My stomach hurt as her words played on repeat in my memory. *My family hasn't healed, and you are not to call here anymore...* It really pained me because all of this was my fault. I was bad luck, a disaster, a bad omen, and I'd ruined everybody's lives that I've touched. As far as I was concerned, whatever bad things that were going to happen to me... I deserved it wholeheartedly. I was a nothing, a let-down, a failure, a snake, an addict. I was nothing more than a secret hiding, sneaky low life; a child murderer. I sat in front of Barnes and Noble and cried as much as I could get out. I cried until I couldn't cry anymore; cried until those tears turned to rabid anger. I cried until I was furious at myself, until I was seeing red and couldn't deal with life anymore.

I knew I needed to pray for my sister. I wanted to see her, but I didn't want to make things worse for her. I needed to pray for the words to speak to her and pray that our sisterly bond could pull her out of that mental asylum. However, I wasn't strong enough for any of that at that moment. All I could do was cry.

17

ZAEDAN

I sat outside of my Buckhead *Free Wi-Fi* location under the umbrella as I waited on everybody to pull up. It was a warm and breezy day despite it being the middle of winter, and as always, the FBI were parked across the street in an hourly paid parking lot. I took a deep breath and shook my head. It was amazing how much time they'd dedicated to following my moves, yet still hadn't been able to get any information about anything that was going on. It made me wonder how long they were planning on wasting time on me.

Each Monday evening me and my family met here. Bullethead, Brizzo, Wilburt, Antonio, and Maclente. We discussed pressing issues, resolved conflicts, and came with new ideas to help us grow as a family, or as a business. I knew the FBI had the area bugged, so not only did we speak in code, but we also had a live DJ on Monday evenings with loud reggae music providing the vibes. I smiled once everybody started making their way to my table. It was like clockwork– and we all smiled as we looked at the FBI's car– it was customary of us to give them a smiling group photo; and we did.

"It's a beautiful day." I yelled over the loud bass and instruments.

I pulled my notepad out of my suit, as did everybody else. We watched as Maclente opened his briefcase and pulled out a document. He had a concerned look on his face, but I was relaxed because I was assuming, he was going to lecture me about how I was keeping the books or reporting they money. Him and Antonio were particular about every detail, and it seemed like I always messed the details up. I made a mental note to allow them more control over the reporting until I could clear my mind about the Tarralla situation. To my surprise, that wasn't the situation at all.

"The phones belonged to our brother family."

I glanced at the paper and was confused on what he was talking about. I frowned. "What?" When I looked up from the paper, Wilburt was shaking his head and had a look of distress on his face.

"Lemme see that." He stood up and walked to where I was and looked at the paper.

"Fuck!" He said and balled his fists up. "Fuck! Fuck! Fuck!"

I didn't have time for talking in code because I was getting pissed that I was left out of the loop. I stood up and put my arm around his neck, as if I was hugging him. I pulled him close to me and whispered in his ear.

"What's going on?" Our *brother family* was the Solumbert Mafia– and although we didn't get money together, we also avoided stepping on each other's toes; we did our best to stay out of each other's way. I was trying to stay calm, but my anxiety was really working itself.

Wilburt exhaled. "Boss... I arranged to have a high value truck secured. I handled it all, I got the money and everything."

Initially I thought nothing of what he was saying, but after a moment I put two and two together. "How much was the truck worth?"

"$27 million."

My heart dropped to ground. "What? What the fuck did I tell you Wilburt?"

"You said if it's anything over $3 million to hit you up before you do it. I know you said it, but I swear nobody ever knew this company had anything to do with the Solumbert Mafia. I mean... I didn't even know until just now. Everything checked out, and I was trying to bring you a gift to close the year boss."

"What the fuck? I told you I didn't wanna go to war with these fuckin bastards man. What the fuck? I'm tryna get money and live. Why the fuck would you think it's ok to hit a $27 million truck on a Monday any damn way? Fuck!" I was livid.

"Maclente what the fuck. How you even find out this shit?"

He shook his head and frowned. "They said the moment the police left from questioning the driver at the hospital, the Solumberts went and questioned him. He told everything within five minutes."

"Shit!"

The Solumberts were an extension of a crime family based out of Chicago. As far as I knew, they were all either brothers or cousins, and had been putting some heavy-duty business moves down behind the scenes. The difference between me and them, I didn't mind putting my murder game down; but them... They thought all people had value and would rather kidnap a person and sell their organs to whoever wanted to pay. I'd talked to the Atlanta-area boss a few times, but our conversations never got too far because of how dark his vibe was.

"No worries. I'll handle it." I exhaled. Even though Wilburt had made a bone-headed mistake, I was going to stand behind him regardless. I was going to call and first see how we could reasonable work out the issues, but I was sure they were going to tell me they wanted the truck back. I didn't want to go to war with them, but I definitely wasn't about to give back a heist of that size. If I did something like that, my reputation was sure to take a hit.

"I got the cash right here in bitcoin. You want me to send it to your wallet?" Wilburt hesitated because he didn't want to say the wrong thing. He had already been messing up and wasn't trying to mess things up further.

"Lemme see that." We all crowded around Wilburt and stared as he opened the crypto currency app and showed us the current balance. I wasn't even pissed anymore. Me hearing him say he secured a $27 million truck, and me seeing an $8 million bitcoin balance was two totally different scenarios.

"Yea, well... Maclente, the Solumberts can go fuck themselves. They ain't getting no $8 million back no matter how they beg for it. They're going to have to charge this one to the game."

Everybody smiled except for Maclente and Antonio. Bullethead nodded his head and locked his balled fist into the palm of his left hand. Technically, Bullethead was the only person I needed on my side in the event of any potential life or death drama. I already knew what type of man he was– saw him keep his word and stand on it with his life on the line several times. That's the one person in the world whom I would never question and always trusted in any scenario other than my wife.

Brizzo had a huge smile on his face, and I had no idea why. "The hell wrong with you?" I asked as he nodded his big ass head.

"Because..." He started. "I've been felt that way about the Solumberts. Fuck them fake ass crackers. Ain't no white man in the world got balls big enough to go to war with us."

Wilburt smiled at him, and I glared at them both. I exhaled deeply and went and sat back at the table. "We don't intend to go to war with anybody on this planet." I said. "However, we will always defend ourselves and will use whatever action is necessary in order to properly win our defense."

"Hell yea." Bullethead nodded as he sat down beside me.

"If you had only $100 left to your name, and somebody walked up to you and tried to take it from you, what would you do?" I asked them as I looked around the table. They had all sat down and seemed to be in thought about the answer.

It was no surprise to hear Brizzo answer first. "Shit... It depends."

"On what Brizzo?"

"On if I have a Glock or a revolver on me. They're going to get one of them for sure."

I shook my head. He was partly right though. "It's like this... You wouldn't allow a person to take your last from you, and as men; you have to always remember that the $100 is never our last. This means that the $100 will never be the point. The point will always be that the last thing we will ever have to our names is our respect. In allowing a person to come snatch your respect from you, you'll no longer be considered a man but a bitch. As men... We will always have a tight grip on our respect, even if we have to die with it in our hands."

Maclente flipped through his folder and pulled out another sheet of paper. He handed it to Antonio, and I watched as he read the paper silently. I checked the time and was shocked to see that 35 minutes had already passed since the meeting started. We hadn't discussed but one issue, but I guess time always passed fast when you were in the presence of family.

"Right... So... Yea... I prepared this document to hand to Zaedan, but then I changed my mind about it. Where did you get this from? You got my house bugged or something? Somebody would have had to come in my house to get this shit. What the fuck?"

I frowned. "What's going on?"

"Tell him Antonio." Maclente said with a smirk on his face.

He shook his head. "For what? It's pointless. It was just a thought, but a thought that I thought better of later."

"What's up man? What was the thought? Talk to me." I prodded.

Antonio had a regretful look on his face and then seemed to say fuck it. "Man Zaedan... So, I was thinking that maybe you could let me take other clients outside of you. My wife... She says she thinks I'm not being paid what I'm worth."

My eyes widened at his words. I paid him an exorbitant amount of money each month, and even on months when I didn't profit as much for myself, I still made sure that the crew got their money no matter what. Antonio was the one who approached me and begged for me to allow him to be the family's second attorney. He told me he saw the vision and he was loyal and going to be down until the end. These were words he offered me; not words I gave him.

"Damn... Antonio, I pay you $35,000 a month... Even on months when you don't do anything. You only have one client... Me... That gives you all types of free time to do whatever you wanna do in your life. I don't understand. You don't feel like I'm paying you enough?"

"Not me, my wife."

"So, let me get this straight... You feel like I'm paying you enough, but your wife doesn't think I'm paying you enough?"

He seemed uneasy but answered the question anyways. "I mean... Yea, I'm good Zaedan... My wife. She– "

Maclente interrupted him. "Fuck all that. Hand the letter to Zaedan."

I was taken aback. I reached out and grabbed the letter, but Antonio held it tight. I stared at him, and he shook his head.

"Zaedan this letter was in my office getting ready to be discarded. I thought me and Maclente were on good terms, but for him to have someone break into my house and steal this... It's awkward, not to mention illegal. I thought you all trusted me. Is this something you told Maclente to do? You don't trust me?"

I narrowed my eyes, and it caused my eyebrows to narrow as well. "Antonio, from the beginning I've always known that Maclente has had my best interests at heart and would do whatever it took to ensure that I'm protected. If you say you were going to discard it, then I'll read it and I'll mentally discard it. I won't hold it against you."

He finally accepted my words and released his grip of the paper he'd typed up. I read it silently, but some of the key points were too good not to read out loud.

"So... I see you've written out what you think Maclente's salary is per month– $45,000. First thing I need to know is where are you getting your information, and secondly, why is his salary any of your business or have anything to do with you?"

I watched as anger took over his face and knew at that moment that his wife had nothing to do with the notion that he wasn't being paid his worth. "We're doing the same amount of work, sometimes with me doing way more work, and you're not paying us equally. I'd like a chance to grow as well. I don't want to be stuck at $35,000 per month when he's getting an extra $10,000 per month to play with."

I nodded. "I get it. It's not an issue. You want $45,000 per month? Then I'll give you $45,000 per month."

He had a surprised look on his face. "Are you serious?"

"Absolutely serious. It's time for a raise for everybody anyways."

"Wow. Thanks, Zaedan. My wife is going to be so thankful when I tell her the news. Me and my family are forever grateful."

"Don't mention it Antonio. Bring her down to the church tomorrow when you come help us pass out the turkeys and hams."

"I think she has to work tomorrow. I don't know if– "

"Bring her tomorrow when you get to the church I said. End of discussion."

He nodded his head, and I scanned over the rest of his paper he'd written without reading anything else out loud. One of the points of the paper was causing me to have doubt and concern about Antonio. He'd addressed money first, and then mentioned in the second paragraph that he should be getting paid more since the FBI were always questioning and trying to coerce him. In his letter he said that he feels like he should get paid more so that the FBI's coercion would never work.

I balled the letter up and looked at Maclente, who had an angry smirk on his face. I glanced at Antonio, but he had his head down staring at the table. I was boiling inside from what I'd just read. He was trying to blackmail me into giving him more money so that he wouldn't snitch on me to the FBI. I was pissed, but I wasn't going to show it. I was going to show him though. I didn't play like that and never would.

"Anything else anybody wanna bring to the table? Good job on what you did Wilburt, it means a lot to me honestly. The more I think about it, the more brilliant your idea seems to me. I'ma have to promote you to another level in this family. Brizzo what's up with that Pretty Tony situation? You got him locked in for the weekend?"

Brizzo was stuck in space listening to Wilburt be praised for the truck full of iPhones he'd pulled off. It was neat because the truck was something Zaedan had been against, but once he saw the profit of it, he was all in and all for it. To add insult to injury, he mentioned promoting Wilburt to another level. That was all he needed to witness in order to put his plan in motion and keep it quiet until he had the money to hand Zaedan the same way Wilburt had done.

"Brizzo? You hear me?"

"Oh yea. Pretty Tony is locked in. He said he was bringing all of black Hollywood to the casino this weekend. The who's who of Atlanta. It's going to be a lot of millionaires present this weekend."

I nodded. I actually believed him. For all of the flaws that Brizzo had, I knew his top quality was that he didn't give up. He would keep trying until he got it right, and as a man that was something that had to be respected in itself. I watched as the guys in the FBI surveillance vehicle got frustrated from the loud reggae music and finally drove off. I suppressed a laugh because they were wasting their time anyway if they thought I was the damn plug to some drugs out here. They couldn't be dumber if they tried.

"Aye Zae... I meant to tell you..." Bullethead said as he pulled his phone out. He scrolled for a few seconds until he found what he was looking for. "We got invited to the club on Friday night. You know it's– "

I cut him off before he could even finish. "Nah, I'm not with that Bullethead. You know I'm not the clubbing type bro."

"Nah hear me out Zae. This is Big Purk's birthday party. He told me to make sure you come support him the same way he supports the casino."

I knew he had me then. I couldn't turn down Big Purk's invite, because he was one of the biggest drug dealers in the city and supported all of my business ventures without question. He even donated money to our church. Helped out whenever we needed an extra hand– aside from his occupation, he was a model citizen. His crew was the complete opposite though. His crew was flamboyant, and any event they attended was sure to cause a shootout just because of the arrogance of them as a whole. It wasn't my duty to give him any advice on how to run his crew. That would be an insult from a boss to a boss. I could only support or choose not to, and in this instance, I had to.

"Aight cool. Tell Big Purk we'll be there." As soon as I could finish the sentence, Brizzo balled his fist up in celebration like he'd just hit a game winning shot.

"Yes! Hell yea! We gon be the talk of the party!" Brizzo said excitedly. It was something about Brizzo that had started to make me really wonder about him. It seemed like he was changing into somebody else completely, and if he continued to do so, I was going to have to let him change way the fuck away from me. I couldn't afford to throw my life away because of another person's errors. It was something I was going to have to think about deeply over the next few weeks.

"So, look... Maclente you already handled the money from the casino right?"

"Yea I did that earlier."

Antonio looked up with a surprised look on his face.

"What Antonio?" He was starting to piss me off at that point.

"It's just... I wasn't aware that Maclente had already done it. I thought it was something we were going to do together."

"Aye listen man... Which one is it? You're underpaid for your work or you don't have enough work?" I snarled at him.

He shook his head but didn't reply. He didn't have to reply honestly. He'd already written his death certificate when he decided to blackmail me into giving him a raise. I was going to handle him, but it was going to be so under the radar that even Bullethead wasn't going to know. I was going to be patient until the perfect time... And then...

"I'm sorry Zae. I've been under a lot of pressure lately dealing with my family and all. Well, my wife... You know... She said an FBI agent approached her one day and gave her a business card. She doesn't really know anything, but neither do I honestly. Especially the types of questions they ask."

He was digging his hole further and further and didn't realize it. "What type of questions do they ask Antonio?"

He looked up at me and was either surprised that he'd made the error of getting himself caught up in his story, or surprised that I spotted the error. Either way, he was going to get axed the moment I had the opportunity.

"I wouldn't know what questions they ask though. I'm just guessing I guess..."

"You wouldn't know? You mean your wife wouldn't tell you? Or you didn't ask her?"

He looked down at the ground like a little kid. "Zaedan she was fussing at me when she was telling the story, and my anxiety got the best of me. I can barely remember what–"

"Yea don't worry about it. Well look y'all... I'm about to go to the house and spend some time with Ayoki. Probably going to surprise her with a dinner date or something. I won't be out too late though because of the church event tomorrow. I hope you all are able to come help out. It's truly a blessing when you help those in need. You know... You never know when you yourself could be that person in need."

They nodded their heads without replying, but they didn't have to. I knew they were going to be there to help, as they did with all other events I was involved with. I was thankful for them all, as they were the brothers I never had. I stood up and dapped each of my brothers, telling them to drive safe, watch your back, and call me if they needed anything– those words were routine for me, as I always wanted the best for everyone. I don't know what I would do if something happened to any of them. My wife, my church, and my brothers... That was exactly what my life was comprised of.

18

BRIZZO

My sleep had been off ever since I used that cocaine Pretty Tony gave me. I know it wasn't still in my system because I wasn't happy at all. I sat in my car outside of *Free Wi-Fi* and leaned back in my seat. I'd been the last person out of the crew to leave, since I was busy flirting with one of the waitresses. I'd been trying to fuck Leteya for months now, and she still didn't seem to wanna give a nigga no play. I knew what it was though. It was because I didn't have that boss presence that I really needed. I was sick and tired of looking like a follower in the crew and had made up my mind that I was going to start running some shit.

Zaedan would never have a problem getting whatever chick he wanted, but he was so caught up in love with my cousin that it made no sense. To me, I thought my cousin was just average, but I guess because we're related, I could never see her the same as other people did. However, since we were related, I also knew other people could never see her the same way I did. Others may have seen her as a church-going good-girl, and maybe she has changed her ways slightly, but I knew for a fact that she was still just a rugged ass street chick just like me and Zaedan.

I think Zaedan's attraction to her probably comes from him liking the real her that he didn't know yet. Maybe he felt a magnetism that he was unaware of, and just couldn't stay away from her. How crazy was it that he didn't want us selling drugs, yet his wife always made me go out and get her drugs? She was sneaky, but just like she made me promise her not to tell Zaedan, I'd made her promise that if she ever got caught, she couldn't mention that it came from me. So far everything had been on the up and up between us.

We'd had a great working relationship. She wanted LSD, I gave her LSD, she gave me the money; I profited double the cost of it. That's not how I set it up, that's how she wanted it to be. I didn't approach her with the drug, she approached me to get more of it. I had no idea how she started with that shit, but I did have an idea of how she was going to get started with the next drug.

The guy I was getting the LSD from for Ayoki was a Mexican named Tony, but of course I couldn't help myself from calling him Tony Montana. He hated that shit, but it was funny as hell every time he reacted to it. I sent Tony a text, letting him know I was headed his way. It didn't take long for him to reply. That's probably because he was always on his damn phone. I put my seatbelt on, turned my music up, and slid my Camaro into the heavy Atlanta traffic. It was evening, so there were a lot of drivers headed from one destination to the next; causing the traffic to be extra stiff on Peachtree Street.

There were no FBI agents following me, which was a great thing because there was no way I could explain some shit like that to Tony. As I drove, I tried to envision how that conversation would be.

"Yo what the fuck? Who the fuck is in that unmarked car and why the fuck are they following you?"

"Oh, it's all good Tony. That's just the FBI. They always follow me."

Nah... I could never have that conversation with Tony and expect to wake up the next day in good health. Hell, I was spooked when the FBI *first* started following us. I thought for sure I was going to go to prison that same day, but after long, Zaedan explained to me how things worked when you really had an organized crime ring. He explained that by him having a lawyer that only worked for him, and who was always around that it made it nearly impossible to just get arrested for some random shit without excellent probable cause.

He told me that Maclente was like a scarecrow. Told me that as long as he was amongst us, it made the FBI weary of messing up a potential investigation. I had doubt initially, but eventually I discovered that he was right. It had gotten to the point to where the FBI were treating us the way TMZ treated celebrities. They were always waiting somewhere off in the cut, always showing up at our public appearances, and always asking us questions when they walked up on us.

Well not always. They never spoke to us whenever Maclente was around. I made a mental note to hire my own personal lawyer to ride around with me the deeper I made it in the drug game. I pulled up to the quiet sub-division and parked my car in his driveway once I made it to his house. The street was empty, and there was a red bicycle on the side of his house with a helmet laying on the ground beside it. I didn't even know he had a child, and I'd been doing business with him on the low for at least a couple of years. I wondered why the hell the bike was on the side of the house though. It was like he was trying to hide it, or maybe that's just where he kept it put up at.

I checked my pistol and made sure it was loaded and ready. I never anticipated anything going wrong dealing with him, but at the same time... when you dealt with and in the streets, you better look twice at your own shadow. I walked to the side door and he opened it before I could knock.

"Hurry. Come in."

I walked in quickly and moved aside as he locked the door. He had 6 locks on the door, so this was different from the last time I came. He had two AKs sitting on the table, and a camera system that I'd never seen before also. After he secured the last lock, he looked out of a peephole and sighed, but didn't budge. I didn't even realize he was holding a pistol until I saw him scratch his thigh with it.

"Damn migo. The fuck. You got fleas?" I joked.

He didn't reply but kept looking, breathing hard, and shaking slightly. He was starting to make me nervous, and that was rare. It took a whole lot of shit to make a nigga like me nervous, but Tony was absolutely doing a whole lot of shit. I didn't say anything, and instead went and sat at the kitchen table. I was starting to feel like I'd caught him at a bad time, and maybe I should get the fuck out of there. I stood up and he turned around and exhaled. He walked up to and shook his head.

"Sorry man. I'm going through some shit right now. What all do you need right now?"

I frowned. He couldn't be going through more shit than I was going through, but of course he wouldn't have known. "What kind of shit are you going through? Maybe I can help?" I offered.

The truth was, I was able to help a lot of people with a lot of shit these days. All I had to do was bring it to Zaedan, and I was bound to have a solution to whatever the issue might be. Tony was sweating like he'd just came back from the gym, and he smelled like his water was off. That was nothing new though. I once came over and Tony had a half million dollars on the table and hadn't taken a bath in a week.

"Maybe you can help. First what do you need from me?"

"Shit you know I need the usual, but what I wanted to holla at you about... I'm trying to get plugged in on them bricks."

"Bricks?" Tony looked at me warily.

"Hell yea man. Listen Tony... I know you think I'm just talking here, but the way I see it... I'm ready to start king pinning some shit around here. Shit... I mean why not me. You know I'm legit for it. You know I won't fuck you over. We can get to the point where I'm the only person you gotta deal with. You know– "

"Enough enough." Tony said and shook his head. "I tell you what... I need some help. You help me out, and I'll see what I can do to help you out with that later."

"Hell to the naw Tony Montana. If I'm gon' help you, then you help me. This ain't no buy now pay later shit. Same time migo."

Tony looked at me with a scowl on his face. "Well I don't need your fuckin help man. You offered me– "

"Ok wait... Wait... We're getting off on the wrong foot. What you need me to do?"

"Nah don't worry about it man. I'll get your stuff. Wait right here." He said and walked away.

"Hey Tony. I'll help you. Seriously." I said as he walked down the hallway. "Yo you hear me?"

He didn't reply and instead kept walking. I got up from the table and followed him down the hallway. "Tony." I shouted right before he was about to walk into a room.

"What the fuck? I told you to sit down until I got back. What the fuck are you following me for?" He said as he pulled his pistol out of his waist.

"Nah I was just saying I would help you man."

"Fuck your help." He said as he took his gun off safety and walked towards me. "Get the fuck out of my house. I don't have shit for you. Get the fuck out now."

The fuck? As long as I'd known and been doing business with him, he'd never acted like that towards me, but I wasn't about to give him a chance to ever act like that again.

"Aight aight Tony. My apologies." I stepped back with my hands raised as he ran up to me with his pistol in his hand.

"Yea your apologies get the fuck out." He said as he waved his gun towards the door. I walked to the door and reached in my pocket to pull my keys out. Once I got to the door, I dropped the keys on the floor on purpose, but didn't move.

"Yo you mind if I pick my keys up?" I asked him.

"Get your keys and get the fuck out."

In one motion, I reached down, drew my pistol and shot him twice in the chest. He dropped his gun and grabbed at his chest, blood covering his hand as if he'd poured a bucket of paint on it. He coughed and staggered, his body struggling between the willpower to remain standing or collapse to the ground. He kept his eyes trained on me as if he was trying to get a good description of me to give to the police in hell. I watched as his legs finally gave way. He fell against a small table, knocking it over and the lamp which once stood atop it.

He wasn't dead yet. He was still twitching, laying on his back against the broken table, hand still on his chest, blood still pouring out, still trying to speak. I walked over to him to finish putting him out of his misery, but once I stood over him, he took his bloody hand off of his chest and pointed to the hallway I'd tried to follow him down. I looked up and didn't see shit in the hallway. I put the barrel of my pistol against his forehead and was about to pull the trigger when I heard a siren in the distance.

It scared me for a second, but I could tell that the siren was headed in the opposite direction; as the sound of it grew more faint with each passing moment. By the time the noise of the siren faded, he was no longer breathing. I was still going to shoot him one more time for good measure. If I didn't trust him when he was alive, then I damn sure wasn't going to trust him if he was almost dead. He needed to be all the way dead, with no room for return. I stood back from him so that his blood wouldn't get on my clothes. I aimed my pistol at him and froze in my tracks.

In the hallway was a young Mexican boy, all of about 5 years old staring at me. *Fuck!* I couldn't leave the kid in the house by himself, and I couldn't bring myself to kill him. He was innocent in the situation. I put my gun down and walked towards him. He started shaking as I walked close. He was frightened. "Is anybody else here?" I asked.

He just stared at me, and he too smelled as if the water was off. "Do you speak English?" I asked.

He stared at me as if he was trying to figure out what I was talking about, but he didn't say anything. I kept my pistol in hand and walked past him down the hallway. I walked in the room that Tony had been about to walk in, and my eyes lit up. There were packages stacked from about six feet off of the floor, and gallons of what looked like water sitting around the packages. I hit a light switch and as I walked closer, I saw that half of the packages were heroin, and half of the packages were cocaine.

The gallons were LSD. I did a quick count and I knew I'd hit the jackpot. Based on what I was spending for the little bit I was buying for Ayoki, I estimated a gallon of it had to cost about $120,000. There was at least ten gallons of the shit, and at least 60 kilos of cocaine and heroin. In the corner of the room were two sleeping bags, one for an adult and one for a kid, and I suddenly felt horrible about what I'd just done. The little sleeping bag had Paw Patrol prints all over it and there was a little plastic toy truck on the floor beside the bag.

I picked up two gallons of the LSD and made my way out of the room. When I got back in the living room, I felt even worse. The kid was standing over his dead father shaking. I shook my head because I felt like a damn fuck up. It was eating at me something serious that I'd taking someone's father away from him. I put one of the gallons down to unlock the door, and then I walked over and grabbed the kids' hand.

"Come with me." I said.

I pulled his hand as I walked and let go of his hand once I got to the door. I picked up the other gallon and made my way to the car. He walked with me silently. I put the two gallons in the backseat and made him get in the front seat. I locked him in the car and ran back in to get more jugs of LSD out. I was going to have to come back for the coke and heroin, but I was about to get off of that LSD for half price and profit something nice.

I started the car and put my seatbelt on. "Put your seatbelt on." I said to the kid. He didn't budge, just sat there looking at me. I leaned over and put his seatbelt on for him and cracked the window to let some of the odor out. I stopped at McDonalds and ordered me something to eat and a kid's meal until I could figure out what the fuck I was going to do with him. I made it home and handed him the kid's meal, and he just stared at me holding it. I took his truck out of my pocket and handed it to him, and he dropped the kid's meal bag on the floor and took the truck out of my hand.

I exhaled. I wasn't no damn babysitter and I didn't have the first clue on what to do in this situation. I opened the kid's meal bag up and pulled a burger out. I unwrapped it and handed it to him. He grabbed it and ate it so fast I don't think I saw him chew it even once. I could tell that he'd never had a kid's meal before in his life, and it seemed as if he hadn't eaten anything in at least a few days.

I pulled the fries out and handed it to him, and he ate that just as fast. After he was done eating, he walked into the corner of the living room and sat down. I felt so bad for him because clearly that's what he was used to. I had an extra bedroom in my apartment, so I led him to it and turned the tv on for him. Disney Jr held his attention while I tried to brainstorm how I was going to get rid of the kid.

After a few hours of thinking, my best idea was to get help from Zaedan regarding the situation. But before I did that, I was going to have to bring him the money first so he wouldn't have a fit about the drugs and shit. And if I was going to bring money for drugs, I needed to go back and get the coke and heroin as well. Ayoki had been texting me all afternoon, but I'd told her she had to give me another day or two because I had a lot going on. She didn't wanna hear that, but there was no way I could pull up on her with a whole child.

Since the kid was sleep, I figured that was the perfect

time to go back and get the cocaine and heroin from the house. I figured I could hurry up and handle that and make it back to the house before the kid woke up. I hopped in the car and beat the streets up as I drove back to the house. I was going to put as much coke and heroin in my trunk that I could fit and take another trip back to get the rest if I had to.

As soon as I reached the street, I had to keep going. The whole street was crawling with police officers, agents, and K-9 dogs. I drove down a few streets and did a u-turn so I could get the fuck out of the area. As I was driving past the street again, I had to yield at the stop sign so that a news van could make its way down the street. Fox 5 News. I made a mental note to check the news later so I could find out what the hell was going on. In the meantime, I was going to need to get rid of that LSD like yesterday.

19

AYOKI

I was still devastated regarding the phone call I'd had with my mother but remembering the words that Ms. Irena had given to me calmed me down a lot. I was going to try my best to forgive myself, but I knew in order to do that I would have to come clean with my husband about what was going on. I was going to do it soon, but I knew I had to first come clean with my sister about how bad I was feeling. I was going to see my sister in the psych ward after the event with the church, and I was going to continue to work on my bond with her even if it took me the remainder of my life.

I WAS GOING to get deep in the Bible tonight, as there were questions I needed answers to and only God had the answer key. I wanted to be a better woman, a better Christian, a better person all-around. I was sorry about my past. I'd made a mistake and that could never be changed. I'd beaten myself up about it for years, and my family had beaten me up and outcasted me as a member. However, I was still a woman with feelings of my own. They were just as fragile as any other human on God's green earth, and I needed to stand up for myself as a person while I was still breathing.

WHAT GAVE others the ability to look down on me when they themselves were not perfect? I didn't like that, and I wanted my life to be different heading into the new year. I was going to fight for that because I knew the devil wasn't going to allow it to happen without me waging war. The stakes were high in this one because both me and the devil were fighting for my life, my soul, my everything. I refused to lose.

20

ZAEDAN

The conversation with Arcielly Solumbert couldn't wait another minute. I'd called him after the meeting at Free Wi-Fi and tried to schedule a sit-down between us, but the urgency in his voice let me know that this matter had to be handled immediately. As such, me and Bullethead were being patted down at the backdoor of a small strip club that I didn't even know they had ownership in. They let us in after patting us down, being clear about who was in charge right away.

There was a code in the mafia that revolved around respect of each other bosses. I knew they would uphold the code, so I wasn't worried about not having a weapon for a mutual meeting, but I was worried about what was going to happen later after the meeting. There was no way I could give up $8 million no matter how it was cut, unless they were able to really convince me otherwise.

I sat down at the end of the table and Bullethead sat next to me. Arcielly sat at the other end, his lawyer sat behind him smoking a cigar, and his right-hand man sat in the middle of the table with his gun in plain sight. There were two other guys standing on opposite ends of the room, no doubt each of them carrying, and there were two men standing at the door. Even if I was armed, there was no way me and Bullethead could take them all out even if we had been strapped.

"Zaedan... How long have you known me?"

"Quite a while. What, around 3 or 4 years?"

"Exactly. We've known each other since when you first decided that you wanted to join this thing of ours, this circle of families. I've always applauded you for how you've moved over the years... You know... the families refer to you as a boss amongst bosses."

"Well thanks Arcielly... But that's not my ultimate goal in life. I don't want to be the baddest boss or anything like that. All I want to do is to get into position so that I can make bigger moves for my future generations to come. Everything I do today I never intend to do forever."

Arcielly lit his cigar and took a quick puff on it, let it out, and then took a deeper pull on it. He opened the carrying case he had in front of him and offered me a cigar.

"No thanks."

"No problem." Arcielly placed his cigar against his ash tray at an angle and sat back in the chair. "See how it's no problem that you didn't want a cigar?"

I stared at him without reply. I was assuming it was a rhetorical question. I lifted my right eyebrow briefly, and sat up straight in my chair, staring him directly in the eyes.

"See... the reason it's not a problem that you don't want the cigar is because that's more cigars for me. The other reason it's not a problem is because if you leave out of this room and leave me with my cigars, there are no consequences with you knowing that I myself has a box of cigars. The reason I have a problem with you only using this thing of ours for financial gain and then leaving to do something else with your life... See... You'll then have too much information, you'll know too much about me and all of the other families involved. Let's just say... I don't see that going too well."

I shook my head. "I get it, but that's a pipe dream for now. It's no different than any other dream that any other criminal may have in the back of their minds. It doesn't mean it's going to come true. In the event that it does, we can address that then. I didn't come to discuss things that haven't happened yet."

Arcielly looked at his lawyer and they both started laughing. Then his right-hand man joined in on the laughter. I didn't see anything funny, but I didn't care to address laughter at that moment. I had tough skin and a sharp mind, so I wasn't one to cancel myself out by making irrational chatter. Arcielly seemed irritated that I didn't ask him what was so funny. He was getting angry because I was choosing not to engage or enable. I sat stoic.

"So... Zaedan Montez... That is your last name right?"

I didn't reply. He'd done great research, but I wasn't surprised. I never told people what my last name was, and when I did I used my fake driver's license under Zaedan Smith.

"So I know you don't want to be labeled or go by any certain name, but you know what? A couple of people... I won't say any names... But a couple of families think that you think you're better than everyone else."

I didn't react, but he was pushing it.

"With your different languages, your education, your businesses, your involvement in the church... Then you refused to label your family by any particular name... Well what that does is create confusion when you do things out here in the streets. By you not attaching a name to your family, you bring unnecessary heat onto other families who don't want or deserve that heat. You see?"

Everything he was telling me were things that I'd already thought out and was the reason I operated the way I did. I looked at Bullethead and he grunted quietly. I shot him a smirk and eye roll and stared back at Arcielly, waiting on him to finish his point. He pulled his pistol out and sat it on the table beside the cigars.

"So, with using a name for your family, when a $27 million truck full of iPhones got robbed, it didn't take long to identify the culprits as the Montez Crime Family. It didn't take any effort for me to avoid confrontation with all other crime families and reach out to the person with balls big enough to steal my truck. And here we are, me and you, two bosses with one problem. So how soon before you can return my truck?"

I exhaled. I wanted to resolve it, but not the same way he wanted to resolve it. "So... first let me just add that I haven't put in motion any targets towards you or any of your trucks. So, with saying that, I want you to be clear in understanding that I didn't rob you nor do I know anything about any of your trucks. As far as I'm concerned, this could just be a ploy of you trying to extort me for $27 million– "

"Don't fucking play with my intelligence Zaedan. I'm going to give you 48 hours to return my truck in its entirety, and there better not be so much as one phone charger missing out of a box. In the event that the truck is returned, we shake hands and acknowledge the error; but in the event that the truck is not returned plus an inconvenience fee of $500,000; there will be funerals to attend."

I continued to stare at him through his thick cigar smoke. His words didn't move me, they excited me, but he probably didn't know that. I showed no emotion whatsoever, and instead I stood up from my seat so that I could leave. Bullethead stood up right after I did.

"Wait... I'm not done with you. Have a seat, we still have something extremely important to discuss."

"What? You coming to the church tomorrow to help pass out hams and turkeys?" I smiled at him, actually hoping he would say yes.

He stared at me like I was crazy. "You're trying to be a comedian, and here I am trying to help you so that your killer jokes don't get you killed."

I'd been trying to lighten the mood since I walked in the room, but it was only getting darker by the moment.

Arcielly put his cigar out. I was glad because it wasn't like he was smoking it anyways. It seemed like he only had it lit for effect, but that effect would never work on me. I wasn't intimidated in the least bit. I didn't feel like sitting down, and neither did Bullethead. I sighed. "Aye... say what you gotta say Arcielly." My temper was building up pressure like a damn about to explode, despite the good job I'd done of trying to suppress it.

"See... that's what irks me about you people. You have the nerve to step on toes inside of my world and have an attitude. My world that is organized crime. See the difference? Your world is bloods and crips, pick one."

I turned to leave, and I wasn't stopping. Bullethead walked behind me, and I knew that if it came down to it, me and Bullethead would take on the world back to back until the end. He was really my best friend in this world beside my wife. I made it to the door and glared at the guy holding his gun until he moved aside.

"Zaedan serious... You really wanna hear this." Arcielly yelled sarcastically from across the room.

I turned to face him. "What?" I yelled, clearly irritated.

He shook his head slowly as he got up and walked towards where I was standing. "Listen. The only reason I'm about to tell you this is because I need you to stay alive long enough to deliver my fucking truck." He was talking as he walked and stopped in front of me and Bullethead.

"You need to lay low. I don't know what type of shit you've done to the cartel out of Mexico, but I caught word that they were pissed about whatever robbery your family put down on them. I don't know why you're robbing every-thing as of recently, out here behaving like a group of erratic criminals, but this hasn't been like you Zaedan. You've always operated with finesse, and I hate to see you let greed consume you. Robbing drug cartels? Kidnapping the son of the leader of the cartel? I didn't even know you dealt with drugs."

"Don't fuckin insult me." I was furious. "You know got damn well I don't fuck with drugs no type of way. Miss me with all the rumors and let me think about what I can do about this truck that I clearly don't have, yet you're begging me for it as if I have it."

Arcielly's white face turned a rich shade of red. "No, you will have my truck. You will return it with interest, or you're going to deliver me 27 and a half million dollars. It's really that simple."

Without another word, we turned and left out of the meeting. It's an unexplainable weird feeling that comes over you when you walk away from your enemies when you know they have guns. It's eerie, and with every step you take, you're expecting a hot bullet to pierce your back or enter the back of your head. Me and Bullethead walked briskly away from the crowd of men as they stood outside the door to their office.

Bullethead got in the car with me and we both exhaled the moment we shut the car doors.

I leaned back in my seat and groaned. Lately it had been problem after problem in my life and with no end in sight. One minute it was the FBI, another minute it was Brizzo fucking with my anxiety, one minute it's Tarralla with some child that was allegedly mine, another minute it's the Solumbert crime family and now the damn cartel.

"Fuck." I spat as I laid my hand against my forehead. Regardless of how many problems that were causing thorns in my side, it didn't mean that I got a chance to take a moment off. It didn't mean that I could give up and it didn't mean that I wouldn't have to face the problems head on. I had people who followed and trusted me to make decisions, even in the times when I no longer had the answers myself.

"Zae I can just go in there and give them a good talking to, and it would all be over with." Bullethead said, sensing my mood.

"Nah... We don't have to do that. All that's going to do is put way more heat on us. If word gets out to the other crime families that we were operating with no respect, then our days would be numbered. It would be an all-out war. It's kind of like how the United States government would go to war if one country took out another country. The reason the US couldn't allow it to happen is because if they didn't go to war, then they know they could be next if they allowed the bully to continue to operate freely."

Bullethead nodded his head slowly as he listened to my words. He rubbed his chin in deep thought, and then looked at me with a confident look on his face. "See that's why I follow your every word Zaedan. You're more than a brother to me. You're a genius. It's nobody I know who's smarter than you in these streets. That's why I rock with you so hard.

Because I know one day, you'll be on top of the world legally. The day that happens, we won't have to worry about these streets anymore."

His words hit home because I knew he meant what he was saying. He wasn't saying it to kiss ass or be fake or funny, that was the truest thoughts of my truest friend, and I knew I couldn't fuck up with my decision-making when it came to the situation at hand. I drove in silence, replaying my best friend's words in my head over and over. The drive gave me time to think, and by the time I made it back I'd had an idea.

I dropped Bullethead off at his car and dapped him up. "Bro go home and get some rest. I'll see you tomorrow at church."

He hesitated for a second and stared at me. "You don't need me to do anything?"

"Nah, I'll handle everything. If it gets to be too much or too messy, I'll give you a call." As I spoke, I saw the distraught look on his face, and it made me look away.

"Zae I really think I should ride with you for whatever it is you're about to do. You know I got your back, and if I slip then I don't mind taking a bullet for me slipping than for you to take a bullet for me not slipping."

"Bro it's all good. Everything is going to be fine... I'll see you tomorrow at church for the giveaway." I repeated.

AFTER DROPPING BULLETHEAD OFF, the first phone call I made was to my wife. I let Ayoki know that I was going to be a little late making it home because I still had a guy who needed a good talking to. I could hear a little sadness in her voice, but I vowed to myself that I was going to take her on vacation the moment I cleared up some of the drama that was taking place in my personal life. After I got off of the phone with her, I jumped on the expressway and took 85 South for about 40 minutes to a small city called Newnan, GA.

Bullethead had given me some advice earlier and didn't even realize it. When he referred to me as the smartest guy in the streets he'd ever known, what he didn't know was that some of my most brilliant ideas had come from a guy whom I thought of as the Godfather. I'd never discussed the Godfather to nobody in my crew, had never even discussed him with my wife; and as far as I knew, nobody who knew me never would have thought that I even knew a guy of this caliber.

He was about ten years or so older than me and was considered crime family royalty to everybody who knew his name. Every time I'd gotten myself in a jam, I knew there was nobody better to help me get out of it than this guy. Other crime families might consider me the boss of all bosses, but I knew that that was an exaggeration. The most powerful people in the world always moved in the darkness. Control and power weren't anything that could be seen, and that's why most flamboyant criminals had none.

I made my way to the Godfather's address and knocked on the door. It was getting late, so I was hoping that he wasn't too busy to help me out. He didn't have a phone number or email address, so anybody who wanted to talk to him had to speak to him face to face. The door unlocked, and one of his soldiers stood in front of me holding a gun so big that I didn't even know what it was.

"What?" His soldier asked rudely.

"I'm here to see Malcolm Powers." I said as I looked him in his eyes.

"Ain't no Malcolm Powers live here. Get the fuck on." He said rudely.

I knew the soldier wasn't new, but I'd never met him before, and that's probably why he was acting the way he was. I don't blame him though, because Malcolm was top 5 on America's Most Wanted, and he couldn't afford any slip-ups.

"I understand. My name is Zaedan Montez. I'll come back in about 20 minutes." I said, and then walked away from the door and got back in my car. I drove out of the neighborhood and stopped at Chik Fil-A to grab something to eat, and by the time I'd returned, around 25 minutes had passed.

When I saw that nobody had been following me, I jumped out of my car and walked back to the door. I knocked again, and the same soldier opened the door. This time he didn't speak, and instead unlatched the screen door that separated us last time and let me in the residence. He didn't have the gun in his hand the second time he opened the door, and I made a mental note to ask Malcolm what kind of gun it was.

He locked the door back, and I didn't realize how many locks, bolts, and bars were attached to the frame of the door until I saw him secure them. "You can go to the living room." The soldier said as he waved me off and continued with the locks.

I paused a second as I looked a little closer at the door locks. One of them was an in-house fingerprint lock that I'd never seen before and when he put his thumb on it, a sliding metal shield slid across the door from the inside. The entrance was state of the art, but it wasn't surprising, as everything Malcolm Powers did was advanced; which was exactly where I drew my motivation from. I wouldn't have been inspired to go to college and lead a crew if I didn't see Malcolm Powers do it successfully.

I walked into the living room and sat in the chair I normally sat in whenever I came to visit him. After a few moments, Kyla and Malcolm walked out of the room wearing matching pajamas with Christmas trees printed on them, each of them holding a cup of what looked like hot chocolate. It was such a happy sight for me to see. I stood up respectfully, my hands folded before me, understanding that I was just a mere mortal kid in the presence of Malcolm and his wife.

"Would you like something to drink?" Kyla asked me, her tone direct, her stance aware, but her face still as beautiful as the face of any super model. She had the vibe of a woman who'd been through plenty, but the face of a woman who hadn't been through any.

"I'm fine. Thank you." I said, not wanting to inconvenience them in any way or form.

Kyla leaned over and kissed her husband gently. "I'll be in the room if you need me. I love you."

"I love you too." He said before turning back to me. "Have a seat."

He sat across from me in a recliner, a small table sitting between us. He sat the drink down on the table and shook his head.

"Good decision on not wanting anything to drink Zaedan. That stuff tastes horrible." He said with a smile on his face.

I smiled back. Patient with my time with him, but cautious not to take too much of it.

"The only reason I drink it is because it cured my cancer."

Startled, I looked in his eyes with a confused look. I

looked at him, and he seemed as healthy as anybody I'd ever known. I didn't recall a time when he was sick. It wasn't in any of the newspaper articles, nor did it ever show up in any research I'd done.

"I didn't know you had cancer. When was this?" I asked curiously.

"I don't have cancer." He said matter of factly. "But I did have it once. It's really how I escaped the federal government's claws, but I'll tell you that story some other time. You're going to love it." He smiled as he took another sip of his drink.

"What's that drink?" I pointed to his cup. I'd never even known there was a cure for cancer, but if anybody would know, it would be Malcolm Powers.

"It's a ground rhino horn drink, blended into a hot chocolate."

"Rhino horn? Wow. What's the price of a rhino horn?" It was all foreign to me.

"Well a kilogram of rhino horn powder would cost around $75,000 right now, maybe more since it's so much outrage regarding it right now. You know... governments can't afford for people to have cures to their most profitable diseases. That's why every time a person claims there's a cure, they always use a private group of scientists to debunk each claim. Why do you think there are so many people who continue to stand by the cures regardless of what these private scientists claim?"

"I never thought about that."

"It's true. That's like if you were to tell me that you could magically make a $100 bill appear out of thin air. If I saw you do it, then I would stand by it and tell another person, and before long, there would be common knowledge that you had that type of talent. At some point, there will be a fake researcher who claims that he sat down with you and found out that you were unable to do it. See... the public is always waiting on that researcher to debunk what's too good to be true, and once they see that, they continue to believe in the lies that control them."

I sat back in my chair, much the same way Bullethead did when I spoke earlier. Malcolm Powers had been a sheer genius, and I was honored to be in his presence. He'd been on America's Most Wanted list for years at that point, and at that point the reward leading to his arrest had topped $2 million worldwide. I was one of only a handful of people who knew of his whereabouts. Every person who knew had just as much to lose as he did, if not more.

He sat his cup down and cross his fingers as he stared at me. "One of your crew members... the young guy... He took out a dear friend of mine earlier today, and he interfered with some business."

My mouth dropped to the floor, and my heart was beating frantically. "Wait what?" I asked, my face filled with concern.

"I knew you didn't know, but I'm letting you know right now. I've been deep in with the cartel for over a decade and a half, so of course even though I'm inactive, they still reach me to find out things when I'm able to."

"But- but- how do you know it was somebody from my crew?" I asked, concern overtaking my mind.

Malcolm Powers picked up a remote control and turned the television on that was on the wall. "They had surveillance in the house, and they sent me a copy of the tape. Apparently, he had been doing business with this guy for a while now, but today it didn't go right."

He pushed play, and as soon as I saw Brizzo, I closed my eyes, unable to see any more. What the fuck was his dumb

ass thinking? I thought to myself as I opened my eyes to see
him execute the Mexican in cold blood. "What the fuck?" I
said aloud.

"Yes. Tony was good people. Tony asked me about your
guy when they first met each other, and I feel bad because I
vouched for him." Malcolm said, his eyes filled with worry.

I didn't even know that Brizzo was dealing with cartel
members at all. What was the purpose? He had no reason
because we didn't sell drugs. I knew I was going to have to
make it right. There was no other way. I hated it, but it had
to be done. "Malcolm I'm going to handle it. You let whoever
know– "

"Zaedan listen. The cartel will want blood. They're
extremely offended, and blood is the only thing that will
satisfy them."

I heard him loud and clear. "Ok. I'm going to handle it."

"How?" He asked.

"I'm going to take him out."

"You're going to take out your own family?" He asked
with a frown.

"Yes. He offended you, and he offended the cartel, and
he didn't act under my orders, so I have to do that to make it
right."

Malcolm shook his head. "Of course, I can't tell you what
to do in this situation, but I can tell you that if you take out
your own family, it'll make it seem like you have no honor.
Men who can't stand with their family either right or wrong
don't deserve to have a family stand with him whether right
or wrong."

I was so lost that I didn't know what to do, and that's the
entire reason I'd come to Malcolm in the first place. I really
needed guidance. I sat there in silence, allowing his words
to echo in my mind. How could I make things right with

everybody and still keep my reputation and qualities as a stand-up leader? The pressure was getting to me, and I felt a sick feeling come over me as I watched Brizzo walk the kid to his car while holding something in his hands. I was going to get to the bottom of it, no doubt about it.

"I know you didn't come here for me to tell you that type of news, so tell me what's up. What brings you here today?" Malcolm said as he pressed the stop button on the remote.

I exhaled. I was suddenly feeling like a burden, and that was never my intended goal. Malcolm always told me to show up whenever I needed help, and he knew I would always do whatever it took to help him had he ever needed it, but so far it had been completely lopsided. I was the person always crying about help for this and help with that, and it was starting to be embarrassing. How could I be a leader if I couldn't lead. Maybe I'm not cut out to lead like I initially thought.

"Talk to me. You're here now. No need to hold it in." Malcolm said as if he could read my mind.

I exhaled. "Ok... So... one of my other guys hit a truck full of iPhones. It's a $27 million truck, which turns out that it belonged to the Solumbert Crime Family. The driver told them everything, so I went to speak to the acting boss, Acielly Solumbert; and he was pissed. He gave me 48 hours to return $27 million and wanted me to toss in $500,000 for his troubles."

Malcolm looked at me with a smirk on his face. "And you believe him?"

I was confused. "Believe who?"

"You believe the Solumbert Crime Family owned that truck?"

I hadn't questioned it before, but when Malcolm asked me, I was suddenly curious. I hadn't asked many questions, and instead I'd just went along with the idea that we'd robbed and stepped on the toes of the Solumberts. "I'm not sure." I said as I shook my head.

"I think if I was still active with the Bankroll Squad, no criminal entity would be able to steal a $27 million truck from me. You know why?"

I shook my head. I really had no clue.

"Because I'm a criminal myself, so I know how criminals operate. So, I'm going to take the correct precautions when I transport $27 million worth of goods. I'm not going to have a driver joyriding with no added security in the truck, in the trailer, behind him, and in front of him. I'm not going to send a $27 million truck to pick up and drop something off the same way I would send an Uber. I'm going to take extra steps because that's too big of a loss to take. If I were a legitimate trucking company, I wouldn't take extra steps because then I'd have legitimate insurance. So, you think long and hard before you act upon the Solumberts' claims."

I suddenly felt like a fool. I'd been worried that I'd crossed the Solumberts, when in reality it had been me who'd been crossed.

"What did you tell Arcielly when you saw him?" Malcolm asked as he looked at me carefully.

"I told him I knew nothing about any truck."

"Right. So, what I'm thinking is... He saw the heist on the news and sent his men to the hospital to beat the information out of that driver of yours. Or he could be pissed about something and is attempting to take it out on you in that way. Was there any type of tension between you and them?"

"Not that I know of."

"Right, so you need to go know of it."

Malcolm Powers was the real genius in the situation. I'd never met a man as smart as he was as long as I'd been living, and that included college professors both in America and abroad. That's why I was willing to do anything to help him had he ever needed me. Judging on the way he moved and thought though, I couldn't see a scenario in where he would ever need someone like me to help him. The FBI would never be able to find him, and he was hiding in plain sight.

"Zaedan, don't take your achievements for granted. Just because your crew is able to pull off $27 million heists, doesn't mean that every crime family had access to $27 million heists. The hard part has been done by your crew, so at this point it's nothing preventing them from trying to get over on you."

"But that would be violating the code. That would be blatant disrespect amongst bosses." I said, my naivety showing with my every thought.

"Those Italians look at you like just another nigga. They don't look at you like a boss, even though they'll tell you they do to your face. Don't get swept into their words, because they'll betray you for the sake of their family's well-being without so much as a second guess. The only thing those Italians care about is Italians. If they valued you, then they wouldn't have made you leave when you helped them out overseas. They detest you for coming to America and starting your own mafia, and so every win you have, you better believe they're going to be jealous that it's not them pulling it off."

I took in all his information and knew that I had to get stronger mentally. Things like that shouldn't be able to get past my attention so easily. I guess I wanted the respect of the crime families so bad that I accepted their lies because it sounded like what I expected to hear.

"The only person you can trust should be your family

members, and as such, you should be the only person your family members trust. The criminal world is unforgiving, and if you're a black man, it's downright unfair. Look at all of the scapegoats they've used over the years, think about all of the kingpins from Frank Lucas to Big Meech who've always taken the fall. Realize that there was always a white man selling the product to them who always got away."

Malcolm Powers' words were worth more than gold to me, and I was glad to be his student. I always learned more in ten minutes of speaking to Malcolm than I could learn in a semester of college.

"Stay focused young boss. Don't let anybody trick you out of position. Because you and I both know... the position you're in is one of the greatest of all." Malcolm said as he stood up, signaling the end of our meeting.

I stood up quickly and shook his hand. His grip was firm, and it made me feel like street royalty just being in the presence of a guy like him. Right as I stood up, his soldier came in the room with that gun in his hand.

"Hey. What kind of gun is that?" I asked Malcolm as I pointed to his soldiers' weapon.

"That's a heat-seeking split-grenade launcher."

"Wow. That's incredible" I said as I stared at it in amazement.

"Yea it is. If there were three military tanks outside and 100 FBI agents, they wouldn't stand a chance against one shot from one of these. Having one of these was the equivalent of giving yourself 3 weeks to prepare for a standoff even if the standoff happened 3 minutes into your deepest sleep."

I gave Malcolm a hug before walking out of the Newnan house and told him I would see him again as soon as possible. The soldier walked me out without speaking to me and closed the door the moment I stepped both feet outside of the house. The door was shut, and locks were being applied and secured so fast that if I'd left something, I probably wouldn't be able to get it for a while.

I got in the car and thought about what type of improvements I needed to make as a leader. I knew I needed to get stronger and more advanced weaponry, and I needed to upgrade my living situations. I was well aware that anything could happen at any given moment, but if I was to get raided by the FBI in the next hour, I would be ill-prepared because of my naivetes. I wouldn't be able to force my outcome the way Malcolm Powers could, but the more I thought about it, the more that seemed like it was a necessity.

I thought about the sit-down I'd had with Arcielly earlier, and how he'd tried to rope me into thinking that I needed to resolve it with him. The fact is, I didn't make $27 million off of the truck anyways, so there was no possible way I could return $27 million and he knew that. Or did he? The more I thought about it, the more I saw through his scheme, and the angrier I'd gotten. I was going to handle him appropriately, but first I needed to make a few more stops.

I called Brizzo, and he answered on the first ring, which I expected, because he had to know he was in hot water with me.

"What's up Brizzo?" My voice was calm as I spoke, and his was just as calm in his replies.

"Nothing much Zae. Just chillin. What's good?"

His nonchalant voice on the phone was infuriating me, but I held my composure regardless. "You have something you wanna talk to me about?" I asked.

"No."

I was quiet. He had officially crossed the line with me. It was one thing to have me in hot water with Malcolm Powers, but it was a whole other epidemic for him to lie to me. I closed my eyes briefly, thinking that maybe he was just being that way because we were on the phone, and if that was the case, then I understood him. I forgave him temporarily, but I needed to see him immediately to get to the bottom of it all.

"Let's meet at my cigar bar in about an hour and a half." I said as I glanced down at the speed limit to make sure I was complying.

"I would, but I have something I really need to do Zae. I'll see you tomorrow at church if it's cool."

He was truly testing my patience. "You don't think this is a little more urgent than waiting until tomorrow?" I asked.

"No. Not at all." He responded.

"Look... I don't give a fuck what it is you think you have to do today, you cancel that shit, and you be at my cigar bar in 90 minutes. You hear?"

"Sure. Ok." He said before hanging up.

I turned the music up as loud as I could stand it as I maneuvered back up I-85. Once I made it back, I pulled up to Wilburt's house and called him from the driveway. He didn't answer, and instead I saw him peep his head out of one of the windows. Once we saw each other, I hung my phone up and got out of the car. There was a light rain starting, but I was hoping that it stopped soon so that the church even would be a success. Me and my wife had run advertisements on radio and social media, and I was going to have it rain, sleet, hail, snow; but I preferred nice sunny Georgia weather for the larger crowds.

Wilburt unlocked the door and I walked inside. I told him everything that me and Bullethead had done after the meeting, as well as my thoughts on the situation, which were technically Malcolm's thoughts, but I would never use his name in any situation.

"So, they were lying about it being theirs?"

"From the looks of it, that's how it seems. I have no reason to doubt you when you told me you did your research and it all checked out. I probably should have put my trust in the situation at that point and left it alone, so for that, I apologize. However, I'll have to treat this as if it was a $27 and a half million robbery attempt from us." I said as I looked him in the eyes.

"Damn... but with it being the mafia and all... What about the code?" Wilburt asked as he sat down in a chair and rubbed his hands across his knees.

"The only code is for them to never cross us, and never try."

Wilburt nodded his head. "Damn right."

"So, look, I'm going to send you $5 million of the truck proceeds, and I want you to keep some for you, and spend at least $2 million getting our security stronger. I want more advanced weapons, I want better security, I want our technology to be more advanced than anything out here. Put together a small crew, one of the smaller guys who are trying to get promoted up in our organization, and I want you to give Arcielly Solumbert a good talking to, but make it smooth, be careful, and make sure the Solumberts know it was the Montez family who did the talking."

Wilburt's mouth dropped open. I'd never used that term before, but if it was anything I'd taken from the meeting with Arcielly, it was that I needed to put a signature on a lot of the things I had going on. As much as I was against branding my crew, things were still coming back to me whether I branded us or not. I wasn't going to advertise us like I was promoting a club event however, just for certain situations I was going to make sure there was a signature on it.

I was at the cigar bar 20 minutes before it was time for me to meet with Brizzo. We didn't open until late night, so I was the only vehicle on the premises. I'd had black boards installed around the back fence so that nobody could see anything that took place behind the building. Despite the light rain, I was leaning against the hood of the car waiting for Brizzo because my anxiety wouldn't allow me to sit inside of the car without suffocating. He'd pissed me off to his maximum ability, and I wouldn't stand for it any longer. He had some explaining to do, and I didn't care that he was Ayoki's cousin.

My phone vibrated, and I checked it immediately thinking that it was him. It wasn't, but I'd been waiting on that text as well.

Tarralla: What are we going to do about child support?

Me: Child support? I told you to give me an address so I can meet the kid that you claim is mine. You still haven't done it.

Tarralla: Nigga I told you what's up. That will never happen. If you wanna meet the kid, it's going to be in a public location.

Me: Ok. When? I'm ready when you are.

Tarralla: Ok. Now. Meet me at the Publix on Peachtree.

Me: Not right now at this very moment, what about in the next hour?

Tarralla: Fuck that, don't worry about it then nigga.

Me: You're disrespectful as fuck. You do a lot of cussing and expect to have your ass kissed. I'm trying to meet you halfway on this shit, but you seem like you just want conflict.

Tarralla: You got damn right I want conflict nigga. You fathered this baby and you went back to your wife like you ain't did shit. Nigga I want all the smoke. I'll be at your giveaway tomorrow since you've been advertising it all over Atlanta. You can meet the baby then.

I didn't reply. She'd been constantly threatening me by telling me she as just going to show up in the presence of me and my wife, and at this point I was going to just have to let her do it. I'd made a mistake as a man by cheating on my wife, and I was sorry for it, but I couldn't be held hostage by my errors. I would pray that Ayoki would forgive me, but I couldn't allow Tarralla to black mail me and get away with it. Just seeing how strong Malcolm and Kyla's relationship was made me want to man up and come clean.

Tarralla: So you ain't gon say shit?

Me: What do you want me to say? I'll see you at the give-away tomorrow.

Tarralla: Nigga I want $5 million. That's what I want you to say. Say you got it nigga.

Me: Nah, I wanna meet my child. I wanna introduce my child to my wife.

Tarralla: She gon leave your stupid ass and take half of everything you own. By the time she gets through with your ass, Free Wi-Fi gon damn sure be free. You gon lose more money divorcing her than you would by paying me $5 million, so just pay nigga.

Me: LOL

It was clear what type of shit she was on from the beginning, and the one thing I knew for a fact, is that my wife was going to be able to see straight through it. I had no doubt about it that once my wife met this lady, she would see the lies, deceit, and the set-up, and that will no longer be held over my head anymore. I was at the point to where I doubted I was the father of the child since she'd been so money hungry in her conversations. She seemed like she was all about money, but she couldn't be all about mine. It just wasn't happening.

My alarm went off on my phone, signaling the time I told Brizzo to meet me at the cigar bar. I called his phone and got sent straight to voicemail. I closed my eyes and held my head back as the rain picked up bounced across my face and throat harder. I sent Brizzo a text letting him know that I wasn't happy with his behavior and opened my car door. I got in the car, and when I drove around the building, my eyes nearly fell out of my face.

I was surrounded by police, and there was no way to go at all. Cops were on their knees with weapons drawn, officers were perched atop buildings across the street with rifles trained on my car, officers were hiding behind car doors, behind cars, and behind trees with guns trained on me. Bulletproof vests aligned the front line, and all I could think about was if Brizzo had tried to set me up.

"Get out of the car." The officer shouted through the megaphone.

"Get out of the car with your hands above your head." He continued to yell out instructions.

I quickly text 222 to Maclente, letting my lawyer know I was in trouble. My location was on so he could track my phone and be to me in no time. I got out of the car and followed the officer's instructions. I looked across the street and saw two of the FBI agents who had been stalking me for the past few months, and they seemed to be happy about the situation, but I wasn't sure what for. They didn't have anything on me.

"We have a search warrant to search your car and the premises sir." The officer yelled through the megaphone.

I didn't have anything in the car, but I knew that Brizzo knew... that I kept lots of money and a few guns stashed inside of a few boxes inside the cigar bar. The guns had bodies on them, and I could kick myself in the face because I was supposed to discard of them months prior and kept forgetting about it. I didn't have proof that it was a set up, but I did have a gut feeling about it. My entire life flashed before me as I exited the car and followed their instructions.

I knew once they found those guns, that I was going away for quite possibly the remainder of my life. I would never get a chance to grow with my wife, and never be able to reach the dreams in life that I desired. Regardless of my consequences, they were consequences that I'd earned, and I was ready to accept my fate as a stand-up man. I was never going to implicate anybody in my crimes, and I was going to accept responsibility knowing that I was giving my life up for my principles.

The officers rushed me from all angles with their guns drawn and handcuffs out. Another set of officers rammed the door of the cigar bar in, and another group of officers started searching my car. Handcuffs were placed on my wrists tightly, and within minutes Fox 5 News was on the scene with reporters and a film crew.

"We are on the scene live where a local business owner has been alleged to have mafia affiliations. Authorities say this man, the man you see in handcuffs has been rumored to be a leader of an organized crime family. Again, all of the details aren't clear, but I will update you live as soon as we hear more information regarding the business raid."

I tuned out all of the noise around me. I could barely breathe knowing how bad I'd fucked up by leaving guns with bodies on it sitting in a damn box. I had no defense or possible explanation for how I possessed weapons that had killed at least four people. Not to mention that the gun had probably been used in multiple crimes prior to the ones I committed myself. There was no escaping this situation, I thought as I remained on the ground while the officers took pictures of me and cracked jokes.

After about 30 minutes, the lead officers walked out of the building empty handed. The FBI had confused looks on their faces as the lead officers walked up to me. "Listen... If you help us, we can help you. You're a church-going man, you know right from wrong. You know God will forgive you, but you know what you need to do. Tell us where the guns and drugs are. We've already received the intel that there were murder weapons here, and we plan up tearing this place up until we locate it. If you cooperate with us, we'll make everything more lenient for you, and help even get you a lighter sentence. If you don't cooperate with us, you could get the death penalty. Do the right thing Zaedan. Tell us where it's at."

I stared at him like he was the scum of the earth but didn't say shit. He shook his head and looked at one of the FBI agents with a confused look on his face. "I thought you said your intel was good. We've searched every box thoroughly, and nothings there."

The agent appeared to be pissed off. "What? You're probably overlooking it. I'll find it. We have to find it, it's mandatory for this case. We can't misstep right now, we absolutely can't fuck this up." The agent and the officer both walked back in the direction of my cigar bar, determined to find the murder weapon.

I had no idea why they weren't able to find it, but the guns and money had been sitting directly on the desk in plain view. I'd left it sitting there as a reminder to myself to throw the shit away the next time I saw it. I couldn't imagine what my wife was thinking as this news made its way across the city. She'd never known that I was this type of person, so no doubt the evidence they were about to present to her regarding me was going to crush her. They led me to the back of the police car, but they still hadn't read me my rights yet, and since I hadn't been read my rights, I wasn't yet arrested.

This let me know that it was all Brizzo's doing. And the agents and officers had been wanting to bust me for so long they didn't even investigate his claims before coming with handcuffs and Fox 5 News. After about another half an hour, the officers and agents walked out of the building empty-handed again. As they were making it out, my lawyer finally arrived. Maclente was a walking hurricane when it came to the police officers, and although I couldn't hear anything that he was saying, I could see his mouths moving a hundred miles per second. It didn't take long after his arrival for them to come remove the handcuffs off of me and let me go.

I was stunned, but I didn't say a damn thing.

"I'm going to have your ass tomorrow agent. Most of you all will not have jobs by the time Christmas comes in a few weeks. You can bet your bottom dollar on that."

I watched in awe as the agents and officers quickly removed themselves off of my property without speaking another word. Fox 5's reporter was trying to get to the bottom of it, but she couldn't get the officers to speak. She was confused and so was I. Maclente saw her scrambling for a story and salivated at the opportunity. He was made for the spotlight when it came to legal fights. He waved them over for an interview, and I walked off into the building to see what type of damage they'd done.

The first place I went to was the office so I could see how they missed the guns in the boxes sitting on top of the table. But when I got in the office it was sparkling clean, and there were no boxes in sight. I knew the manager didn't clean the office up, because he barely gave a fuck about his own job. I couldn't see him taking the extra step and cleaning up when it wasn't in his job description. I sat at the desk and dialed Blue's number, but he didn't answer.

I called again, but he still didn't answer. I figured he wasn't going to answer on his offday because he probably thought someone wanted him to come to work on his day off. I grabbed my cell phone and text him.

I just have a question really quick. That's it Blue. Answer the phone.

I called back, and this time he answered on the first ring. "What's up? Why you at the cigar bar today? It's not even supposed to be open today." His voice sounded groggy, as if he'd been sleeping all day, and was out of whack.

"I just wanted to know what made you clean up in the office?" I wasn't going to tell him my business, because as far as he knew, I was just a legitimate businessman trying to run a cigar bar. He was quiet on the phone for a second as he thought about the question he'd been asked.

"Is something missing? I swear I thought I saw that new bitch you hired in there moving boxes around and shit. I told her not to fuck with your shit, but she kept claiming the office needed a woman's touch. What's missing Zaedan? I'll go hunt her down right now and get it. I'm sorry, I should have been paying more attention."

"Actually, don't worry about it Blue. That's all I wanted to know."

"You sure? Please don't fire me man. I still need this job to help out with bills."

"Nah, you're good. But come by the church tomorrow and help me pass out– "

"I'm there. Say no more Zaedan."

After I hung up the phone with Blue, I breathed a deep sigh of relief. I'd hired Ares on the spot, and she'd already saved my life. She must have been an angel sent to me from God himself. I knew I was a sinner, but I was praying daily for my heart to be healed from evil and for forgiveness so that I can be a better person one day. One day, one week I was going to be healed, but I knew it wasn't going to be that day or that week. That week there were going to be bodies dropping. Too many people had taken my kindness for weakness, and I was about to teach them that I was not to be played with in any manner whatsoever.

Maclente walked into the office and held his finger up to his lips. I stared at him confused and watched as he pulled a small box out of his suitcase. He flipped a switch on it and walked around the room. He stopped several times, each time shaking his head before continuing his walk. He walked over to where I was sitting and motioned for me to stand up. When I did, he squatted under the desk and shook his head again. He pulled what looked like a magnet off of the desk and sat it on the table.

"What's– "

Before I could complete my question, he put his finger back up to his lips. He motioned for me to follow him. We walked outside of the building, and he kept walking until we'd made it about 2 blocks down the street. We stopped at a crosswalk, but he continued to stand there even when the light turned white to allow us to cross.

"Your office is bugged. Your car is bugged, and I think there's a tracking device on it. I wouldn't be surprised if your phone calls are being tapped, both home and cell phone. I wouldn't be surprised if your home is bugged, I wouldn't be surprised if your wife's car is bugged. They have it out for you, and they think you're some type of big-time drug kingpin."

"Well I'm not."

"You sure about that?" Maclente's question startled me. I couldn't believe he was questioning me like that.

"You know I don't fuck with drugs Maclente. Don't try me."

"I hear you, but for some reason, there's an awfully large suspicion that you have a major hand in the drugs that are coming in and out of Atlanta."

"Because they see the money, the power, the success, and they know I deal in the streets, but they don't know to what extent. Since they have to clue about what the story is, they've been trying to create a story."

Maclente closed his eyes for a brief second. "Zaedan, but even I don't know to what extent you're involved in the street. How can I advise you or defend you if I'm caught off guard and not knowing what I'm stepping into?"

"Maclente... Do you think Brizzo snitched about the guns?" I asked, changing the subject.

"Well, did the guns actually exist? And are they tied to any murders?" He asked me.

There was no way I would ever admit some shit like that to him or anybody else, unless they were involved in the crime with me. Even then I probably would still deny it. To be a good criminal, you needed to always deny involvement. I don't care if you were caught on camera doing it, the answer is no it didn't happen, and it wasn't me.

"The guns existed, but why the hell would they be tied to murders?" I asked.

"Alright. Well did Brizzo know about the guns?"

"Yes."

"How did he know about the guns?"

"I told him."

"Why did you tell him?"

"It doesn't fuckin' matter why I told him, the question is did he fuckin tell the FBI about the guns Maclente?"

Maclente got quiet for a brief moment, as if in thought. "I don't think he did."

"Why? He was the only person who knew. I'm almost certain it was Brizzo."

"No... It had to come from somebody higher up than a common criminal. A tip from a common criminal or average person might get the local police involved, but it would take a more solid tip; one from a higher up to involve the FBI."

What fuckin higher up? I thought as I stood at the crosswalk. I was going to get to the bottom of that shit if it was the last thing I did. "Alright, well are you coming to the church tomorrow?"

"Wouldn't miss it for the world. I'll send someone to debug your office and car tomorrow. In the meantime–"

"Yea I know. I know."

21

———

BRIZZO

I'd had a few minutes to spare before my 6 PM meeting with Zaedan, so I decided to stop at Wal-Mart to grab the kid some clothes so he could take a bath. I felt bad for the kid, and I knew it was a traumatic experience for him to see his pops dead like that. I was certain the kid hated me, but the least I could do is help him clean himself up while I figured out what to do with him. I'd gotten so carried away at Wal-Mart that by the time I realized it, I was already late for the meeting.

I hurried up and paid for the items I'd picked out and ran to my car without even getting the items bagged up. I jumped in the car and tried to maneuver as best as I could through the snail-speed Atlanta traffic. I was easily doing the dash, pedal to the floor trying to see what my car was made of. I didn't slow down until I'd made it to the street where the cigar bar located, and even then, the only reason I slowed down was because the entire street was blocked off. Cops were making sure no traffic entered the street, and I assumed it was because there must have been a movie being filmed, and they couldn't allow the scene to be interrupted.

Black Hollywood. I shook my head and turned off down a traffic-filled side street. There I sat in even slower snail speed traffic behind cars who didn't know alternative routes to their destinations. I called Zaedan's phone, but he didn't answer, and I figured the moment he saw the police officers, he probably went home and went to sleep. He did mention that he was exhausted earlier, so I wasn't tripping when he didn't answer. Instead I left a message letting him know that I was at least making an attempt to attend the meeting.

I drove back to my house, but I was prepared to keep going if there would have been any suspicious vehicles or activity anywhere in the area. It seemed like the coast was clear, so I parked my car in the garage and took the items in the house for the kid. When I walked in, he was still sound asleep. I grabbed a washcloth, towel, soap, and woke him up. He woke up with a confused look on his face, but I handed him some of the items and made him follow me to the bathroom.

"Take a bath. Clean yourself up." I said as I did a washing motion with the washcloth, in case he didn't understand me. I put all his stuff on the sink so he could change once he was done, and I walked out and called Antonio.

"My main man Brizzo. How are ya?" Antonio's cheerful voice made me feel better. Even though I knew Maclente and Antonio were both lawyers for our crew, it was Antonio who I felt most comfortable talking to about stuff. He always listened to me without judgement, and sometimes he gave me advice to help me elevate my position in life. I felt confident telling him most stuff simply because of the client-attorney privacy thing. I knew he couldn't repeat it to anybody.

"I'm good. Man, I had a rough day." I said as I sat back in the seat.

"Really? How so? I know you told me you had a meeting with Zaedan at 6, how did that go? It's over already?"

"I didn't make it to the meeting. I had to pick up something from the store, and when I made it over there, the street was blocked off by the police."

"Really? So, you weren't with Zaedan at 6?" He asked, and for a moment I thought I heard concern in his voice.

"No... I told you..."

"When are you going to see Zaedan again? Is he still supposed to give you those guns?"

I got silent. The way he was pressuring me on the phone about Zaedan, and now about some guns... It was beginning to fuck with me mentally. My stomach just didn't feel good, and I didn't feel like I could continue the conversation with him as I'd intended.

"Antonio, let me call you back in a few. I have to– "

"Are you home right now? Where are you? Is Zaedan there with you?"

I hung up the phone. Antonio was acting weird as fuck, and I wasn't about to sit on the phone and act like he wasn't acting weird as fuck. I definitely wasn't about to act weird right with his ass. I paced my living room, walking back and forth while replaying the conversation I'd had with Antonio. He was clearly up to something, but what it was I didn't quite know. I was about to sit down when I thought I saw a headlight flash through my curtain.

I walked to the window, looked out, and nearly shit on myself. Zaedan was staring dead in my face as he walked up the steps towards my door. There was nothing I could do or say at this point, I was caught red-handed. As much as I hated it, me being caught red-handed was probably a good thing for me because I was beginning to get more confused as time went by. I had a whole bunch of problems that I needed answers to, and I knew Zaedan had every answer I could ever need. I unlocked the door and opened it, and Zaedan walked in with his pistol in his hand.

"Hey Zae, what's good?" I asked, but he didn't reply to my friendly greeting.

"Look boy. You got 1 minute to come clean or I'm about to chop your body up into a hundred thousand pieces." Zaedan was pissed and I didn't even know where to begin.

"Yo... I was trying to impress you the way Walter impressed you. The way everybody else brought money to you, I was trying to get a revenue stream going so I could be a benefit to the crew instead of a liability."

Zaedan pointed his gun at my head slowly. The look on his face told me that there wasn't anything I could do to alter his mindset. I really didn't want to die, and I was hoping he had some compassion to see that everything I did was out of admiration and love.

"Nigga you tried to set me up with the cops? You're the only one who knew about the murder weapon. You a real fuck nigga for that."

"Huh? Zaedan I don't even kick it like that." I was confused.

"Kick it? You think this is about kicking it?" Zaedan asked as he pointed the gun down at my foot while staring in my face. "You think this shit is about kicking it?"

I could never explain to you the pain I felt when he pulled the trigger of his pistol. The pistol blast was louder than normal, and all I remember afterwards is me laying on the floor screaming in agonizing pain. I'd told myself that I wasn't going to scream loud because I expected him to shoot, but since I'd never been shot before, I didn't really know what to expect at all. I screamed so loud that I was sure several of my neighbors were about to call the cops.

He then stuck the pistol in my mouth and that's when I knew to shut up and deal with the pain as silently as possible.

"Quit screaming boy, I shot the edge of your foot. That's a damn flesh wound if I ever saw one."

I heard him, but I was in shivering pain. My body was shaking like I'd just had the greatest orgasm of my life. Zaedan's voice was active, but I didn't understand or hear a word he was saying to me. I tried to focus when I saw him point the pistol at my other foot. I tried to listen just in case he was saying something that would prevent him from finishing me off. Just as I was trying to focus on his words, the boy came out of the bathroom wearing the change of clothes and holding his old clothes in his hand. He stood there in front of me and Zaedan, staring, but there was no fear on his face. I glanced down and my foot and it didn't seem as bad as it felt. I only had on a pair of socks, and the hole from the bullet was accurately placed on the edge of my foot.

Zaedan put the gun on his waist and stared at me with a disgusted look on his face. "Get up and explain this shit Brizzo."

I stood up, and surprisingly the pain had already started to subside. It was like I'd gotten a bee sting and then the moment was over. Maybe it was the sound of the gunfire that hurt worse than the gun itself.

"Zaedan I didn't know what to do. I couldn't leave the kid after shooting the father. I just figured I was going to figure it out later, which is what I've been trying to think out."

"Yea but you don't think well anyways, so what made you feel like that was going to be successful? Why don't you ask the kid where his parents are?"

"I tried, but he won't speak to me."

Zaedan looked down at the kid, then knelt down so that he was at eye level with the kid.

"Cual es to nombre?"

The kid didn't say a word. He stared at Zaedan the same way I was doing. I couldn't resist an I-told-you-so right then. "I told you bro. I– "

"Esteban."

Zaedan glared at me as I stared at the child in awe. I didn't even know he could speak at all, and I never would have thought to try a different language. I felt just as small as the kid did. "Man, I'm sorry bro." I offered an apology but Zaedan ignored it and kept probing the child with questions. I went and sat on the sofa so I could see if I was going to need stitches or just a good wound cleaning.

I took my sock off and looked at it, and it looked like the bleeding had already stopped. I was going to put something on it just so that it didn't become infected. After a few minutes, Zaedan came and sat in front of me with the kid beside him. I really felt like shit, because it seems that all I was able to do for the family is fuck things up worse every time I tried to do something.

"Brizzo, this is Esteban. The person you killed was a part of a human smuggling ring. He was helping families get over here, charging them one price to get them here, and then after he got them here successfully, he raised the price, and kept a child hostage until they paid his new price."

"Wow." Was all I could say. I had no idea what types of shit Tony had been into, as I only knew that he was the person to buy the LSD from for Ayoki. I figured I needed to come clean about Ayoki as well to avoid getting shot later.

Esteban reached in his old pants pockets and pulled out a piece of paper. He gave the paper to Zaedan. Zaedan looked at the paper and handed it to me. I took it and frowned. "What is this?"

"That's where you're going to drop Esteban off at so he can be with his family." Zaedan said as he glared at me. "Then you're going to throw all the drugs and shit in a dumpster and never look back. How many times do I have to tell you that I don't fuck with drugs? Furthermore, about this police shit... Brizzo you were the only person who knew... So, if you didn't, then who tried to set me up?"

I was really at a loss for words. I didn't want to get rid of the drugs after I'd done this much to get them. I really wanted to make it pay off at this point. I was just so damn close. And as far as the setup shit... I would never do such a thing.

"Zaedan, I really don't know about that one." I said, then I thought about Antonio's voice. His probing. His questioning and the tone he used when he asked me questions regarding me and Zaedan. But it couldn't be him... He was a lawyer and...

"What are you thinking?" Zaedan asked, his patience wearing thin.

At that point I knew I would have to tell him. Because if Antonio really was working with the police, then it was some shit I definitely needed to know immediately.

22

ZAEDAN

I was going to kill Brizzo, there was no way around it. The only reason I didn't kill him the night I went to his place was because I needed him alive to accept blame for most of the shit he'd done. A dead body would only leave me to accept the blame for his fuck ups, and I had enough problems already piled atop my plate. I was a block away from my house when I received a phone call from Maclente, and I answered it quickly, eager to hear what he had to say.

"Zaedan, call me from the 1-800 line."

I hung my cell up and grabbed the private customer service phone that only a handful of people even knew I owned. I turned the power on and called Maclente's 1-800 number.

"Get this. So, a contact I have at the FBI slid me some information. Looks like Brizzo isn't your snitch after all. I think Antonio is trying to cut a deal. Seems like the FBI caught him up on some charges unrelated to us, and so now he's trying to find something concrete to give them so that they can get a conviction out of you."

"Are you serious?" I was pissed, but I was still going to kill Brizzo. Nothing was going to change that. He'd violated my orders and went against the rules I set, embarrassing me in the process.

"I'm dead serious, but that's not all. You may want to also make sure your wife isn't doing any talking to the FBI."

"What??" I screamed through the phone. "She doesn't even know shit!" I yelled.

"Yea, she might not, but in the files, it said the FBI had a conversation with her recently. It didn't say what was said, but just be careful."

I hung the phone up and tossed it back in the glove compartment. I was seeing red. I was so pissed that I almost called her phone and blacked on her, but I knew I had to keep my composure regardless. I was praying that my wife wouldn't do me like that, because then I was going to have to kill her, Antonio, and Brizzo. Three people who I had real love for prior to these new revelations. I parked the car and walked towards my front door.

I glanced down the street and saw an FBI van parked at its normal post. I stood there for a moment, knowing they were taking photos of me through the darkness. I posed, gave them three different poses, and a smile. I was tired of them bothering me at that point. They were constantly waiting on me to slip up, but the reason I didn't run, hide, or avoid them was because I knew they simply had no clue about me. When I walked in the house, my wife was sitting in the living room in front of a lit candle with her Bible open. She was still dressed from earlier that day, which was good because suddenly I didn't want to talk to her in the house anymore.

"Ayoki. Let's go see a movie." I whispered in her ear.

She looked up at me, tears in her eyes, and I was praying

that she hadn't really betrayed me like Maclente said. Ayoki was my soulmate, and I couldn't imagine life without her; unless she was going to force me to imagine it. "What's wrong?" I asked, genuine concern on my face.

I sat beside her on the sectional and put my arms around her as she continued to cry softly. I felt tears start to rise in my own eyes as I realized that that moment could easily have been the last time I acknowledged her as my wife. It hurt me to think like that, but the reality was raw. Everybody I knew understood how I felt about loyalty. They know I didn't play with it and would die for it. They also knew that anything I was willing to die for; I was also willing to kill for.

"I haven't been completely honest with you Zaedan." Ayoki's tears soaked my shirt as she spoke. Her voice was cracking, and I could sense her pain and fear as she tried to force her words out. "I love you so much." Her tears seemed like they had magnets on them because for every tear she dropped, it made me drop one as well.

"Zaedan... I told you I didn't have family, but I do." She said as she continued to cry. "I told you I didn't know why I couldn't get pregnant, but I do. I told you I don't know why I get depressed so much, but I do. The bad dreams... I said I didn't know why I was having them... but I do know."

My forehead wrinkled up as I stared at her in confusion. My heart beat twice the speed as I realized suddenly that I didn't even know what the hell she was about to tell me. At first, I thought she was about to come clean about the FBI, but this didn't seem like a conversation about any police. "Talk to me Ayoki... I'm sure we can get through anything. We're a praying family, and there's nothing–"

"I killed him Zaedan!" She screamed. Her body was

shaking uncontrollably, and as much as I was trying to comfort her, her words were scaring me to death.

"You killed... who?"

"I killed a baby!" She cried harder. Many questions flashed through my mind. I didn't know what she was talking about, and my anxiety was through the roof.

"You had an abortion?" I asked, staring at her with concern.

"I killed my sister's baby. I was 18. He was only 3 years old Zaedan! That's why I'm cursed! That's why I say I have no family. They disowned me! They hate me! They want me to suffer like that little baby! I'm cursed Zaedan! My womb is cursed! God will never give me a baby after I've done something so terrible! We can try and try, and I'll never be able to get pregnant! I've really fucked my life up, and I think it's time to let you know so you can move on and do better! I'm cursed Zaedan! I'm really cursed!"

I never heard my wife cry as hard as she was, and my feelings were hurt as I thought about how many years she'd been holding that secret inside. She'd fought to keep that secret away from me, and I knew it was my fault because of all of the secrets I'd kept back from her. I never discussed difficult stuff with her, so she must have felt that I never endured anything of difficulty, but that was far from the truth. She cried into my chest and I held her as tight as possible, my way of letting her know that she was loved and not disowned.

I kissed her on the neck and kept my arms around her as if to protect her from judgement of the world. She was distraught about accidentally killing someone, but if she'd have known how many people I'd killed in the streets, she would lose her mind. I knew I had to present her some of my flaws as well. Me hiding my flaws were going to create a truly unhappy marriage, and before long we would just be two strangers living together.

"Ayoki... Baby... It was an accident... You didn't mean to kill the baby. It was an accident. God knows it was an accident, and He forgives you for it."

"Nooooo. He won't forgive meeeee!" She cried harder and I held her harder. I couldn't imagine the mental anguish that she had to have been dealing with. She'd been holding in her biggest secret from me for years, and honestly it made me love her that much deeper. Now that I knew that I wasn't the only fuck up between us two, it allowed me to understand why we found happiness in each other.

"Yes, He will forgive you Ayoki. Have you asked for forgiveness?"

"Yes. All the time I ask for forgiveness but it's not a forgivable act Zaedan. I know He's not forgiving me for it."

"You have to first forgive yourself."

"That's the same thing Ms. Irena said Zaedan, and I'm trying! That's why I'm coming clean with you right now."

My palms and forehead were both sweating as I fought to find the correct words and thoughts to give her to calm her down.

"Baby it was a mistake. Mistakes happen. I've made mistakes. We will both make mistakes as human beings. We do stuff that we don't mean to do, hurt people by accident even though we love them. Our hearts don't intend to hurt people, but we are flawed, and that's how we make the mistakes."

"No Zaedan. See... That's the lie I've been telling ever since I ran the baby over."

My mind blanked out. The more she talked, the more confused she made me. She pulled away and stared me directly in the eyes. Her tears slowed down and her tone changed. She took a deep breath and shook her head. "Zaedan you're the first person I'll ever tell this to, and you'll be the last."

"Ok baby. Talk to me. We can get through anything."

"I was high Zaedan."

"High? Off of weed? You smoked?"

"Off of LSD…"

"What? What the hell do you mean?" To say I was at a loss of words was an understatement.

"I started doing LSD when I was 15-years-old Zaedan, I started doing it for fun after my friend gave me some after school one day. On the day I ran him over… I wasn't myself. When I looked in the rear view, all I saw was grass. Everything was grass, including him. Even when I think back to the incident, I heard everybody screaming and crying, but I still didn't know what I'd done. My sister was holding grass in her hand, and then she turned to grass.

My mom turned to grass, and then the truck I was driving turned to grass. The LSD had me confused and hallucinating bad. I passed out and woke up in the hospital. That's when the doctors told me what I'd done. They told me what happened, and I was in disbelief. I could never tell my family I was high, but it really wouldn't matter because they disowned me anyways. They hate me Zaedan."

She stood up and walked through the kitchen and into the bedroom. I sat there staring in silence at the candlelight, confused and lost. Several times my wife had told me that the people who attended church the most *needed* church the most, but I always thought about myself when she said things like that. Never in a million years could I ever have imagined what she'd been through. Yet, I still loved her. I couldn't help but to love her because I was no better than her. Even with her telling me it wasn't an accident; I was still worse than she could ever be.

I'd made way more mistakes in my life than she'd made in hers. Compared to me, she was flawless in sin. I got up and walked into the bedroom and froze in the doorway. That moment was easily was the most afraid I'd ever been in my life.

"Baby please don't leave me." I spoke to her softly.

She had her back turned to me and was staring out of the window into the darkness. In her left hand was a pistol and she had it pointed directly at the side of her temple.

"Baby please... Understand that I love you no matter what, and I'm going to continue to love you regardless of what obstacles we have to get over. I'll help you heal baby, but please don't leave me. If you leave this earth, then who's going to help me heal? I'll be broken beyond repair. Please don't do this to me."

She started sobbing as I spoke, and just imagining my life without her had me panicking and twitching. "Please Ayoki. Please." I begged as I stood in place, careful not to move. I didn't want to trigger her into making a mistake. "Please put the gun down baby. You're not the only person who's made mistakes baby, I've made plenty. Please baby grow with me, keep building with me."

"I don't deserve you." She managed to muster out through her tears. "You can do so much better than me. I'm poison to you and I'm only going to bring you bad luck."

I couldn't let her think I was perfect. I was far from perfect. I was the scum of the earth. I never would have thought that me keeping a secret would potentially cause my wife to leave this earth, but I was ready and willing to tell her about every mistake I'd ever made in my life if it meant I could keep her alive.

"I'm not perfect baby. I go through plenty of things that you don't know about. I deal with them silently because I'm the one who sees you as perfection baby. I don't wanna ruin the way you think of me by telling you the stuff I go through."

She put her gun down on the table, and I ran to her and put my arms around her. "Baby I love you. Please don't scare me like that again. Don't think about leaving me on this earth alone. Not as much as I love you. I want you forever, and there's never been so much as a moment of where I felt otherwise. Let's work through our flaws and mistakes and be better people. I'll help you, and you can help me, but baby no matter what... Please don't scare me like that again."

I pulled her away from the gun and lay back on the bed with my arm around her. I held her tight through the night, as silence wrapped around our bodies and kept us warm and protected. She fell asleep in my arms, and I got up only to go hide the gun so that she never saw it again. I set the alarm on my phone so that we could get up and make it to the church for the giveaway, and I prayed for strength on how to come clean with her about my many inhibitions and flaws.

There was no way I could tell her things that could get me a life sentence, no matter how bad I wanted to come clean with her. I was going to tell her about the loan sharking and let her know that we punished people for non-payment. I thought about the other bad things I had going on and knew that I couldn't express them to her no matter what. I definitely couldn't tell her I had a baby on her by Tarralla, not while her emotions were near suicide level like they were earlier. I guess the good thing was that I was definitely about to tell her more than she knew previously, and since she didn't know anything previously; at least she would know I wasn't perfect.

As far as the LSD... I still had several questions about that. I prayed that she wasn't still using, but even if she was still using, I could still help her move on from her addiction. Me helping her get right was way easier than her helping me get right. I was going to have to do what I needed to do to get us a fresh start in a fresh place. I could feel in my heart that if we remained in Atlanta, GA; it was going to be the death of us both. The pattern of her heartbeat against her chest relaxed me.

Soon I was sleep, my eyes and mind happy to be taking a break from such a rigorous schedule of life. I had to make boss decisions all morning, day, evening, and night; had to call life or death shots on a regular basis. Had to deal with the FBI like it was normal. I had to maintain a clean public eye, make sure I'm never associated with drugs, all while trying to build a future with a woman who was addicted to LSD. When there were so many things against me, it was a much-welcomed blessing for me to be able to experience the small things. Like sleep.

23

BRIZZO

I was fucking pissed dog. I'd done a great deed by reuniting a kid back with his family, but what the hell was my reward going to be? Seems my reward was getting shot in the foot by my boss and being ordered to throw away a million dollars' worth of drugs. That just wasn't going to happen on my watch. Hell, Zaedan must have known I wasn't about to throw away a million dollars' worth of drugs the moment those instructions left his mouth. He probably should have seen how much of it I had. Maybe if he'd have seen how much dope I had he would have changed his mind. He got out of my house so fast it was like he was running from something. I figured he didn't want to be around that kid though, so I made it my first order of business to drop him off as soon as Zaedan walked out of my spot.

I glanced at my watch and made sure my pistol was cocked as I sat in the parking lot of Kroger. I had the LSD in my trunk, and after making a few phone calls earlier that evening, I finally had a buyer who wanted to get it all from me. I didn't know the guy, but since he came well-vouched for from some boys who was really getting money, I knew he was legit. Even if he wasn't legit and the deal fell-through, I had another buyer from Gwinnett County who wanted to buy it, but he was only willing to pay 80% of what I was asking for. I needed the whole million so I could break Zaedan off half and show him that this dope money wasn't so bad after all.

I was crouched down in the front seat of my car, studying every vehicle that drove into the Kroger parking lot. The guy didn't know what I would be driving or what I looked like for that matter, so I was expecting him to drive into the parking lot and give me a call. He told me he was driving a navy-blue Suburban, so that's what I was on the lookout for. The moment I saw the Suburban he sent me a text letting me know he'd arrived.

I had a terrible feeling about it though, so I didn't reply. Instead I watched trying to see what type of shit he was on. When he drove straight to my car I damn near shit in my clothes. What the fuck? He wasn't supposed to know shit about me. I sat up and rolled the window down.

"Can I help you?" I asked, acting confused.

"Yea. Ain't you Brizzo?" The guy on the passenger side asked.

"Huh? Hell no."

The driver leaned around the passenger and asked again. "You ain't the guy with the stuff?"

"What stuff? I'm sitting here waiting on my wife to come out the grocery store."

"Yea? You're sitting pretty far back from the store to be waiting on a broad."

"Because I was on the phone with my other bitch. I didn't want my chick to creep up on me. I'll drive up there when she's ready. Why the hell y'all pressing me? Who the fuck are y'all?"

The guys seemed to buy my story. They didn't reply, and instead they drove into the middle of the lot and parked. The tag told me everything I needed to know though, and I was definitely about to get the fuck out of there. SLMBRT. I sent them a quick text letting them know that I was 3 minutes away, then I blocked their number, put the car in gear, and snuck out of the exit on the side of the building. I took a deep breath once I got out of the parking lot, and quickly made a series of turns to make sure they weren't following me. But they were. *Shit!* I didn't have time to be beefing with them. I called the nigga who plugged me in with them and to my surprise, he answered the phone.

"Damn nigga what you on?"

"Huh? What you mean what I'm on? Nigga what you on?"

"I ain't on shit. But damn, you setting niggaz up to get hit by the mob? What type of shit you on?"

"Man, I ain't set you up nigga. I found you a buyer. If you got beef with that nigga, then that's between you and him." He started laughing through the phone. "You say fuck the Solumbert Mafia didn't you?"

I hung the phone up and hit the gas. I dived onto the expressway and sped down 85 going at least 110 miles an hour for ten minutes straight. I couldn't believe them lil niggaz really told the mafia I said fuck them. Niggaz really wanted to use whatever source they could to eliminate other niggaz in the streets. It was a sad epidemic, but it was what it was. I dusted them mafia niggaz off something serious on the expressway because I hadn't seen them niggaz behind me in at least 20 minutes. I still had business to handle, so I looped back on the expressway to do the deal with plan B.

Plan B was an old school nigga on the westside who went by the name Nike. I'd never done business with him, but he had a solid reputation in the city as one of the niggaz in the streets getting money. I text him and told him I was on my way with it, and he text me back and let me know he was ready for it. After about 30 minutes, I pulled up to the address he'd given me and backed into a parking spot. I felt way more comfortable doing business in the parking lot of run-down apartments instead of doing business in front of a Kroger. I had my pistol on ready, and I leaned against my car as I waited on him to come down the steps.

I felt even more comfortable doing business with him because he was by himself. He was old school for real and didn't come with an entourage of niggaz just to make one purchase. He walked up to me and shook my hand.

"Peace yo." He said as we greeted each other.

"Peace. Bro you brought the cash?" I asked. I didn't see a bag with him, and I didn't have time to be playing around.

"Brother calm down. I have everything I need with me. Let me check the product out."

He could sense the hesitation and shook his head. "Brother if you do business, you have to do business the right way. I don't have any guns or anything. If we're doing business, then let's do business. Otherwise I'm about to get back to what I was doing."

He was right though. I couldn't be scared doing business if I was going to get in the dope game. I was going to move with confidence. I popped the trunk and handed him a gallon of the LSD. There was a seal on it, much like the seal off of a milk jug. Nike peeled the seal and put his nose to it. Then he stuck his tongue in the jug. He smiled.

"Damn boy you weren't bullshitting." He said with a big

smile on his face. He looked in my trunk and counted the gallons and shook his head. "And all of this is the same quality?" A look of astonishment formed on his face, and for a moment I was feeling like I was being severely undercut with regards with how much money I was making for the load.

"Yea, all the same."

Nike unzipped his windbreaker and pulled out a large, clear, air-sealed plastic container loaded with $100 bills. He tossed the bag of money to me and I nearly dropped it from the weight of it.

"That's half. I'm about to take half of the jugs upstairs and come back with the other half of the money."

I watched as he walked off, and once he got to his stairs, I took a knife and cut the plastic to check the money out. I had a counterfeit pen in the car, and as I swiped it, all of the money was coming back legit. He didn't fake me at all, it was all hundreds, no 50s and no 20s or 10s to be found anywhere. I already loved doing business with him. Pretty soon he came back downstairs with the other bag of money. He took the rest of the jugs of LSD upstairs, and I was on my way.

AFTER GETTING OFF THE LSD, the first thing I did was go get a room the Peachtree Plaza Westin. Just knowing I'd made that much money in one night was an unbelievable feeling. $800,000 just like that. I ordered room service and a bottle of wine and watched a pay-per-view movie until I fell asleep. I woke up at 8 in the morning with no alarm clock. I sat there looking at my surroundings, trying to make sure that what I'd done wasn't just a dream. I reached inside the paper bag next to the bed, picked up some of the cash and flipped through it in amazement.

I couldn't believe I was about to be living the life I'd dreamed of just like that. I went downstairs and called an Uber; I wouldn't be needing my car anymore. I took the Uber to Lenox Mall, and even though I knew it was closed, I wanted to be in the area the moment it opened. I sat on one of the benches and started flipping through Auto Trader. I went to the For Sale by Owner section and found a nice Bentley for sale right there in Atlanta for $97,000. I text the number to see if the owner was awake.

YOU STILL GOT THE BENTLEY FOR SALE?

I DO.

YOU ACCEPT CASH?

SURE DO.

CAN I COME BUY IT NOW?

RIGHT NOW? SURE. I'LL HEAD BACK HOME.

I couldn't even contain myself. I called another Uber to take me to the address to where the guy was selling the Bentley. When I pulled up, the beautiful red car was sitting in front of his house as if it was waiting on me and me only. That car screamed my name and I had to have it. I'd counted out $97,000 in the back of the Uber, and already had it separated by the time I got out of the car.

A white man came out of the house with a big smile on his face. I smiled back at him as we approached one another.

"Do you have any questions for me? I mean, the car– "

"I have no questions. Here's the money." I handed him the bag and he stood there with a startled look on his face. "I just need you to sign it over to me and hand me the keys."

"Alright... You mind if I count the money real quick?"

"I don't mind, but it's all there, and I'm kinda in a hurry."

"This won't take long." He said as he quickly flipped through the cash. I could tell he'd had a lot of experience dealing with cash, but I didn't feel like talking to him about a damn thing. I was ready to go.

"Well, here are the keys. I'll sign it over and I guess that's that."

He signed the paper, I snatched it up and got the fuck out of there. I'd never had a luxury car on that level before, and I couldn't wait to hit the streets to shit on them niggaz who was talking all that shit to me earlier. I was going to the mall to get fresh first, then later I was going to grab me a new spot to stay in. I was going to go harder in the dope game and build my way up to the top. Since Zaedan didn't want me to have the dope, then I figured he wouldn't want the money, and I was just going to keep it. I'd been trying to get him to get in the dope game the whole time, and every time I mentioned it to him he acted like he was too good for it. If he was too good to sell dope, then he definitely had to be too good for the money. I was keeping all of it. Fuck that.

24

ZAEDAN

Me and my wife made it to the church around 11 AM that day. She was in a much happier place mentally since she'd told me her darkest secrets, and I think that was exactly what she needed to be able to forgive herself for what she'd done in her past. She asked me when I woke up when I was going to tell her my flaws and secrets, but I couldn't bring myself to tell her anything that early in the morning. I told her I was going to tell her later, and she seemed fine with that.

The deacons were already at the church before me, and some of the ushers had begun to set the event up so that it was attractive to the public. Bullethead arrived around 11:15, along with Blue; and Maclente arrived at around 11:35. I'd gotten a text from Wilburt saying that he would be a few minutes late, but he was on his way too. I continued to set up as I waited on Wilburt and Brizzo to pull up and join us. Me and Bullethead carried pans of cupcakes that we were taking from the church to the food tent. I stopped in front of my wife holding my cupcakes and smiled at her.

"Baby make sure you bring one of these cupcakes home so I can eat it off of you."

She laughed. I loved the fact that she was in such a better mood. "You so nasty. I love you. Go handle your business bae, the people will be showing up any minute now."

We continued to set up the event, and I smiled when I saw Wilburt walk onto the church grounds. I knew he wasn't going to help set things up with us, but I was happy that he was at least going to help us give out some of the hams, turkeys, and toys for the kids. That's all I asked for from my crew, just a little support for things I really cared about, and the community was one of those things in a major way.

My wife was giving a speech with the microphone as the crowds made their way from the parking lot onto the church grounds. I tuned her out and sent Brizzo a text.

WHERE YOU AT BRIZZO?

OH YEA, I AIN'T GON MAKE IT.

I couldn't believe he'd sent me that text, but I wasn't about to allow him to ruin my vibes. It really didn't matter anyways, because he was a dead making walking as far as I was concerned. I guess a part of me wanted him to at least try to be a better person. At least attempt to salvage our friendship. I could see that wasn't going to happen though.

The moment I tuned back into my wife's speech; I was interrupted again. This time by WIlburt. He walked over to me and whispered a few things in my ear that would have me on alert throughout the day.

"I tried to give Arcielly Solumbert a good talking to last night, but it seemed like they had the heads up. They had double the amount of security, as if they were prepared for something."

"It's cool. We'll give them a good talking to later. It's a beautiful day, let's enjoy it."

He walked away and the deacon walked over and shook my head. I stood up and he smiled with genuine tears in his eyes. He nodded his head as if to thank me for doing this for the community. The happiness on everybody's faces was the reason I did things like that.

We were giving away thousands of dollars' worth of food and toys and enjoying every single minute of it. It felt amazing to give back to people who weren't as fortunate as we were. Just *trying* to make a difference in everybody's lives always made a difference in my life. It was so fulfilling in such an empty and cold world.

The moment my wife's speech was over, I went to my post and officially began the giveaway. I loved seeing the smiles on people's faces as they received their items. Humanity was not kind, so just adding a sprinkle of joy to a small community went a long way as far as I was concerned. I'd gotten caught up giving away turkeys that I didn't realize there were two detectives in front of me.

"Would you like a ham or a turkey sir?" I asked the first one sarcastically.

"Let us speak with you for a second." The second one said.

I glanced over at Maclente, and he made his way over to where we were. I knew he was going to run them off, but I was honestly curious to what they wanted to talk about. Not that I was going to talk to them, but I just wanted to know which drug angle they were going to come with outside of the church.

"Do you mind if we have a word with you alone?" The first detective asked gently, but Maclente must have overheard it.

"Absolutely not. Anything you have to say, you can just say it freely." Maclente said as he walked up with his hands in his pocket. "Furthermore, do you have an arrest warrant of any type?"

I whispered to Maclente and smiled. "I can handle it bro. I got this."

"Are you sure? They don't have a right to ask you any questions unless you're under arrest, so just know that– "

"I got it Maclente." I followed the two men about 35 feet away from the furthest food tent, and we stood on the opposite side of the church where nobody could see us or hear us. I stood there with my arms crossed, waiting on them to tell me whatever it was they wanted to tell me.

"So... Are you going to act like you didn't have anything to do with those deaths last night?"

"Huh?"

"Don't huh us. Your fucking lawyer... Antonio and his wife. You found out he was cooperating with the FBI and had them killed. You may think you're getting away with this shit right now, but I promise you, all this shit is going to come piling down over you in the worst way ever."

"The question is... Would you like turkeys or hams? Or both?"

The detectives smiled at each other and then smirked at me. The taller one exhaled and stared me in the eyes. "Yea... See we're not the FBI. We don't need to build a case to arrest you. All we need is to collect the evidence, and we're going to give your ass the electric chair. By the time we convict you on capital murder charges, then the FBI might have their case built against you so they can give you life too. One thing about it... We already know you're behind a slew of murders, with this being the latest one. We also know you're moving a large quantity of drugs into the city, and it's only a matter of time before you slip up and your world comes crashing down."

"Well if you knew so got damn much, why didn't you tell the FBI so they could do something about it? I don't even need an attorney present to talk to you two rooty poop officers. You two don't have the power to do shit except keep your nose the fuck out of a federal case. You and I both know this."

"Murder in this city falls on us, and we will convict you. We're on to you. You can make it easier on all of us and just confess. Think about it Zaedan. We know you're trying to turn your life around. We see you're out here giving back to the community. We know you mean well, but we also know that you've made some bad mistakes. Why not set the ultimate example and confess right here on church grounds? Why not turn yourself in and give God His due for the sins you've committed? You're an honorable Christian, aren't you? So, stop this cycle of hurt and violence, stop the flow of drugs and set an example for all of those who look up to you."

"I'll ask you again... Do you want turkey or ham? Or both?"

The detectives sighed and their body languages slumped in defeat. They looked at each other with a loss for words, and I just stared at them in silence. The taller detective walked away, headed back towards their vehicle, but the other one continued to stand beside me in silence. He didn't speak until the other detective had gotten in the police car.

"Zaedan my bad man, he made me come out here with him."

"Nah, it's all good lil cuz. Where the fuck he get all that information from though?"

"Honestly there's no evidence nowhere regarding anything Zae. They're bluffing at the precinct because all they have is a hunch and some confidential informants. I've been trying to get ahold of the files to identify the informants, but I haven't had access to the files in private yet. Of course, I'm guessing the lawyer guy was one of the informants, so I'm guessing the FBI will be bothering you later today as well. Don't quote me on that because I'm not sure."

I nodded my head. "Thanks, lil cuz. But make sure if they do find any type of evidence, to call Maclente's 1-800 number. If you find out the name of any informants, same thing; call Maclente and let him know, and he'll let me know. You better get back before this detective start thinking something is up with us. As a matter of fact, push me."

"Huh?"

"Push me hard in the chest. Push me."

He pushed me, and I fell backwards on the ground. I got up as if I was furious and pointed my finger in his face. "Put your hand on your gun but don't pull it out." I mumbled under my breath.

"Partner is everything ok?" The taller detective yelled as he started running back towards us, his hand on his weapon.

"I'll see you later lil cuz, get his ass off of the church grounds, and you'll have your money later."

"Say no more. Love you cuz."

He walked off, cutting the taller detective off halfway before he could reach me. I could tell he was trigger happy and searching for a reason to shoot me. It seemed like he was angry that I wouldn't say the dumb shit he wanted me to say. It was a shame that he'd come onto the church grounds and tried to force me into confessing by using my faith as bait. I know I've done plenty bad, and God knows I know because I've begged for forgiveness for it several times. But I also know that I didn't hurt innocent people, nor did I wish hurt on anybody who didn't deserve it. If I ever hurt a person, it was because they chose to go down a certain path that they should have never walked down.

The detectives got in the car and pulled off, and I walked inside the church so that I could use the bathroom and get myself together. That was a low moment for them to come question me while I was at church, but I thought about it while I washed my hands and realized that those orders to come question me must have come from the FBI. They had to approve it because they knew how stupid they would look by questioning me in a public place during their so-called investigation.

Local police knew not to bother me, so I knew that order came from a higher clearance. It was like they were trying to make me be this big-time drug dealer and weren't going to stop until they could figure out how to prove that I was. As far as Antonio, if he was indeed dead, then he got what he deserved. I hadn't checked the news that day, but I couldn't wait to catch up on what I'd missed that night.

25

AYOKI

y senses were heightened. Ever since Zaedan told me he wasn't perfect, that he made mistakes and was full of sin as well, it had my mind racing. When I told him my darkest secrets, he acted like it was nothing major, as if I'd just told him that my favorite color was purple; as if what I said didn't scare him at all. If what I told him about my past didn't scare him, then I had to wonder what was in his past that made him strong enough to accept my words with a grain of salt.

I thought about the rumors and things that I'd heard about him in the past and tried to picture him being that person. I couldn't see it. Rumors about him running a gang or a mob or being involved with the mafia... I couldn't see it. I looked at Bullethead as he helped give away hams and turkeys and toys. I looked at Wilburt as he made hot chocolate for some of the kids, and I just couldn't see them being anything but good men of God. I thought about my cousin Brizzo and felt bad because I had him bringing me LSD when I knew Zaedan didn't approve of anybody even being in the same room as drugs of any type.

I was curious as to why Brizzo wasn't there with us, but that wasn't my place to ask questions about my husband's business. I thought about all the times Zaedan had been questioned by police officers for no reason. I always knew that they were jealous of his success as a black man and wanted him to be a drug dealer so that they could justify his success and say that he took the easy way out as opposed to earning it dollar for dollar.

His Free Wi-FI chain was the perfect business, and there were many people angry that they hadn't thought to create that chain of cafes before Zaedan did. There were many people upset because of Zaedan's intelligence. My husband was multi-lingual, and not to mention he was absolutely stunning of a man to look at. Jealousy would always exist.

I watched as the two police officers got in the car and glanced over to see Zaedan walking into the church. I stopped worrying and started back focusing on the task at hand, which was me making plates for the women and kids who stood in the line. Time always went fast for me when I was helping people. It was something I naturally enjoyed. Before long, my line was finishing up, and Zaedan was right behind me with his arms around me. He turned my head towards him and gave me a kiss on the lips.

"I love you Ayoki."

"I love you too." And I meant that. When I told him my darkest secrets, the way he forgave me made me realize that it was ok to forgive myself. I think not knowing his reaction was what had been holding me back from my mental growth for so many years. I turned around and started working on another plate when I felt Zaedan's body tense up as he leaned against me.

"You ok?" I asked as I continued to work on the plate.

"Nah he ain't ok." A sharp voice from the other side of the table pierced the mood with rudeness.

I looked up and my heart caught in my throat. I stared at her, speechless, lost, in a daze; my whole life flashing in front of me like emergency lights. She stared back at me holding a baby in her arms, her eyes like daggers, her mood a deadly tornado. I tried to gather words to speak, but none of the words I could put together could shock me the way Zaedan's did when he spoke.

"Tarralla! So, you really wanna play huh?" His voice was venomous, his tone more tense than his stance, and it was the angriest I'd ever heard him since I'd known him.

"Y'all two know each other Zaedan?" I asked, taken aback by the moment.

"Yea Zaedan, answer her question nigga. Tell her the fuckin' truth nigga."

Zaedan glared at her, and I glared at him. The moment was too surreal. There was no way this was happening to me.

"I'm sorry Ayoki." He said to me and hung his head.

"You're sorry about what?" I asked him, my voice equally as venomous as his was.

He stared me in the eyes and shattered my heart into a million pieces. "I cheated on you Ayoki. I cheated and got her pregnant. I'm sorry."

I was at a loss for words. Not just because he'd stepped out on his marriage, and not just because he'd had a baby on me. No... the hurt I was feeling was deeper than life itself. It wasn't just the hurt simply because he'd taken my heart and crushed it, nor was it the pain of all of my dreams turning into a nightmare right before my very eyes. This pain hurt five times as hard as any hurt I'd ever felt before. It hurt me so bad that I didn't even know I was crying– didn't even recognize my tears for what they were.

"I can't believe you Zaedan."

"I'm sorry."

"You're sorry? You cheated on me with my sister and you're sorry?"

"What? Your sister? What the fuck?"

"Zaedan this is Eyoki Tarralla Sanders. This is my sister."

"I'm not your fucking sister bitch. You killed my three-year-old son and thought you were just going to get away with it? That's not how life fucking works bitch! But don't worry, I won't let you kill this one bitch. A son by your husband, and you will most definitely be paying me for the next 18 years."

"How could you Eyoki?"

"No! How could you Ayoki? How could you destroy me like that? How could you get so high that you took my life away from me?" Tears were falling down her face as she stared at me. I knew I'd hurt her, but she'd also hurt me as well; even before sleeping with my husband.

"Eyoki... You were the person who got me addicted to LSD. You were the person who wanted me on drugs. All I did was look up to you as my big sister. I loved and admired you, and I still do to this day." I couldn't stop crying. I'd been holding on to her secrets for years too, but nobody deserved to hear them except for her.

"So what? I gave you LSD when you were 15, you killed my baby when you were 18. There's no excuse for that."

"Eyoki I was just a child when you gave me that stuff. I couldn't even say no because I was afraid to disappoint you. I'm sorry I ran him over, I truly am sorry; and Lord knows if I could go back to the day, I would trade places with him. I know I hurt you, and I know I hurt the family, but I'm sorry. I've been praying you would one day forgive me, and instead you're behind my back sleeping with my husband? You used him as a pawn to hurt me?"

"Bitch I told you, you're not my family. My family is standing beside you. Now if you'll excuse me, I need to speak to my baby daddy in private."

I continued to stand there, absorbing her words. It was easy to blame my husband for cheating, but I also knew that Eyoki had revenge on her heart, so she definitely targeted him. This wasn't some random thot that he'd found off of the streets, this was a woman who knew exactly what she was doing, and fully intended to hurt me.

"I'm sorry Ayoki. I'm so sorry." Zaedan kept whispering. I wasn't concerned about that though, there was something else I was seeing.

I held my head high and looked at my sister in her eyes. She was right. In her heart she didn't think of me as a family member anymore. She thought of me as an enemy. I could tell that she wasn't exaggerating when she said I wasn't family, and the reason was because I was suddenly able to see into her life the same way I could a stranger's. It sent a tingle down my spine because that was the first time I'd ever been able to see into a loved one's life. I froze and my eyes narrowed.

"Zaedan that's not your baby." Words were leaving my lips faster than I could process them.

"The hell it ain't." Eyoki said defiantly. She just didn't know how she'd set the stage for me. By her disowning me as family... She was just an empty stranger at the moment, and I was about to tell her about herself.

"Zaedan that isn't your baby sweetie. It's absolutely not." I said as I stared at her and the baby. "She was so angry when she didn't get pregnant by you... She went and got pregnant by the first person she could find and put it all on you. This was her plan. She wanted to hurt me, to try to drag me out for years because she thinks that's what I did to her."

Eyoki and Zaedan were both silent. She stared at me with her mouth wide open, not saying a word, yet all of her secrets spilling out before me.

"You broke out of the psychiatric ward when you looked me up on social media. You thought I was living good, so why not try to ruin me? You've always tried to ruin me Eyoki, going back to us as kids. Why? Because you thought I was going to get more guys attention than you? You wanted to ruin your own sister because of that?"

Eyoki stuttered as she barely managed to force her words out. "Y-Yes. I-I was so intimidated by you growing up. I- I- I'm sorry. I- I don't know what to say."

She sat the baby down in the car seat she was carrying and walked around the table to where I was. We were both emotional and highly upset. Both of us were crying, both of us expressing sadness and hurt. She stood in front of me and shook her head.

"I'm so sorry. I forgive you."

Those were the words I'd been longing to hear forever. Her words sent a wave of relief through my body as she wrapped her arms around me to give me a hug. I took a deep breath as I inhaled her sweet perfume. I'd always admired her, always looked up to her, always wanted to be like her. Anything she told me as kids, I went for it because I loved my sister just that much. There was no wrong she could do in my eyes, and I would always forgive her. I would always see her as my sister, even though she didn't see me as family.

"Ayoki no!" Zaedan yelled as he ran towards us.

I watched as he ran toward us, shock and panic covering his face, but I wasn't aware of why he was panicking. Then I felt it. A sharp knife ripped through my shirt, straight through my mid-section. I stood there staring at the knife, lost, trying to figure out how it got there. Who would stab me? There was quite the commotion going on around me, and I was trying to piece together the words and sentences, but soon everything was spinning, and I was dizzy. I saw people running and scrambling, saw Zaedan pinning Eyoki to the ground. I saw the trees spinning, and when I looked at my sister's face, I realized that she would never be my sister again, no matter how bad I wanted her to be. She wanted me dead and was prepared to hurt me however she could. As I lay on the ground, I figured the least I could do was grant her request. Maybe if I left this world, she would forgive me once and for all. I blacked out.

26

BRIZZO

I was having the greatest day of my life. I was having money, pushing a Bentley, and my wardrobe was fresh from shirt to shoes. I'd pulled up on several people who I really needed to shit on and done just that. Pretty Tony for the way he tried me at the studio that night. I pulled up on him and let him know I was *having*. Shit I'm having whatever he wanted and needed. If he wanted coke, weed, syrup; I could get any of that shit. Starting my empire with the amount of money I had, there was no way I could ever fail.

By 6 PM I'd already spent almost $400,000 on everything from jewelry, clothes, a new $200,000 crib, to a new Bentley. I was on top of the world for real, but by the end of the day I realized that I was going to need a plan in order to stay there, and throughout the day, I'd put together a strategy that I was happy with. My phone ring while I was at the red-light, and it pissed me off because it seemed like the nigga couldn't take a damn hint.

"Hello."

"Well hello to you too Brizzo."

"What's up?" I didn't even have enough patience to hear what Zaedan had to say at that point. I was on the way to be the biggest drug kingpin Atlanta had ever seen.

"What the fuck you mean what's up? You were a no-show for church this morning, and you're answering the phone sounding real cocky. What's up with you?"

"Nigga I'm good." I couldn't even look at him the same after I'd made that much money in one day. I couldn't believe he was struggling coming up with difficult ass ways to make money when money could be made with the snap of a finger. That type of behavior irked me for real. I'd lost respect for him instantly.

"Nigga?"

"Yea. Nigga. And matter of fact... I'm good on the crew. I'm rocking solo going forward bruh. Starting my own shit."

"Alright. Well I only called you to let you know that your cousin is in the hospital. She got stabbed at the church event... By her sister. I guess you weren't planning on telling me that Tarralla was my wife's sister?"

"Nigga them your problems. I told your ass you should let me handle the shit way back then. I could have put big cuz in her place and stopped all that shit. But nah, you wanted to be in control like always. So, nigga all that shit is on you. I'm good. You don't need to use this phone number ever again bruh."

I hung the phone up and turned the music up. The glare of the Bentley headlights beamed against the vibe of the city traffic. I was done fucking with Zaedan, and with me letting that shit go, I shouldn't have to worry about the FBI following me and shit every day. Fuck that type of life. Who the fuck wanted to knowingly deal with the FBI on a daily basis? That's some sick shit to comprehend each day.

I pulled up at my new spot so I could take a shower and

get dressed for the night. I'd met a Mexican guy at Lenox Mall earlier who was pushing a brand-new Ferrari in the valet area. His name was Horrez, and I knew the moment I saw him that he had a heavy hand in the streets, and I definitely needed to connect with him; which I did. I'd hit up Nike and asked him if he wanted another LSD load and sure enough, he told me to come on with it the moment I got it.

Doing a deal with Horrez wasn't as simple as I thought it was going to be though. I was under the impression that we would negotiate a price, I pay him, he gives me the shit and it's over. He wanted to kick it with me first. Had I been broke I would have turned that offer down, but with the type of money I was having, I deserved a night out on the city. The city deserved to see a young nigga shining when he came from nothing.

I finished getting dressed and text Horrez my address. I told him earlier that I was going to drive my Bentley, but when he told me I could ride with him and his boys in the new Rolls Royce truck, it was a no-brainer. I was guaranteed to be the talk of the city after tonight. We were going to hit up the hottest new spot in Atlanta that night, *Chic Lounge*; and I was definitely dressed to the nines. I'd spent $4,500 on my outfit, easily the most I'd ever spent on clothes in my entire life.

Horrez pulled up in his white Rolls Royce Cullinan with a set of white 26-inch rims on it. That shit could win any car show, and it was sure to shut down the parking lot. I'd spent $97,000 on my Bentley earlier that day, but that truck he was pushing set him back close to $500,000. I was excited about building my bond with Horrez and his homeboys. That was the type of life I was trying to live on a regular basis. Fuck all that mafia shit.

When we made it to the lounge, all eyes were on us. It

was as if we were the Kings of Atlanta the way we commanded attention. Horrez already had a section reserved, so we walked in through the VIP and went straight to our area. I followed his lead as he sat up on top of the couch. I relaxed and tried to look as important as he was. He motioned for a waitress to come over and whispered something in her ear. The music was perfect. Chic Lounge had two of the best DJs in Atlanta providing the greatest vibes possible. The sound system was immaculate, and I had to admit I was feeling good as hell.

It wasn't long before the bottle girls were bringing us bottles of Don Julio 1942 and Hennessy Master Blender. I counted 12 bottles. They had sparklers atop the bottles and since it was just four of us in a huge section, it sent a message to every woman in there that our section was the place to be.

"You drink light or dark?" Horrez asked me as he leaned over and grabbed a cup from one of the bottle girls.

"Light."

"Good choice."

He poured us both shots of 1942 and held his cup up. "Toast to new business."

Hell yea. That was exactly what I wanted to discuss. "Toast to new business!" I took a shot of the drink and nearly spit it out. That shit was disgusting, but it definitely didn't take long for the effects to kick in. It seemed like it was kicking in immediately. I loosened up and relaxed a bit more.

"So... What prices are we talking Horrez?" I asked over the loud music.

"Well. What is it you want?"

"LSD and coke."

"It depends Brizzo. The more you buy, the better the

deal is I can give you. If you're a big spender, then I really gotta take care of you. Know what I mean?"

I had close to $400,000 that I was trying to flip like yesterday, so I knew he was going to give me the best deal possible. It was important that I show him that I was a valuable friend with valuable business. I didn't want him treating me the way Zaedan did. I wasn't some incapable child; I was a man with a helluva hustle about himself.

"For now, Brizzo, let's not worry about business. Let's have fun."

I nodded my head and took another sip of my drink.

"Here." He said as he handed me a small paper square with a cartoon face on it. He gave his friends one each and put the remaining square under his tongue. I copied them, thinking they'd given me Listerine strips. I didn't taste anything, and it dissolved pretty quickly.

"Let me know what you think of my LSD quality. I'm sure you'll love it." He said as he stood up and started nodding his head to one of the new songs by Gunna and Young Thug.

I didn't intend on taking LSD, nor did I even know LSD came in solid dissolvable forms. I had only been exposed to the liquid, but I'd never tried it myself. I guess I was going to find out what Ayoki was so excited about. I didn't really care what I had to do to get in good graces with Horrez, because the only thing that mattered to me was, I was going to be pushing Rolls Royce trucks right along with him. I leaned over and whispered in his ear.

"One more thing... When you sell it, you sell it in liquid form right?"

"Yea. Wholesale in liquid unless you want wholesale in tabs."

"Liquid."

"Aight say no more. Just relax Brizzo. I got you. Chill. It's our night to enjoy life." He waved a group of girls towards us, and it seemed like they had been waiting for any indication of an invite to our section. They cut through the crowd like it was a fire drill and stood in front of the VIP security guy who was guarding the entrance to our section.

"We're with them." The first girl said as she pointed to us. The security guard looked back for confirmation, and Horrez gave him the thumbs up. Just like that our section went from 4 guys to 4 guys and 6 girls. I was about to have the time of my life. Fuck that. I was already having the time of my life. This was going to be a night Atlanta would never forget. The story of the underdog who made it to the top.

27

WILBURT

I hated seeing Ayoki in the hospital like that. It was unbearable to watch Zaedan in so much pain and hurt. We all knew how much he loved her, and things would never be the same if he lost his wife. I didn't want that cold path for him. I prayed for them, me and Bullethead both did. Not that our prayers were strong enough to make a difference, but because in the offcase they were... we'd done our part in faith. We were sinners with hearts. Killers with respect for mankind, and a sharp appreciation for love and loyalty. We were complex criminals.

After me and Bullethead left the hospital, I pulled out a scrambler and plugged it into his cigarette lighter. In the off chance that his car was bugged, the scrambler made sure that none of our conversation got picked up by anyone who was listening.

"Damn family." Bullethead was distraught. "I keep feeling like it's my fault bro. If I wouldn't have left them alone then she wouldn't be in that hospital right now. I wouldn't have let anybody touch her."

"Nah man. It's not your fault. You gotta remember... Zaedan was right there. The girl was her sister. It was a vulnerable moment for everybody."

"That's what I'm telling you though Wilburt. It was a vulnerable moment for everybody except for me. I wouldn't have let that bitch hurt Ayoki if I was over there bro. I'm serious about that."

"I get it bro... But what can we do? It's done now, and the bitch is locked up for attempted murder. Fuck that bitch. Speaking of attempted murder... I think the Solumburts are on to me bro. I don't know how... I got a funny text about an hour ago that said TRY AGAIN. I was trying to give them a good talking to last night but couldn't pull it off."

"Nah, we won't trip over that shit. We good. Fuck the Solumberts and fuck that bitch."

Bullethead drove in silence for a few miles, both of us reflecting on what would have otherwise been a successful day. There was no FBI trail at all that day, which was extremely rare. Since we hadn't seen them all day, we figured they must have been busy harassing some other successful black men who they wanted to wear the drug dealer label. When we got close to where I'd parked my car, I broke the silence.

"You got the black box for the month?"

"Oh yea. I almost forgot. It's in the trunk. I'll give it to you."

The black box was a small black computer bag full of murder weapons for the month that needed to be melted and evaporated.

"You got the gun in there from the Antonio murder last night?"

Bullethead smiled. "It's in there. I had to take out his

wife too, because he'd been telling her everything. If he wasn't here to work for the FBI, then she would be doing it."

"I knew his time was coming. I could feel his vibe. It was like... Unspoken... Like I knew someone was going to do it."

"Let me tell you how funny Zae is bruh. Zaedan got up early this morning while his wife was sleeping and drove over to Antonio's house. That nigga had a damn double barrel shotgun with a double barrel silencer on that shit. Talking about he's been dying to use it. Dying to try it out he says. But I was leaving Antonio's house when Zaedan was pulling up. I beat him to it. Use that crazy ass shotgun some other night. Not tonight."

I laughed at Bullethead's story. I remember when I first ordered that shotgun for him and was glad that he really liked the gift even though he hadn't been able to use it yet. We both checked to make sure the coast was clear when we pulled up to my car. After confirming, he popped the trunk, got out and grabbed the black box; and handed it to me. I took it from him and put it in my back seat on the floor. I shook his hand and saluted him before he got back in his car and drove off.

We had a system that worked. Bullethead had my back, Zaedan had my back, Maclente had my back. I had Bullethead's back, I had Zaedan's back, I had Maclente's back. Anybody who stepped against the grain was an outcast, and all outcasts deserved to be treated however they got treated. Zaedan told us how Brizzo had crossed the line, and there was definitely a green light on his head. The moment we found out how Antonio was rocking, there was a green light on his head as well; but it didn't take long for his situation to be wrapped up. He'd had a good talking to while sitting on the couch in his living room. Sometimes that was the best place to have a good conversation.

I put my seatbelt on because I couldn't afford to get pulled over for anything; then drove to the compound so that I could melt the murder weapons. I'd been doing the same thing for the crew for nearly two years, and it gave everybody a peace of mind once they handed the black box over to me. They knew that those weapons would never be found ever again. Bullethead had once joked that my hands were like the black abyss. He said the moment that bag of guns touched my hand it evaporated like a magic show. He was right about that because I would definitely lay my life down and die in order to protect those that I loved.

For me, Zaedan was my family. Bullethead and Maclente was my family. Ayoki was my family. To protect those that you loved, it required the maximum level of loyalty available. It was no secret that I'd kill for them, had killed for them, and would kill for them all again at the drop of a dime. Zaedan's style of how he ran shit was different than every other so-called street boss I'd ever bore witness to. He was understated, quiet, secretive; and most of the things he had a hand in, he never even admitted it to himself.

Truth be told, that's why the FBI was furious. That's why they wanted him so bad. Zaedan moved like a magician in the streets. He was so smooth with it, that even I had to question if he was getting money in the streets or if it was all coming from Free Wi-Fi. I know it was ten times as hard for the FBI because if I had to question it, and I was one of those people contributing to the street money; then the authorities had no chance. It wasn't just the way he moved in smooth silence; it was also the way he treated others.

I've never witnessed a scenario in which Zaedan treated people like he was above them. If he didn't treat people with respect, he didn't speak at all. All of those traits, and on top of that he was loyal to the ones he loved. There had never been a scenario in where one of his people got arrested and lost a trial. He was gutsy. He'd put the fear of God in several juries, prosecutors and judges, but he only had one rule: *Don't make any gigantic mistakes.* He used to joke that he could fix all large errors, but a gigantic mistake couldn't be repaired.

I'd heard him say this several times over the years, yet there I was; in the midst of making a gigantic mistake. Every time I was handed the black box in previous years, I always sprayed a capecitabine solution on the weapons immediately. Capecitabine therapy was used to treat cancer patients, and as a side effect, it removed their fingerprints for 2 to 4 weeks. The solution I had was from the black market, and there was a compound added into it that accurately morphed fingerprints as opposed to removing them. Accurately morphed being the keywords– this solution didn't morph the fingerprints into prints that didn't exist, instead it created a brief scientifically correct morph so that the prints turned to prints that actually existed.

Since the FBI were constantly bothering us, we never applied type of solution to our hands. If we were to be fingerprinted for any reason, there would be no reason to give them any extra ideas– our prints would always come back as our prints. Instead, I always sprayed the solution onto the weapons the moment I received the black box. That way, if I ever were to get pulled over before having a chance to melt the weapons, at least the fingerprints would come back as a match to someone we've never met before instead of coming back as a match to Zaedan Montez. It was a pattern. It was something I'd done for years and never made the error of forgetting.

Except for that night. With all that had been going on, I

forgot to place another order of the solution. The black box I had contained murder weapons from who knows where. I was almost certain Zaedan's prints were in there somewhere. I was near certain Bullethead's prints were on a few of the weapons. They never told me who was killed, but it didn't matter. We all just kinda knew things without ever expressing it to each other. I'd known Antonio was going to get caught a long time ago. I just didn't know that I was going to get caught slipping on my job.

My car was surrounded the moment I pulled up to the gate of the compound. There were so many police officers behind me that it looked like they'd brought the entire academy out to arrest me. The fact that I didn't see any police cars when I turned on the road must have meant that they had been setting up at least a half mile down the street. But how did they know I wouldn't take a different route to the compound? What if I would have spotted them first? Would they still have surrounded me? I couldn't help but to wonder if I'd been set up by anyone, but I knew that couldn't be true. That would imply that the person who set me up was Bullethead, and I knew for a fact he didn't have a snitching bone in his body. So, no... I wasn't set up... But maybe they'd bugged my car and I forgot to check my own car since I was too busy debugging everybody else's. A host of thoughts flushed my mind as I sat there stunned.

"Step out of the car with your hands up!"

The megaphone was loud and direct, and it only highlighted the intent of the officer who was speaking. I could hear in his voice that he wasn't going to allow me to get out of there alive. There was no escaping, and it was the end of the road for me. Literally. I thought about my odds of winning a trial and shook my head. It was impossible. That was the type of gigantic mistake that Zaedan always said avoid. I couldn't beat a trial if they recovered that box because it would probably get the whole crew indicted. I couldn't go for that. My crew were my brothers, and that would be fact and gospel until the end of time.

I quickly checked the glove compartment to see if I had another gun, but it wasn't there. I thought about taking the guns out of the black box and shooting my way out, but when I checked in the rear view, it seemed like even more patrol cars had showed up since they had me cornered. I looked on the floor for another gun when I remembered something. I knew exactly how to get out of the situation, but it was certainly about to be risky.

"We have you surrounded. Step out of the vehicle with your hands up. Now! Keep your hands in plain view!"

I ducked down instead and crawled into the back seat of the car. I pulled down the back seat and pushed the small subwoofer out of the way. I crawled through the hole that housed the subwoofer until I was in the trunk. In the trunk I had a bomb package, but it was wrapped in bomb proof wrapping so that I wouldn't blow up by accident. I took the wrapping and created a small wrap around curtain in the trunk of the car. I knew they hadn't advanced towards the car because the megaphone was coming from the same distance.

I quickly crawled through the hole in the trunk and put the bomb on the armrest in the front seat. I covered the hole where the subwoofer once was with bomb proof wrapping and slid back as far back as I could. I couldn't allow law enforcement the opportunity to recover the guns, and I couldn't allow them to arrest me either. I wasn't expecting the bomb proof wrapping to save me from the blast, I was just hoping that once the blast was over that I died in one piece instead of a million pieces. To be able to have a funeral in one piece was the ultimate peace for me.

I listened carefully trying to figure out where they were and what they were doing. There was silence for a moment, and then I heard the sound of heavy equipment getting closer to my trunk. There was a rattling of keys and footsteps getting closer, so I used the only option I had left. I squeezed the button on the remote to the bomb, but nothing happened. One of the swat team popped the trunk like it was already open, and suddenly I'm staring down the barrels of 6 guns.

"Hands up! Hands up! Hands up now!" They screamed at me.

I squeezed the remote again, but nothing happened. The bomb didn't even go out, and I had no idea what I'd done wrong to prevent it from working correctly. Out of all the gadgets I'd ordered from the black market, that was the first one that failed when I needed it the most. I was doomed.

"Open your hand and face me with it! What's in your hand? Drop it! What is it?"

There was all types of commotion, but then I realized things were about to get even worse once they realize it's a bomb in the front seat.

"Drop it! Drop it! Whatever it is drop it!"

I dropped the remote as they wished, and suddenly it seemed like 10 to 12 more officers were running up to the trunk with their weapons drawn. I closed my eyes and kept my hand outward facing them, trying not to piss them off further. I knew they wanted to kill me; I could see it on their faces. But what they couldn't do is see the equal emotion that I had on my face. Everything they wanted to do with me, was exactly what I wanted to do with them, if not more.

"Put his ass in cuffs so we can see if this is the ware-house, they keep the drugs in."

"Yes sir."

The moment the officer pulled his handcuffs out, the bomb remote made a beeping noise as if the battery was dying. I shook my head. Why didn't I think to replace the–

28

ZAEDAN

Ayoki and I first met at the state fair. We weren't even old enough to drink, hadn't had any experience making adult decisions; yet our souls knew it was going to be permanent from day one. The crazy thing is we were both on dates that night, and both of us had been dealing with difficult relationships. The girl I was dating at the time, Rhynda; was one of the evilest women I'd ever known. She was the type of woman who laughed at sick people, made fun of people who couldn't help themselves, gave people the wrong directions and thought it was funny, kicked dogs in the head while they were sleeping, and constantly tried to deceive anybody who tried to love her.

There were a few reasons that I dated her back then. Her popularity and beauty for starters. I was popular, and I needed someone who wouldn't be intimidated by me feeling good about life. Another reason was that when it was just me and her alone, I would often see glimpses of the great woman that she could be. I knew a lot of the stuff she was doing were cries for help, and I figured I could work to help her change and be a better person.

It was a full moon the night I met Ayoki. 75 degrees on a beautiful fall night in Georgia. It was the type of night where you could sit on the porch and admire the stars and be content doing nothing else. I always enjoyed the looking at the stars. Always enjoyed spotting constellations and shooting stars. Always enjoyed making a wish when I spotted the north star. Always wondered if there was life beyond the stars.

Even though I'd had lots of experience star gazing, the first time I saw Ayoki was the first time I got starstruck. The fact that a woman could exist and look so stunningly perfect had me at a loss of words. From the very moment I saw her, I knew I desired to be her friend. Even though I desired it, I knew it would be impossible. She had her boyfriend there with her and I had my girlfriend there with me, besides; even if we didn't have significant others with us that night, I couldn't have imagined that she would even give me the time of day.

Me and Rhynda were in line to play one of the games called Pop Darts. The goal was to throw a dart and hit the one red balloon in the middle of all the yellow balloons. The twist to it was they would give us a bigger bear depending on how far back we stood before throwing the dart. We'd stood in line for 25 minutes to play that game, and right when it was my turn to win her a bear, a guy came limping in front of me.

I wasn't offended because I could see that something was wrong with him. He could barely walk, and it took a lot of patience to understand what he was saying. I smiled at him and moved back to allow him to talk to the operator. The moment I did that, all hell broke loose.

"Get yo' retarded ass back!" Rhynda screamed at the kid. She embarrassed me so much that if I had the option to disappear, I would have done it without second guessing. Everybody was frowning at her in shock that she was downing a kid who can't help himself. He turned around and looked at her with a sad look on his face.

"I awry."

"You what?"

"I awry."

"Be awry and get out our way retard."

I couldn't take it anymore. I grabbed her by the arm and walked her away from the line. We took about 5 steps and she snatched her arm away from me. "Let go of me soft ass nigga. How you gon take that retarded ass kid side when you know we been waiting in that line all damn night?"

She had my blood pressure boiling, but being that we were in a public setting, I tried my best to prevent myself from blacking out. I took a deep breath. "If we waited 25 minutes, we could wait 26 minutes. The kid can't help himself, but your grown ass knows better. You gotta stop being that way. That's never gon get you anywhere in life."

"What? Nigga you don't tell me what to stop being like. The fuck. You a soft ass nigga for real. That's why..."

"That's why what?"

"Don't worry about it Zaedan."

"Nah say it. That's why what?"

"That's why I gave Kelvin my phone number. I already see we won't be able to last. I need a real nigga, not no soft ass nigga who gon let people run over him."

Her words didn't hurt me. What hurt me was the fact that she thought I cared. Truth be told, I'd mentally checked out of the relationship after knowing her for a week. The only reason I still dated her was because every time I tried to dump her she would change the subject. There would be no subject change after that night.

"That's what's up. Well I wish you and Kelvin the best."

"Oh yea? So, you just give up that easy huh? You didn't give a fuck about me anyways."

I stared at her silently. She had her hands on her hips, a small coat of sweat beginning to form on her forehead. Who was I to argue about her? She was right in so many words, and there was no need to debate the truth.

"You know what? Nigga fuck you!"

She walked off after her outburst, blending in with the happy people as if she was one of them. I waited by the fence in case she needed a ride home. Despite our differences, I was still a gentleman, and I was going to do the right thing because it's what I would want done for me had the shoe been on the other foot. I sat on the bench prepared to wait until the fairgrounds closed, when I saw Rhynda walk by me holding some older guy's arm. She smirked at me as they walked out of the exit, and I remained sitting there.

Even though I wasn't a jealous person, I did get offended by disrespect; and I felt like that was one of the most disrespectful things a person could ever do. Still I suppressed it, at least I tried to. I remained sitting on the bench even after the fair closed for the night, and the only reason I got up to leave was because I saw security guards walking towards me. If I hadn't seen the security guards, I probably would have just spent the night there in that same spot.

I walked to where I thought I parked my car at, and when I got there, I realized I'd walked to the wrong end of the parking lot. I sighed. I hadn't paid much attention, but I definitely paid attention to how long that walk was. I looked at the other end of the parking lot and shook my head. I guess I had no choice but to get it done. After fighting my mental laziness, I started walking back the opposite direction. I got about halfway when I saw Ayoki standing between a truck and a van, trying to pull away from the guy she was with that night.

Instinctively, I started walking in her direction. I couldn't make out what was being said, I could only see that whatever was being said wasn't being agreed with. As I got closer, I began to make out some of the words.

"Let me go! Let me go!"

"Bitch get in the got damned truck. You think I took you to the fair for nothing? You gon' give me something. Get in the truck."

That shit had my blood boiling. I ran faster, ignoring the fact that I was about to put my nose in another person's business. The only thing on my mind was to see if I could help her. Even if she wasn't mine and never became mine, she still didn't deserve to be taken advantage of anywhere, in a parking lot or otherwise.

"Aye bruh... What's up?" I said as I approached them.

The guy froze. Looked at me like I was the scum of the earth. As if I'd offended him by speaking to him. "What's up nigga?" He said as he glared at me. Just by his demeanor I could tell that he thought he was a bad ass. So, I knew that if I approached him with force, he was going to reply with force because that's all he knew. Instead I approached him with psychology.

"I know you ain't finna go out like that." I said as I walked closer.

"Go out like what?" His voice got louder, and his face twisted up like he was ready to punch me. He still had an iron grip around Ayoki's arm, and I could tell she was ready to get away from that man the first chance she got.

"Shit... go out like a lame."

"Nigga ain't shit lame about me cuz. Who the fuck is you?"

"I'm just saying bro. You supposed to be keeping it player. If a real player can't get none from a chick, he just get another chick. I mean... I'm just saying..."

He instantly let her arm go and got defensive. "Man, bruh I don't even want this broad for real. I was really just playing with her before she started getting serious."

The moment he let her arm go, she took off running. I changed the subject because I knew if I kept probing, that I'd end up boxing him off in the corner, and once he mentally felt like he was in the corner, he was going to try to fight his way out of it.

"Say bruh. Don't you be rapping?" I asked as I got closer to him.

"Hell yea! How you know?"

"What's your rap name?"

"T Zeezy."

"Man, I thought that was you bro. I fuck with your music bro. You got any mixtapes on you?"

"Shit not right now, I sold out... but gimme your number. I'll have some more copies tomorrow."

I gave him my number and he kept running his mouth about some new album he'd been working on. I kept a smile and pretended to listen, but the truth was I didn't even know the nigga rapped or had mixtapes. But since every other nigga had a mixtape and rapped, I figured it was a 95% chance the shit would apply to him too. I nodded my head as he talked, occasionally breaking into the conversation with a "hell yea," or a "oh yea that's gon be hard," but at the end of the day, I don't even know what the hell he was talking about.

By the time me and him got done talking, we were the last two people there. I shook his hand, and he left the parking lot thinking he had a new fan. I started walking through the empty parking lot thinking about how crazy my night had gone. I'd broken up with my girlfriend and broken another guy up with his too. I walked faster since I was starting to get sleepy. It was going to be a lonely trip back to Atlanta, so I needed to save all the remaining energy I had so I could focus.

I walked around my car and nearly jumped out of my shoes when I saw Ayoki sitting on the ground on the driver's side of the car.

"I'm sorry if I scared you." She said as she looked into my eyes.

I reached down to give her a hand. "You didn't scare me... but how did you know this was my car?"

She got up off of the ground and smirked. She stood directly in front of me and looked at me as if she was examining me. "Thank you."

"You're welcome... But seriously... How did you know this was my car?"

She looked at the ground, almost as if she didn't know how to answer the question. "If I tell you, you'll think I'm weird."

"No, not at all... I'm curious..."

She walked up to me and wrapped her two hands around mine. "My name is Ayoki."

"My name is Zaedan."

"Nice name."

"Thanks."

"Yea... Well... I knew this was your car the same way I know you're going to be my husband one day... I just... knew."

It was 5 in the morning when I felt someone shaking me. I opened my eyes and initially didn't even know where I was. I looked up and a nurse was smiling at me. I wiped my eyes and tried to refocus so I could see through the glaring light.

"Did you hear me sir?"

"Huh? No. What did you say? What happened?"

"I said your wife has been asking for you."

I jumped up out of my seat. I didn't know how long I'd been sleep in the waiting room, but I was so excited to hear that Ayoki was asking for me. When I fell asleep earlier that night, she still hadn't come to yet. This was great news. I walked down the hall and turned back around with a blank stare. The nurse smiled.

"Yes, you're going the right way."

I turned and kept walking, went as fast as I could; every step I took reminding me of the first night we met. Every step in the hospital just like my walk across the parking lot to meet my fate. She knew I was going to be her husband before I even knew she was interested in me. Here we were so many years later, just us against the world; us remaining by each other's side through thick and thin, experiencing the ups and downs and praying our way through it all.

She didn't see me when I walked in her room. Her head was turned facing the wall and the bear I bought her earlier from the gift shop was snugly under her arm. I walked up to her and kissed her, and she jumped back frightened. I felt bad for scaring her after all that she'd been through, and I made a mental note to be gentler moving forward. When she realized it was me, she pulled me close and kissed me herself.

"I love you Ayoki. How are you feeling?"

She smiled at me. A happy smile, and I couldn't tell if she was happy because of the pain medications she was on, or if she was smiling like that because of me.

"Good. I feel good."

She was talking slower than she normally talked, but I attributed it to the medication and the fact that she'd had two very difficult days back to back. I knew she had to be exhausted because that was exactly how I'd felt before I crashed out earlier in the waiting room. I sat down on the chair in front of her and stared at her. She was so precious, so perfect, and I don't know what I would do if she ever took her love to Heaven and left me on earth. I would be beyond sick, beyond stressed, just as lost as I could ever be.

After about 7 minutes she fell asleep again. I knew she would be in serious pain from that stab wound if it wasn't for the medicine, so I had to accept that she wasn't going to be herself until she got better. A doctor knocked on the door and walked in the room.

"Hey. Are you her boyfriend or?"

"Husband." I said as I stood up and put my hands in my pocket.

"Alright good. I was just checking. If you would come with me, I'd like to have a word with you."

I followed the doctor outside of the hospital room and into the waiting room. "So, I'll get straight to the point. Does she have a history of alcohol addiction?"

"No, not that I know of."

"Alright, what about drug use of any type?"

I exhaled. "Yes. She said she'd been taking LSD or something like that."

The doctor started writing something on a sheet of

paper, and then adjusted his glasses. "Ah yes, so that explains it. Earlier she was having extreme hallucinations, and I believe the pain that she suffered with the stabbing has stimulated some pre-existing trauma. We gave her anti-psychotics to treat the hallucinations, but after a few hours we had to raise the dosage. We do plan to give her a CAT scan later today because I do suspect that she has brain damage from the LSD and underlying trauma."

"Brain damage? What do you mean doc? Like what? Like she won't be able to function?"

"I'm not sure yet. Brain damage doesn't have to be that extreme, or it could be even more extreme. We won't know until we do the CAT scan."

"But doc the nurse said she asked for me earlier... I mean..."

"Yes. And that's good. It could also be a possibility that she doesn't realize you're real. Her sense of reality is slightly distorted."

My anxiety tuned the doctor's words out as panic rushed through my mind. This couldn't be happening to us, I refused to accept it. I loved that woman with everything in me, and God knows I'd do anything to have my wife back normal. I hated that I'd kept so many secrets, and I knew she hated that she'd done the same. If I'd went ahead and told my wife about Tarralla back when it first happened, we could have avoided all of the events that took place at the church. I was pissed at my decision making.

"Why don't you go home and get some rest, and come back later when– "

"I'm not leaving my wife here by herself. I'm not– "

"I assure you she's in good hands. I really need her to get her rest before the tests I have scheduled for her later. I need to make sure she doesn't have brain damage. How about you come back at 10 AM since the CAT scan is at 10:30? That way you can be with her for the duration?"

I shook my head. "Not happening doc. I'm not leaving my wife. The only reason I was in the waiting room sleeping earlier was because I'm a loud snorer, and I didn't want my snoring to wake her. I'll be here at 10, 10:30, and all the hours leading up to it."

"Alright then. Well I'll have the nurse bring you a pillow and blanket. Do you have any questions?"

"Well I wanted to know if she was going to have any organ damage from that stabbing?"

The doctor flipped open the folder he had and started flipping through the pages. He frowned when he got midway, a confused look on his face. His facial expressions were making me nervous. He took a few steps over to an empty table and placed the folder atop it. He started flipping through the pages, looking at the bottom of every page carefully. By the time he flipped to the last page and shook his head.

"Excuse me. Give me one moment."

He walked to the nursing station and had a few words with the nurses. I couldn't hear what was being said, but he showed her something inside the folder and it caused them all to panic. They started looking at the ground and walking around as if they'd dropped a car key somewhere. Another lady came out of the back holding a piece of paper with a smile on her face.

"Found it." She said as she handed the paper to the doctor. I couldn't help but to expect the worse. Every step he took made me feel another inch closer to my impending doom. He could sense the worry on my face.

"Relax. Everything's fine. She doesn't have any injuries, and the best part of everything is the fact that the baby is ok."

"Baby?"

"Yes. Your wife is 6 weeks pregnant."

29

BULLETHEAD

I hadn't been in the house but for an hour when Maclente called me with the news.

"Wilburt is dead. Law enforcement was acting on a tip of some sorts– They surrounded Wilburt outside of the compound. The reports are that instead of surrendering, he activated a bomb or similar device, and ended up killing himself and 7 officers while wounding at least 5 others. From the information I'm gathering, I think this was initiated by the Solumbert Family as a part of some retaliation."

I was so familiar with death that it didn't affect me when I lost someone. In fact, death was all I thought of on most days and all nights. I participated in the death industry, was a contributor to the funeral home business and a hindrance for insurance companies. If the public were to ever write an article on me, they would label me a monster. The same would go for Wilburt, Zaedan; all of us. But monsters we weren't. We only killed in order to live, protect, and maintain. Nothing was ever going to be given to a group of black men without them applying brute force to obtain it, and that included respect.

If we didn't kill, all of us would be dead right now. That didn't make us the monsters, that made us the monster killers.

I had a moment of silence and reflection as I listened to Maclente's words. I knew the decisions would normally be made by Zaedan, but I didn't want to add more to his plate while he was with his wife at the hospital. I was going to have to have his back on a few issues in the meanwhile.

"I also wanted to discuss something that was brought to my attention Bullethead, but first I had a few questions."

"Aight what's up?"

"Obviously anytime drugs are mentioned to Zaedan he laughs at it or denies it. That's all well and fine, but now is not the time for denial if there's any type of truth to it."

"Truth to what?"

"Zaedan's involvement in drugs Bullethead. I've gotten some inside info from someone who works downtown, and they're telling me that the FBI and local law enforcement are speculating that Zaedan could possibly be a kingpin. My source says that that's why Antonio started acting funny before he died, they had some type of leverage on him."

"How did they have leverage if he was a lawyer? That makes no sense for one, and for two, I don't know shit about no drugs. When have you ever seen me use or discuss drugs with anybody? When have you seen Zaedan use or discuss drugs? It's like the FBI have painted an image and running with it whether it's true or false. That's a damn shame that you would even ask that question to me. I'm not Zaedan, so that's his question to answer, but since you did ask me; now I have to question your IQ at this point. Are you going to be mentally strong enough to represent us or do we need to hire a different lawyer in case real trouble ever comes our way?"

He was silent for a moment, and I understood his difficulty; but I don't see how any questions about anything illegal could help anybody. It made no sense to me regarding the questions, but I understood the position he was in. Maclente was probably afraid thinking that he was going to be killed next, but that wasn't the case. Maclente hadn't violated the way Antonio did.

"You, nor Zaedan will never need another attorney. The reason I ask questions is so that I can start preparing defenses in the case something goes bad. I'm not asking for–"

"Yo you got anything else to talk about?"

"Uhm yea."

I could tell that Maclente was offended, but hell that made two of us.

"Word is... they're supposed to be taking everything to the grand jury in order to officially get an indictment on Zaedan."

"Indictment on him for what? What charges?"

"They're telling me they wanna hit him with the RICO act, and prosecute him under the Kingpin statute."

"Good luck with that." I laughed.

"What's funny? Because it's not a joke to me. It's a nightmare on the cusp of becoming reality. These are serious charges, and they'll most likely be seeking a life sentence. This isn't fun for me Bullethead, so I find no humor in it."

"Well you better find some damn humor in it."

He knew I didn't fucking play. I wasn't about to threaten him on the phone, nor was I going to let him talk to me any kind of way. If he didn't find humor in it, I was going to break his funny bone into a thousand pieces and spread them out in a garden.

"Alright then... Bullethead I'll let you know if I get any more updates regarding things."

"Wait wait. Did they find Wilburt's remains?" I'd forgotten to ask him that earlier, but I needed to know.

"I mean... the entire area got blown to a hundred thousand pieces of blood, bones, flesh, guts and car metal... I'm sure his remains are sprinkled in with the remains of the cops."

"So, he's alive?"

"Fuck no. He's dead. Believe that. They had him surrounded and he suicide bombed– killed himself and everybody around him. You know if he was alive, he would be in custody. They're on the scene as we speak trying to gather evidence, so I guess we'll find out soon if they picked up his remains. I'll be sure to ask them that question specifically in a couple of hours."

"Nah, don't ask them. I only asked you. Leave it."

"Cool. Well if that's it, I'm going to see if I can figure out who's in charge of trying to obtain this secret indictment. Maybe that'll help things if I know in advance. I'm going to speak to Zaedan when I get more information, I don't want to bother him with something that could very well be just a rumor."

"Aight cool. I'm out."

I hung up the phone because I was tired of damn talking. I jumped up and grabbed my keys so I could go to the compound. Wilburt was too smooth and too smart to just blow himself up like that, but then again, I didn't really know the circumstances. I thought about the black box and panicked. Shit... What the fuck? A panic seared through my chest when I thought about the murder weapons in the box. The fact that Maclente didn't mention it must have meant that they didn't find it. If that was the case, then I couldn't allow them to find it. I needed to think of a quick strategy, as time was not on my side.

30

BRIZZO

Cockroaches the sizes of dogs were crawling out of the club speakers. Ants were crawling out of the cockroaches' eyes, and the roaches had snakes on a leash like they were just casually walking their dogs. The strobe lights in the club looked like small flashlights initially, and but with every passing second, they started getting bigger until they began looking like headlights. I jumped up and fell across the table, knocking over the bottles of alcohol as I tried to get away from the truck.

"Yo homes you ok?" Horrez grabbed my arm and pulled me up off of the ground. "You good homes?"

I stood up and tried to answer him, but when I looked into his eyes, I saw a speeding train coming towards me. I ducked and rolled over so it wouldn't hit me, accidentally knocking down one of the women who were standing in our section. I jumped up off of the ground and suddenly found myself in the middle of the expressway with speeding cars honking their horns and speeding around me. I started running and the security guard grabbed me.

"Aye you ok man?"

"He's fine. We'll handle him." Horrez said, a look of concern on his face.

The security guard released me, and Horrez grabbed my arm. Horns started growing out of his head right before my eyes, and I let out a loud scream; causing several people to become concerned about what was going on in our section. I screamed louder as his horns continued to grow, and I could no longer understand what was going on. Horrez opened his mouth and fire came out, causing me to duck to avoid it, but it didn't matter.

My clothes were on fire. I started jumping up and down trying to fan the fire out, but it only got worse. The fire was hot, starting to burn my skin so I started taking my clothes off. The music stopped and people started screaming and yelling, but I was sure it was because they were seeing the devil just like I was. I pulled my shirt and shoes off and the next thing I knew I was tackled by Horrez's homeboys and carried to his truck. They held me down in the back seat as Horrez drove. Everything looked like it was melting, as if I was wearing a pair of 3-D glasses in the middle of a cartoon.

I was paranoid and hot, sweat the only thing cooling me off as they held me back from moving. "Please I need air. Please. Please."

They cracked a window and I saw an airplane flying towards the window. "Aaaaaaaaaagggghhhhhhh!" I screamed as I squirmed and twisted and tried to avoid the impact. Then the truck disappeared, and it was just me in the air, but somehow Horrez was still driving and his homeys were still holding me from moving. I was dying. I was afraid. I was lost. I was crying, and nobody seemed to care that horns were growing out of everybody's heads. The truck reappeared again, and the cockroaches came back, this time out of the air conditioning vent with venomous fangs protruding out of their claws. They disappeared and guns were drawn on me by one of Horrez's homeys.

"Horrez I'm about to kill this muthafucka."

"Not in my fucking Rolls Royce you're not. You do that and I'll kill you for fucking up my truck. Plus, me and him still got business to do."

The next moment I was yodeling. I've never yodeled a day in my life, nor did I even know what the fuck I was doing, but there I was just as clear as the night was dark... yodeling my ass off in the back seat. Horrez started laughing.

"Homes you never had LSD before? I thought you were hip to it. You're going on a baddd ass trip right now."

I kept yodeling, and after my voice got tired, I started making pig noises. Oinking as the truck made its way through traffic, and eventually to my house. Everybody in the car was laughing at me but I couldn't control it. I kept oinking until Horrez parked the car and looked back at me. He turned serious, and when he turned serious, he went from being a man with horns growing out of his head to appearing as a businessman in a suit.

"We're going to stay here with the guy until his trip comes down." Horrez said to his guys.

"What? Why? His LSD trip won't be over until tomorrow sometime. I say we just do what we came to do and keep it moving."

"No, we have to make sure he has a clear mind. Let's go."

They took me into my house and tied me up to a chair in the kitchen. They gagged me so I couldn't scream and tied me tight so I couldn't move. The floor turned into a pit of snakes and they were hissing, threatening to bite me. I started trying to kick at the snakes until I flipped over in the chair. When I hit the floor, my weight broke the wooden chair, and I was only tied to a few pieces of wood. I stood up and started jumping up and down so that the snakes wouldn't bite me.

"Yo, knock his ass the fuck out homes." Horrez shouted. I thought he was talking to the snakes, so I balled my hands up into fists and stared at the floor, daring the snakes to knock me out. I looked up and saw a gun swinging towards my head at a rapid pace. Then blackness.

31

BULLETHEAD

Officer McJacobs walked under the crime scene ribbon with a notepad in his hand. Nobody questioned him since everybody was already busy attending to their own individual task. He frowned as he stepped over a piece of somebody's leg and held his nose as he stepped around what smelled like the inside of someone's intestines. He continued to walk until he'd gotten out of sight of the other officers, agents, and detectives. He walked across the yard and stepped in front of the door of the beat-up wooden outhouse. He put the code in, walked in, lifted the wooden stairs and stared into the barrel of a shotgun.

"You move one more inch and I'll send you to go find missing pieces of the Titantic."

"It's me nigga." Bullethead said as he removed the hat and pulled off his fake mustache.

"What the fuck? Why would you do that? Why didn't you just wait until the scene was clear?"

"Because I wanted to see if you needed help. That's why. I know you got all kinds of gadgets and shit, all kinds of tricks and ways to survive, but a mistake could have fucked you up and you might have needed some medical help. Nigga I had a doctor on standby and everything."

"Nah I'm good bro. I appreciate it. The bomb proof shit is crazy bro. I blew up every damn thing except for the trunk I was in. It blew the trunk across the fence, and I started running fast as a muthafucka through the thick smoke. This outhouse should be called a damn lifehouse. This shit saved my life. Then I saw your ass creeping... My first mind was to put a bullet in your ass the moment I saw your face, but I knew you had to be on my side if you knew the damn code to the door."

"I'm always on your side. We family."

"Bro I'm already knowing. What's the word in the streets?"

"Shit Wilburt... Everybody's saying the Solumbert Family is behind this shit bro. On some real shit, they're saying they found out the identity of the guy who buys the trucks from you, and pressed him for info about the things he knew."

"Damn... The Solumberts? And then they send the FEDS and the police and shit? That's unlike them."

"Nah bro listen. It's not like them to snitch on each other. They don't give a fuck about a black man. They really hate us, and apparently are willing to do whatever it takes to prevent us from continuously having a foot on their income."

Wilburt shook his head. We were both pissed and were both tired of the bullshit. I sat down beside him and unbuttoned the police shirt. I had to get rid of that bullshit attired immediately. "You got any clothes down here?"

"In the back room, there are new jogging pants and t-shirts in there."

"Perfect. I say we try to get some rest and let the police continue to disappoint themselves looking for some imaginary drugs. It's gon be hell to pay because of the dead officers, but as long as they believe that you're deceased, you should be fine. So, I say we get a few hours of rest, and wake up refreshed early in the morning. We get up early and go give the Solumbert Family a great talking to."

"I like that idea... But then what bro? I can't just be out and about and shit.

"Then you get the fuck out of town. I'll talk to Zaedan and we figure that part out. It's been time for us all to relocate anyways, I know he's been mentioning it for months. Now would be the perfect time ya' dig? Get the fuck out, change our lives up, live off of the cash that's been accumulated over the years."

Wilburt nodded his head. "Yea I like that shit family. Say no more."

ZAEDAN

Hearing the doctor tell me that my wife was 6 weeks pregnant did something to me that no other words could do. It calmed my spirit and excited me simultaneously. It didn't rattle my spirit the way Tarralla's words did when she first told me she was pregnant. That's how I knew this was meant to be. That's how I knew this was real and legit, and that's the moment my view of the world changed. I sat in the hospital room staring at my wife as she slept. I looked at the machines and monitors, and even though I was upset because she was in that position due to my secrets; I also felt a wave of happiness because I knew I wasn't going to keep any secrets from her going forward.

I was blessed to be able to get a second chance with the woman that I loved and was committed to be a better person the moment I could clear up all of my current issues in the streets. The truth was... things were bound to be worse before they would be better, that was just a basic law of life. It seemed like my wife was in a daze during the CAT scan earlier, as she didn't say anything to anybody, including me, and after they brought her back to the room she went back to sleep again. It was around 1:30 that evening when she finally woke up from her sleep, and I got up and stood right by her side once she opened her eyes.

"Hey baby." I said gently. My voice was calm although my heart was beating twice as fast.

She smiled at me, and it made me smile even harder. She was the most beautiful woman I'd ever laid eyes on as long as I'd been living, and she was my wife. I was her husband, and we had a baby on the way. Life was amazing.

"Sammy?" She said as she continued to smile at me.

"Huh? Who's Sammy?"

"I don't know. Are you Sammy?"

I leaned down closer to her. "Baby it's me. Your husband. Zaedan." I smiled again, hoping she was just sleepy and in a light fog.

"I'm not married. I'm married?" She asked.

"Yes baby. You're married. We're married, and I love you."

"I don't know." She shifted and tried to turn the other way.

"Baby be careful." I reached over and put my hand in hers. "I can help you if you want to turn– "

"No. I just want you to leave me alone. I don't know you. I'm not married to you."

My heart was breaking. I couldn't lose her right then. I couldn't give up. This couldn't be happening.

"Ayoki. It's me... Zaedan. Remember we met at the fair? You were waiting on me by my car. You told me we were going to be married one day. You remember?"

"I'm sorry."

"No, it's ok. You don't have to apologize. It's ok. Do you remember me now? We were the last two in the parking lot that night. We've been inseparable baby. You remember? It's me." I didn't even realize tears were coming out of my eyes, but it felt like I was trapped in the middle of a really bad nightmare.

"Who are you?"

I sighed and tilted my head back. I closed my eyes for a moment trying to think of the words to tell her.

"Are you trying to kill me? Can you get out of here? Police! Help! Help me!" Ayoki screamed as I stood there in shock.

Three nurses came in the room with concern on their

face. Ayoki was twisting and screaming, as if someone was bothering her. I stood there staring, confused, lost, astounded by the pain that had seeped into my life.

One of the nurses gave her a shot while the other two held her.

"She's bleeding." I pointed out to the nurses as a red stain began to form on her blanket.

"Yes, she must have disrupted some of the stitches. We really need you to let her rest so that she can get better. It seems that anything emotional, even if it's a positive emotion... It seems to negatively stimulate her. Just come back tomorrow and let us keep her in observations through the day and night."

"But what if she never gets back right?"

I was frightened at the possibility of that nightmare lasting forever. It was truly the worst thing that could ever happen to me. I needed her to get back right. I needed that more than I needed anything in the world.

"How about you discuss that with the doctor tomorrow?"

I nodded my head and walked off. She was right just as the doctor had been right when he first told me to leave and go get some rest. When I walked out of the hospital room, there was a lady standing there who looked like older versions of Ayoki. When I thought about it, hell, she looked like Tarralla as well; and I guess by me not knowing she had a sister I didn't put two and two together when I first laid eyes on Tarralla.

The older lady had the same car seat in her hand that Tarralla had when she came to the church to ruin my life. I looked into the car seat and let out a sigh of relief. That baby seemed to be mixed with a white man. It definitely wasn't mine.

"What the fuck are you looking at?" She asked as she glared at me. I know she didn't know who I was, and I was going to keep it that way. I walked away, but not far. I took a few steps and pulled my phone out just to see what the lady was going to do next. One of the nurses came out and the lady stopped her.

"Excuse me." The lady said. "I'm her mother. I was just wondering what's going on with her?"

"Well... We think she's suffering from brain damage of some sort."

"Good." The older lady said as she smiled and walked away. The nurse stood there just as stunned as I was as we both watched the lady walk away with a smile on her face. She didn't look at anybody and didn't care about what anybody had to say or what they thought. For some reason, she wanted to see her daughter ruined, as if she'd prayed for it to happen. I shook my head and left out of the hospital. I needed to clear up all pending business in the street so that I could put my complete focus on Ayoki.

My first stop was at Brizzo's new house. I'd done Brizzo a favor so many times, but he would get no more favors from me. I'd tried to let him slide, just knowing that he was related to my wife, but I knew he was going to be a serious liability if I let him slide any further. I looked up and down the block to make sure I wasn't being trailed by FBI, then I walked up the steps and knocked on the door. I was about to knock again, but Horrez opened the door with a smile on his face.

"What's up Zae? We gave him something to eat and left him tied up in the bedroom. He's all yours."

I dapped up Horrez and nodded my head in a show of appreciation. He whistled twice and his homeys got up and followed him out the door. I locked it and watched them get in the truck and pull off. I saw broken pieces of wood on the floor as I walked past the kitchen on my way to the bedroom.

When I got to the bedroom, Brizzo was still sleep. I took out a knife and cut the gag off of his mouth. He woke up instantly.

"Zaedan thank God you're here! Oh my God man them fucking Mexicans kidnapped me man. Did you kill them? Thanks so much man. That's why I'm forever loyal to you bro. You don't know how much I love you Zaedan."

I stared at him as he lied with no conscious. It was like he didn't even give a fuck about anything or anybody except for himself. I'd always had my reservations about him, but I always chalked it up to him being young and naïve. Being a liar was not excusable.

"Brizzo. I told you to get rid of the drugs. Instead you wanted to sell them."

"No I didn't. I got rid of them." He continued to lie.

I ignored him. "So what I did was... I gave my OG some money to buy them from you, just to see if you were going to keep your word like you said. You said you were going to give me half, I wanted to see if you were real like you claimed to be. You stole drugs from the cartel. Luckily, I was able to pay them back for your mistakes, yet you still chose to say fuck me. You have no respect for nobody, you're out for self."

Brizzo started shaking his head in disbelief.

"Then you started talking crazy to me on the phone. It was like the moment you got what you wanted, you turned into a bitch. See what you don't realize is... Nigga I run Atlanta. I run this city to a magnitude that you could never understand or comprehend. That's because you never paid attention. You were so concerned about bullshit in the streets, bullshit cars, bullshit jewelry– none of that shit matters nigga. Now look at you... You got the car you wanted, you got diamonds on your wrist, and you got a new house. Everything you wanted and desired, but you have no life."

"Zaedan wait! Zaedan please! I'm sorry! I'm– "

The gun I had on me was what was referred to on the black market as a water gun. Not like the big super soakers that kids get from Wal-Mart in the summer, but a different level water gun. The gun had a small refrigeration system attached to the clip that created balls of rock-solid ice. It shot balls of ice twice the speed of a bullet and left no shell casings or bullets to be collected as evidence. The gun cost me $50,000 on the black market, and I always said that if I had to kill someone I cared about, then I would make sure they went out in style.

One shot from the water gun went completely through his forehead and splattered against the wall behind him as a mass of water and blood. The gun made no sound– the only sound being that of his urine mixing with blood and splattering against his wooden floor. I checked his pulse to make sure he was dead, then glanced over at the money that Horrez left on the bed for me. I didn't touch it, instead walked out to allow the police that worked for me to pick it up when they worked the scene.

Then I remembered something and walked back in. I picked up $100,000 of the money and then left back out. I put the money inside of a grocery bag and drove off. The second stop was on the Eastside of Atlanta, at a beat-up looking house with trash scattered in the yard. I parked my car beside the road and walked towards the house, stepping over egg cartons and grocery bags as I made it to the door.

I knocked on the door and waited. And waited. I'd stood there for so long that I was beginning to think that nobody was home. Then I heard someone whisper behind the door.

"Girl don't open that door; it might be a bill collector."

I knocked again, and after a moment with them still not replying, I talked to them through the door. "I'm not a bill collector. I'm Arres' boss."

The door opened quickly and Arres walked out fast so that I couldn't see inside. "Are you ok?" I asked her. She looked like she was stressed out and smelled like it too.

"Yes. I'm fine." She said quickly.

"Alright... Well I'm not going to hold you up for long. I just wanted to know... Well... There was a missing box in the office... And I was wondering– "

"I'm sorry Zaedan. I'll repay you for it. I knocked it over

by accident, and when I saw what fell out, I hid it so that it couldn't be found so easily."

"Repay me for it? Huh? Where did you hide it?"

"I put it in the trash can outside and forgot to get it back out. I meant to get it out once the shift was over, and I forgot. I'm so sorry, please don't fire me. I really need the job. We're struggling, me, Granny, my kids. Our water is off and I just–
"

"Here." I handed her the grocery bag and walked away.

By the time I got to my car, she screamed and started jumping up and down with joy on her face. Her grandma came outside as well as her two kids to check on her. She was shaking with happiness and trying to explain to them what I'd just done for them. I waved at them and drove off before they could have a chance to thank me. A thanks was unnecessary. It was I who owed them for saving my life.

32

BULLETHEAD

We'd been stalking the strip club that the Solumbert Family owned since 7 AM. It was 3 PM by the time Arcielly Solumbert arrived with his top goons. After discussing everything with Zaedan, he greenlighted the hit on Arcielly. Being that Arcielly was a mafia boss– a made man, I knew it could be extreme consequences from other mob bosses after a murder of that magnitude. However, Zaedan said he would talk to the bosses after the murder so he could explain to them how Arcielly was snitching and working with the police. If he tried to speak to them before the murder, he had no doubt they would try to prevent a black man from killing a mafia boss, no matter how much power he held. There was a chance they wouldn't believe him about Arcielly snitching if he came to them first, so he wasn't going to them first.

Earlier that morning, we'd slipped in the building and attached 2 bombs to the corner of every room of the strip club. Once we saw the last of Arcielly's goons go inside of the club, Wilburt took a portable welding gun to the door and welded it completely shut. I was lying flat on my stomach with an automatic rifle covering him just in case I spotted something that he didn't. After he finished the welding, he ran back to where I was hiding.

"Ok. So that's done. I think we should get the fuck away from this area before we hit the button." Wilburt was sweating as he spoke, and I could tell he was having flashbacks from the last bomb he hit the button on.

We walked two blocks to the where I'd parked the car and froze in our tracks. We ducked back to the side of the building out of sight. The FBI agents who always followed us were parked right behind the car.

"Shit! Wilburt, we'll get the Solumberts some other time. For now, just leave their ass welded up in their club. We won't be able to finish the bomb job up because they know I'm in the area. I want you to go catch an Uber and let Zaedan know the FBI is following me."

"Fuck that shit bro. They might wanna arrest you. Let's stick together– "

"Nah. Zaedan will get me out if they arrest me. Plus, if they arrest me, maybe we can get them to stop fucking following us all damn day. This shit might be long overdue. But we can't both get arrested family. I need you out here just like Zaedan needs you out here. Plus, you're dead remember? You blew up in a suicide bombing."

"Right. Right. Aight, well I'll see you soon fam." Wilburt ran the opposite way and cut through a parking lot. He went around a building and then I didn't see him again.

I tossed the rifle into the bushes and walked back around the building like nothing was going on. I walked to the car and before I could open it, the two agents walked up to me.

"We figured you would be back to the car sooner or later."

"What do you want from me?" I was irritated because that would mean they were sitting there all day waiting on me.

"Well, we were expecting a shoot-out between you and the Solumberts, but I guess you changed your mind?"

"What do you want?" I asked again.

"I'm guessing you had something different than a shoot-out planned for the Solumberts? I don't know... maybe a bomb or something?"

"Man, what the fuck do y'all want?" I was annoyed at that point.

"You know we also watch the Solumberts, so I thought it would be two birds with one stone today. This could have been a legendary day for the bureau."

"If you don't want anything, then I'll be on my way."

"Wait. You see this piece of paper?" The taller agent asked as he handed it to me.

I looked at it and sighed. It was an arrest warrant. I stopped reading after the first charge: CAPITAL MURDER. I handed it back to him and put my hands behind my back, but they didn't arrest me.

"What are you waiting on? Let's get it over with?"

"Listen man." The short agent turned me around while he spoke. "You know we don't want you, and we also know that you probably won't turn on Zaedan even though you're facing life in prison."

"Yea it's common knowledge so get the arrest over with, lock me up and throw away the key. Do what you gotta do."

The short agent ignored me and kept talking. "But we also have realized that you really don't even know Zaedan's power. See this whole time we were thinking one way, but after we continued to research, we've realized that you don't even have a damn clue. So now that we know you don't have a clue, we're going to rip this piece of paper up and let you go on one condition."

"What condition?"

THEY'D MADE me come with them to a vacant building. I'd never been there before, so it was all new to me. We all went inside the building and walked into what looked like a small conference room. There was a small school desk in the corner of the room, isolated as if it was used to put criminals in time-out. There was a long table, about eight chairs, four on both sides, and some ink pens. The agents had me hand-cuffed and sitting in a chair facing the door. They sat on both sides of me and put their guns on the table right in front of them.

"What are the guns for?"

"Well you know how y'all get down. I can't risk Zaedan having the place shot up. After all, we're stepped outside of bureau policy trying to get this situation resolved once and for all."

"Man get what resolved?" I was so tired of them fucking with us about some damn drugs that it was getting ridiculous.

"Oh, you'll see shortly." The taller agent said.

After about forty minutes had passed, Zaedan walked into the room. He'd taken a shower and changed since the last time I'd saw him at the hospital. He was wearing a black business suit and dress shoes. He sat down in front of us and clasped his hands together.

"What's up?" He asked the taller agent.

"You know what's up." The smaller one said. "Now that we have solid charges against your best friend here, we *know* that you know what's up at this point."

"I really have no clue what you're talking about." Zaedan responded.

"I'll help you get a clue." The taller agent said. "See what's going to happen is... We're going to release a RING security video from a home next door to where your friend committed a murder. What's going to happen is he won't beat this murder charge, and he will get life in federal prison. Then for the rest of your life, you'll get to live with how you've ruined so many lies with your decisions fueled in greed. Then once you can't bear it any longer, once you think it's all over, then you're going to slip up also, and you'll also do life in federal prison; and this will be all because you're acting like you have no clue about what we want."

Zaedan didn't reply. He just sat there staring at them.

"Zaedan. You wouldn't have agreed to show up without your attorney if you didn't know what we were talking about. There's no way. Let's not waste any more time huh. We're doing you a favor, trying to negotiate with you without this having to become a public spectacle."

"You already tried to make it a public spectacle. Raiding my cigar bar? Looking for some murder weapon that doesn't exist? Why should I ever trust the FBI?"

"That wasn't us. The bureau tried to go around us because they feel like we're not proceeding fast enough. They want you out of the way Zaedan, and you know why. So, let's talk."

"I'm not saying anything. If you know so much, then tell me the specifics. If you can accurately tell me the specifics, then maybe I'll consider."

The short agent stood up and nodded his head. "Fair

enough. At least we know we have your ear now." He walked to the corner where the desk was sitting and stopped. He turned around and faced us. "Look... the only way I can explain it is by giving you the same presentation that I planned to give to my boss this week. There's a deadline on your case, and we have to wrap it up regardless of if we can come to an agreement."

He reached in the desk and pulled out a thick folder and returned to the table beside me. I glanced at Zaedan trying to see if he was going to reach for one of the guns, but he didn't look at me. I was waiting on him to kick my foot under the table to let me know if I needed to distract so he could grab the guns, but it seemed like his mind was elsewhere.

"So, here's what we know Zaedan. We know in the years 2000 to 2005, the Port of Savannah was the fastest growing seaport in the United States with an annual growth rate of nearly 17%. Meanwhile the national average was around 9%. However, in 2003, March specifically– the Iraq War began, and what this did was decrease revenue growth for the seaports. There were a variety of reasons for this, of course the country was around four years away from heading into a recession."

He opened the folder and glanced at the first page before continuing. "Well, we looked deeper into things and we learned that at the time there was a man named James Montez who seemed to have a heavy involvement with the Port of Savannah. Do you mind telling us who James Montez is?"

"You know who he is."

"Absolutely we know who he is. He's your father."

I'd never heard Zaedan mention his father before, so I definitely had no idea where this conversation was going.

Zaedan crossed his arms and sat back in his chair. I watched him out of the corner of my eyes to see what he wanted me to do, but he didn't look at me. Not once did he make eye contact with me.

"In 2003, you were what? Like 11 or something? Anyways... Check this out. A couple of months after the war in Iraq started, there were about 1500 longshoremen who were a part of the union, who were threatening a strike. They got the idea from the west coast strike that cost nearly a billion dollars per day. But we all know that Savannah is an east coast port, so the losses would be far greater if they went on strike there. Anyways... the strike happened... but it only happened briefly for some reason. You know what the reason is?"

Zaedan nodded his head and let out a small laugh. "Thanks for the history lesson, but this has nothing to do with me. So, I have no idea why you're wasting your time."

"The reason the strike happened briefly is because your father, James Montez took control of the union quietly in 2003. There was a lot of bloodshed that month. Lots of cold cases are still being investigated. When he took control of the union, he took control of the Port of Savannah. Zaedan I'm not here to ask you where your father is hiding, I don't even care. I'm here because we know that you run the Port of Savannah today."

My mouth nearly fell to the floor. I had no idea Zaedan's dad was such a gangster. At the same time, I still had no idea where this conversation was headed. Zaedan had his hands in lots of businesses, so it wouldn't be surprising. I watched as Zaedan yawned and shook his head.

"Hypothetically, let's just say I did run the Port of Savannah today... What the fuck are you fucking with me for?"

The agent stopped talking and put his head down in his hands. He passed the folder to his partner, and he took over the conversation.

"Zaedan, we know you're responsible for most of the drug flow coming into the east coast. You've indirectly been one of the biggest kingpins in the United States of America, and it was passed down to you by your father. Every single month, you've been responsible for billions of dollars of cocaine, heroin, and LSD coming into the Port of Savannah. It's the true reason you're able to do so much shit and get away with it. It's the reason the mafia bosses have all considered you absolutely untouchable. The Mexican Cartels think you're untouchable; but you're also the reason that so many people are dying out here in the streets."

Zaedan sighed. I knew he was tired of being accused of dealing drugs, but I also had never heard anything like what the agent was saying. That was some other level shit, and it even had me wondering if it was true or not.

"Hey man. Tell me what it is you want from me. I don't care about your speculations." Zaedan said as he leaned forward against the table. I thought he was going to reach for the guns, so I prepared myself in case he gave me any type of signal.

"Well we know there was a new union boss in 2013, because that's the year your father went on the run. Again, we don't care about any of that... What we want you to do is quietly pay up a restitution of 12 billion dollars, relinquish whatever stronghold you have over the union; and let us arrest you for something like tax evasion, you sign a plea deal for like 8 years."

"What the fuck? What makes you think I got 12 billion damn dollars? And why the fuck you want me in prison so bad? That's not happening. None of it."

The agent shook his head. "The alternative is you and your friend both eventually doing life."

"What I want do know..." Zaedan started as he frowned at the agent. "Why the fuck do you want me to pay twelve billion dollars privately? Why is this not public news?"

The shorter agent took over the conversation. "Honestly because the government is embarrassed about this happening. This won't be the first private negotiation between the FBI and a criminal, but since you've made it so far up the ladder, we've been ordered to negotiate with you first. You have just as much to lose as the government, so my boss feels comfortable that you'll do the right thing."

Zaedan shook his head and pressed his lips together tightly. I could tell he was pissed, but I could also tell he was thinking. I interrupted the silence just in case this stuff was true, and he was weighing the odds. "If it's true, which I'm sure it's not... Zaedan you better keep every dollar and every ounce of control that you own. I can do my time. I don't mind doing life knowing that the government thinks my best friend is one of the most powerful men in the world."

"I'll give you $6 billion dollars, not 12. And I'll do 3 years, not 8. You'll drop all charges against my crew, and I need it all guaranteed."

The shorter agent shook his head. "Bullshit. You're asking for too much and not giving us enough."

"I'm giving you $6 billion privately, not going to fight you on criminal charges; all so you can come out a winner and make you look good, but you can't do the small shit for me? The shit I'm asking will cost you nothing. The shit you're asking will cost me plenty."

"Yes, but that was before you mentioned dropping charges against your whole crew. This negotiation will just be for you and Bullethead. Maclente and Brizzo will have to answer to their charges."

"So how about I give you $10 billion and do 2 years? That's more money, one year less time; and you drop all charges."

The shorter agent shook his head. "One year less time? If you can get us $20 billion, I can arrange for you to do no time at all. How's that for less time?"

Zaedan seemed to think about it for a second and dismissed it.

"Nah. $10 billion and do 2 years in prison and you got a deal."

The taller agent looked at his partner for a moment. His partner nodded his head in agreement. He stood up and took the handcuffs off of Bullethead. "Deal."

I extended my wrists across the table, and they put the handcuffs on me instead.

"Bullethead... My wife."

"Say no more family. I got you."

33

ZAEDAN

2 *YEARS LATER*
It was true.

I wasn't a drug dealer; I was the gateway to drug dealing into the United States of America. The types of assets that I held were so large and valuable that it prevented me from ever uttering a word about it to anyone. Me and Bullethead had been best friends for well over a decade, and even he had no clue. It was why I always condemned my crew from mentioning drugs or even thinking about participating in it. There was no point to it.

When the cartel moved in $50 million in cocaine, I made $5 million. You'd be surprised at how many $50 million loads arrived in the Port of Savannah each week. See... by my Dad having a stronghold on the labor union back in the early 2000s, he was able to hire who he wanted to hire. His people were the ones at the dock checking the crates. My Dad got indicted for something unrelated to the Port of Savannah around 2013, which was a few years after my big brother Catfish got indicted with the Bankroll Squad– but that's another story for another day.

Under normal conditions, my big brother would have run the port; but he couldn't do it while being on the run, so it fell solely on me. The Port of Savannah was moving 51,200 crates per week when my father was running it. Under my leadership, the Port of Savannah brought in 67,307 crates each week. Out of that, there were around 500 crates each week with a minimum of $20 million worth of drugs coming into America. I can't fault my father for this because it was actually something that I was proud of at one point. Whereas some dads passed down old cars or trucks to their kids, my father passed me down a multi-billion-dollar empire.

If you Google 'drug seizures in the Port of Savannah," most of those happened because I wasn't paid properly. Sometimes the truck drivers lose shipments after they pick it up from the dock, and then the cartel tries to sneak another crate in without paying me. It doesn't work like that. I'm not your truck driver, my job is to either allow your shit to come in or have it reported. I was one of the most powerful men in America, and this too, is something that the FBI knew.

The real reason they negotiated with me was because they knew I knew some really sensitive info. See... in 2014, fentanyl started coming in from South America. The government tried to send some CIA agents to the port to make waive it through, but they were denied by me. I seized it, per our company policy, and told them the same thing I'd tell any other wanna be drug dealer or dealer: You're going to pay me first, or I'm either reporting this shit to the author-ities, or if you're the authorities, I'm reporting this shit to the press. Either way, I get 10% period.

So, the cycle began. The United States government had

to pay me the same way El Chapo had to pay me. I received millions from drug lords that weren't even on the United States' radar, as well as drug lords who were. As far as I was concerned, the US government was one of the biggest drug lords I'd ever seen. This is why they initially started trying to find something on me so that they could arrest me. When that didn't work, they followed me for years hoping that I would slip up. I knew they were always looking for a way to link me with drugs, but it would never happen. I wasn't a drug dealer.

One of the things my father told me before going on the run was that if the government ever tried to squeeze me for control, to let them have it. Our family had stacked so much money from the arrangement that we would never have to work again. We'd stacked money behind the scenes in a method so smooth that it took two decades for them to figure it all out. Back when the CIA realized they had to pay me, they also realized that they couldn't report me to anybody without implicating themselves as well. This gave me an extra 7 years of being in power.

I had cash stashed in so many different countries, invested in so many different companies– This was the reason my Dad wanted me to study abroad. He wanted me to learn different cultures because he was certain that the United States wasn't going to be the only country I was going to live in. It was the reason I was able to keep my people paid even when they thought it was no money coming in. They didn't realize that they all served a major purpose in the grand scheme of it all. I knew that anything we did; I could ultimately fix– the knowledge and advantage that I had over the US Government was rare air for a criminal.

I probably would have been number 1 on the Forbes' list of the richest drug dealers... but that would never happen only because I wasn't a drug dealer.

Bullethead was waiting on me the moment they let me out the prison doors. Two years had gone by at a snail's pace, and the only downside about it was that I really, really, missed my fuckin wife. When they first took me into custody, I told Bullethead not to tell me anything about anything I can't control. It would do me no good to know or worry about anything while sitting in a prison bunk, so no matter how big or small the news was on the outside, just handle it for me the best way he knew how.

For two years, instead of me worrying about the goings-ons of the outside world, I took that time to get closer to God. I started becoming more conscious of the errors of my ways and started regretting some of the decisions that I'd made. Since I had nothing else to do, I also started trying to calculate how much money I had stashed around the world. My cellmate had a small cell phone, and I would call the banks that I could remember and get my balance. My net worth was nearly the net worth of the owner of Amazon.com. What's so crazy was that I didn't even realize it.

The money came so fast and consistently, that all I did was stash it the moment it came in. It was so much money coming in that it became a nuisance. Almost like trash that I needed to get rid of because it was all over the place. I was smart, black, and rich, and the most important part of my wealth was the family I had who had my back through everything. These guys also knew that I had their backs through everything as well, so as a team, as a crew, as a family... we would not be defeated.

No matter how much I thought I'd learned while I was

in prison, by the time I got in Bullethead's car, I realized that I didn't know nothing.

"Welcome home family."

"Bro I appreciate that. It's been a long journey to freedom, but I'm here now. What did I miss?"

He looked at me and laughed. "Well for starters..."

Before he could finish, a baby started crying in the back seat, scaring the daylights out of me. I got out of the car and got into the backseat in astonishment. I put my finger in his hand, and he immediately stopped crying. He smiled at me, and when I saw his smile, I knew he was my baby. Tears fell down my face as I stared at him in happiness. I tried to open my mouth to speak, but I couldn't find the words.

"His name is Zaedan." Bullethead said as he handed me the birth certificate. "I've done what I could family. I've had to get your Grandma to help me because I knew nothing about taking care of a baby." He laughed gently, and his laugh quickly subsided.

"Where's– Where's– Where's my wife? Why isn't she helping?" I asked, my heartbeat starting to speed up.

"Well... I'll take you to her now."

We'd made it to downtown Atlanta, and I was still in the backseat with my son. He'd fallen asleep on the ride down there, and I couldn't help but to stare at how perfect he was. He was the perfect blend of me and my wife, from skin to hair, from lips to eyes; he was like a symbol of the greatest love story ever told. Lil Zaedan. I was going to be sure to protect him the horrors of the world and the dangers of the universe. I was going to pass down something more valuable than a criminal empire, so that by the time he became my age, he won't even realize that such a dark and cold world existed.

Bullethead pulled over into a vacant parking lot across the street from a liquor store. He parked and took a deep, dramatic breath. "I'll wait here with the baby... She's... She's... down this street. I just saw her when I was turning into the lot."

"What?" I looked outside to see what he was talking about. I saw a condo down the street, and then I understood. "Oh. Well what unit does she live in? I'm going to surprise her."

"Uhm, just catch her real quick while she's walking. I'm not sure of that..."

I jumped out of the car and started jogging down the street in the direction he'd pointed to. All I kept thinking about was the softness of Ayoki's skin. The smoothness of her voice, the shine of her eyes, the glimmer of her hair. She was a black African queen, a living goddess who deserved daily worship and admiration. She was my wife. My soul-mate, a gift from God and I'd spent every day asking God to send his angels to camp around her and protect her while she slept.

When I jogged around the corner, there was only one person on the sidewalk, and she was leaning against the fence. I looked to the left, to the right, confused, thinking maybe I missed her. The lady on the fence didn't look like my wife, but I was too far away to know for certain. As I got closer, I began to smell a loud body odor; and the closer I got, the more I realized that this lady was wrapped completely in filth. Her head was down, so all I saw was tangled hair covering her head and black dirt covering her arms.

"Excuse me. Do you know a lady named– "

I froze. It felt as though my heart stopped beating and would never beat again. My wife looked up at me with dirt and smudge covering her face, her lips were swollen and bruised and there were bumps under her dark eyes. Her smell was loud, as if she hadn't taken a shower in years. Her left shoe had a hole in it, and her left foot was black and had a large bruise on it as if she'd been bitten by a dog. Her fingernails had dried blood on them as if she'd been scratching a scab of some sort.

"Ayoki... It's me. I'm home."

She looked at me with the saddest look I'd ever seen in my life. "Who are you?"

Tears fell down my face as I stood in front of her in pain. I wasn't ashamed to cry in front of her. I had to let it all out. It was years of pain that had all embedded itself into that one moment. I cried without speaking, cried so hard that I couldn't see her through my tears. When you lost someone that you loved due to death, that was a sad feeling; but ultimately you had to move past it because you knew there was nothing you could do to bring them back. Losing someone who was standing in front of you still breathing... that's a different type of pain.

I wiped my eyes and stared at her. She had a blank expression on her face, stared at me as if I was just another stranger on the streets. I stood there regardless of the situation, and realized I still loved her, and still would love her until they buried me. She was still my wife and was still the most beautiful woman I'd ever laid eyes on, even when covered in filth.

"I love you Ayoki." I smiled as I gave her my truth. "I really love you, and I always will."

I've always known that God was a miracle worker, and I've always known that his miracles required patience. I was willing to continue loving this woman in the midst of her lowest point, because I knew that she would do the same if the roles were reversed. I couldn't give up on her. It was more my fault than hers. I was the gatekeeper to allow drugs into the United States, as my father was before me. I was passed down and forced to deal with the sins of my father, and I wasn't going to back down from it.

Once, when I was kid, I was outside on the porch with my father while it was raining outside. It was around 3 in the evening on a warm summer day, and it had been raining for a good two hours. Suddenly the sun came out while it was still raining, and it was the first time I'd ever seen such a thing. I remember asking my father, James; how could the sun come out while it's still pouring down raining. I never forgot his words to me that day.

"It means the angels messed the schedule up." He laughed, *before continuing. "It's God showing you his power son. It's a simple reminder that nothing is impossible as long as God is in control. When you get used to things being one type of way, he'll*

find a way to remind you that you have no clue how fast things can change."

It would be those words that would prepare me for the next moment.

"Zaedan?" Ayoki said, a look of confusion coming over her face.

"Yes! Yes! Ayoki! It's me! Your husband!" I yelled in excitement. All hope wasn't lost.

"Where am I? Why do I smell like this? What's happening?" Ayoki asked as she looked down at herself in horror.

"Baby, we're about to go get you cleaned up ok? We made some mistakes in life, but it's ok now. God just rescued us. Don't worry about a thing. I'm going to fix everything ok?"

Ayoki started crying. Vicious tears that broke my heart. It was like she'd been in a sunken mental place for years, and finally snapped out of it. "I'm... so... embarrassed..." She was fighting to get her words out through the tears, barely managing to form the complete sentences. "Look... at... me... oh... my... God... I'm... so... embarrassed..."

I wrapped my arms around her and tried to pull her close to me, but she pulled back.

"I'm so... dirty Zaedan." I could hear the shame in her voice, but it didn't matter.

I pulled her close to me until she let go and cried against my chest. I could care less about how she smelled or how dirty she was because nothing was cleaner or purer than our love. Before God we'd made a promise; married each other because we loved one another and promised to stand by our words through richer or poorer, in sickness and in health. I refused to let her fight her fight alone, refused to let her tackle her problems alone because it was us against the world. Me and my wife.

AUTHOR'S NOTE

Normally I use this section to give my readers an update about some of the things that are going on in my world... But I know if I explained it, I would have to relive the thoughts, and the thoughts are what I'm trying to heal from. I'll use this time to ask for prayers. Not selfishly though, because I know there are other people going through difficult situations as well. Instead I'm asking for a collection of prayers not just for me, but for everyone who's enduring difficult times, whether those times are mental, physical, or otherwise.

Thank you Lord that you are victorious over every trouble and obstacle. Thank you that you have overcome sin, and death, and any evil that we may face today. And because of you, we too are overcomers. We too can have victory, and we can walk strong in your peace.

I do wish to thank you all for supporting me. A greater thanks for having patience with me as I fight the multiple wars I've been faced with over time. If you do have the time, I'd like to ask you to leave a review on Amazon with your thoughts about the story, and feel free to follow me on social media: @therealrichforever on Instagram, and if it's your preference: www.Facebook.com/AuthorDavidWeaver.